BUILD
UNIVERSES

Margaret Grant

Three Eleven

europe books

© 2021 **Europe Books** | London
www.europebooks.co.uk – info@europebooks.co.uk

ISBN 979-12-201-0800-3
First edition: March 2021

Distribution for the United Kingdom: **Vine House Distribution ltd**

Printed for Italy by Rotomail Italia
Finito di stampare nel mese di marzo 2021
presso Rotomail Italia S.p.A. - Vignate (MI)

Three Eleven

For all my friends, former colleagues and students in Tokyo and especially for my Middlemarch class.

PROLOGUE
Tokyo, March 11th, 2011

Haneda Airport 6.26am
Katherine checked the departures board. She was catching the 7.30 flight to Sendai to spend the weekend with her mother-in-law. In about nine hours, a tsunami would flood the very airport she was flying into. But Katherine was oblivious to this near future event. She ran her fingers through her pixie cut and looked around anxiously for her husband. She expected him to meet her at check-in. He hadn't come home the night before, but there was nothing unusual in that. Katherine had married a workaholic, a PR Wizard at Mitsubishi Motors who often stayed in his office until dawn. She reached into the pocket of her navy down parka for her phone. It wasn't there. She found it in her carry-on bag, tucked between her cosmetics pouch and her copy of Middlemarch. Middlemarch was her book club's choice for March. She was half-way through the novel and hoped to finish it over the weekend. She dialled her husband's number. He didn't pick up.

The Hibiya Subway Line, 8.05am
Surrounded by salary men in grey suits, Fumiko clung to a grab handle. She was bound for Maronouchi and her job at TY Logistics. With her one free hand, she loosened the plaid scarf at her neck and undid the buttons of her camel coat. The waistband of her black trouser suit felt uncomfortably snug against her bulging belly. Despite training twice weekly in karate, she had gained a lot of weight recently. Middle aged spread, she supposed. Her bag weighed heav-

ily on her shoulder. She shouldn't have brought that book – Middlemarch. Now she would have to lug it around with her all day, to the izakaya, where she would meet her friends after work, and on to the karaoke box where they would sing away the stresses of the week.

She thought of texting Takeshi and inviting him along to karaoke. She could impress him with her rendition of *Stairway to Heaven*. An image of Takeshi's floppy hair and handsome face came into her mind. She sighed and adjusted the position of her bag on her shoulder. God, that book was heavy. Perhaps she should leave it in the office. She would never get through it in time for her book club on Wednesday anyway. She had struggled through the first chapter, but there were eighty-seven of them in total.

The Seibu Shinjuku railway line, 8.16am
Sinéad sat on an almost empty train heading towards the distant suburb of Tokorozawa and "Sunshine" kindergarten, where she taught English. She was reading Middlemarch, her all-time favourite novel. She wondered if she had made a bad choice in selecting it for her book club this month. Fumiko had excellent English, but a Victorian novel might prove too much of a challenge. And it was so very long. She wouldn't be surprised if she was the only one to get through the thick doorstopper of a book. Not that it mattered, books were only an excuse for the friends to catch up and have a nice meal. Next month, she would choose something short, a novella perhaps. Sinéad closed the book, took out her compact and applied lipstick and mascara. Her five-year-old students thought she was beautiful. She didn't want to disappoint them.

Fujimidai, Nerima ward, 11.30am
Lauren carried six-month-old Ken in a sling on her back and held two-year-old Emi by the hand as she trudged down

her local shopping street. She yawned. Ken had kept her awake all night. He was teething, poor little guy. Emi tugged at her hand and raised her free arm upwards, indicating that she wanted to be carried.

'Sweetie, I can't carry both of you,' Lauren said.

Emi stomped her foot and started to cry. She had been clingy ever since Ken's birth. The parenting books said it was normal, it would pass. Lauren hoped it would pass soon.

Kaldi Coffee farm's blue signboard shone like a beacon a mere fifty feet ahead of her. Lauren thought she could probably manage the two of them for that short distance. She bent her knees and scooped Emi up onto her hip. Emi beamed, victorious. She jostled against Ken, who cast her a side-long glance, but didn't protest at her sudden proximity.

Lauren struggled onward. As she approached Kaldi Coffee Farm, she saw a shop assistant in a navy apron place a tray of sample coffees on top of a barrel. As soon as Lauren reached the barrel, she put Emi down, closed her eyes for a moment and savoured the aroma of fresh coffee. She took one of the plastic cups and let the sweet warm coffee soothe and revive her. Then she pursued Emi who had already rambled away to explore the wonders of the coffee and fine food store. Lauren grabbed a packet of Lavazza from a shelf, along with a pack of shortbread cookies. Armed with these treats, she thought she might actually make it through the day.

Thank God it was Friday. Naoto would be home all weekend. Lauren would have back-up and might manage to catch up on some sleep and some reading. Not that she would get through that tome *Middlemarch* by Wednesday. She would join her friends for book club anyway. There would be food and wine and grown-ups. She couldn't wait.

Rikkyo University, Ikebukuro, 12.56pm
Charlotte walked through Rikkyo University's ivy-cov-

ered archway. She had a meeting with Suzuki san of the University's International Education section at one. Dressed in burgundy cords, sensible brogues and a grey wool coat; a quarter inch of striped woollen socks showed between the end of her trousers and the top of her shoes. Charlotte never bought clothes in Japan. Nothing fit. And even in the UK, trousers sometimes weren't quite long enough for her six foot frame. Her battered satchel contained work related documents, a packed lunch and a copy of Middlemarch. She had read the book for A level English nearly twenty years before and hoped to re-read at least some of it before next Wednesday's book club.

The Pacific Ocean, 70 kilometres east of the Tohoku Coast, 2.46pm
Under the sea a magnitude nine megathrust earthquake occurred. It was the most powerful earthquake ever recorded in Japan. The epicentre was more than 300 kilometres from Tokyo. Yet, it brought the city's rail, subway and bus system to a halt, forcing many workers to sleep in their offices and others to walk through the night to get home to their loved ones. And that was the least of the damage it wrought.

Neither Charlotte, Fumiko, Katherine, Lauren or Sinéad was wounded in the disaster. They didn't lose their homes, their families or their jobs. Yet the lives of these five friends changed forever on that day. The ground beneath them shook for six long minutes, during which time they thought they were going to die. The sophisticated and technologically advanced city which they called home was not as safe as they had believed. They lost their sense of stability and with it their balance. It would take them years to regain their equilibrium.

This is the story of those years.

PART ONE
LOVE IN AMED

THE QUAKE

Charlotte clasped the book in both hands, its shiny new cover, and oh, its new book smell. She really shouldn't. Her bookshelves had long since overflowed and she had resolved not to buy any more books until she had found a home for some of her old ones. But this memoir was so very tempting. Besides, Sinéad would be coming over on Sunday and would surely take some books home with her, so perhaps Charlotte could buy this one slim volume? But no. The situation was critical. Stacks of books occupied every spare corner of her rather small apartment. She returned the book to the shelf, hurried to the escalator and descended through Junkado's seven storeys of books, before any others had a chance to call out to her and beg her to take them home.

She exited the bookstore and glanced at her watch. A quarter to three. Tired, after a busy week, she thought how nice it would be to go straight home rather than back to the office. Probably not a good idea though; Griffiths was sure to look in on her section before he left for the weekend. Just the previous week, the deputy director had gathered all the junior managers together in order to harangue them for not pulling their weight. Charlotte rarely left the office before nine, and had worked every Saturday so far this year, yet Griffiths had had the gall to tell them they weren't working hard enough. 'I see the senior managers in the office late at night and I see the junior staff, but I don't see you,' he'd said. Griffiths never saw them because he was never there himself. He always left the office at five. Unfortunately, no one had had the nerve to point this out to him.

She would go back and write up the report on today's

visit to Rikkyo University while it was still fresh in her mind. She could proofread that circular that Hashimoto san wanted to send out too. She stood and waited for the pedestrian lights to change.

She looked down at her shoes. Her feet appeared to be moving towards her head. She felt dizzy and thought she might be going to faint. Then she heard a rumbling, followed by a rattling noise. She looked up. Drivers were having trouble controlling their cars, cyclists wobbling, pedestrians losing their balance. An earthquake.

When the lights changed and the drivers managed to bring their cars to a stop, Charlotte crossed to the traffic island in the middle of the road. It seemed safer than the pavement, a safer distance from the multi storey buildings on either side of the road. Many pedestrians had congregated there. They focused their attention on the structure directly in front of them. Twenty storeys high and swaying violently.

Next to Charlotte, a salary man tried to make a phone call. To his wife or girlfriend, Charlotte presumed. A teenage girl in a school uniform had her phone in her hand too, 'Okaa san, Okaa san,' she called (Mother, Mother). 'OKAA SAN.' The girl started to cry. She couldn't reach her mother. Perhaps Charlotte's network would work. The girl could use her phone. Charlotte didn't need it. It was much too early to call her mother and she didn't have a spouse to call. She rummaged in her bag. Not in its usual pouch, perhaps she'd put it in the front pocket. Not there either, she reached under the heavy files. No. Blast it, where was it? But wait. It didn't matter. No one around her was getting through to anybody. One phone was as useless as another.

Charlotte planted her feet wide apart to stop herself from falling. A middle-aged woman comforted the schoolgirl, told her not to worry, everything would be okay. A small boy sobbed, his arms wrapped around his mother's thigh, his head pressed against her belly. His mother told him there was nothing to cry about, nothing at all. An old lady struggled to keep hold of her bicycle as it threatened to roll away from her. The salary man grabbed onto it and together they held it firm.

Around her, people were talking to each other, helping each other, offering words of comfort. No one spoke to Charlotte. All the hours she had put into perfecting her Japanese, and now here she was on a traffic island in the middle of Tokyo, in the middle of an earthquake, and no one was talking to her. And it wasn't as if they couldn't see her. She was the tallest, the largest person there. Would someone talk to her? Look at her? Acknowledge her existence?

That building. It was going to snap in two. It couldn't hold. It wouldn't hold.

Charlotte knew that these buildings were designed to sway. And she had confidence in Japanese engineering. She had confidence in everything Japanese. But the way that building was swaying, how could it return to its original position? It couldn't. If it didn't snap in two, it would crumble. If it crumbled, would they be safe here on their traffic island? Charlotte didn't think so. The building was too tall, and way too close. This could be it. This could be the end.

Tears rolled down her cheeks. She didn't want it to be over. She didn't want to die. Not yet. She thought of all the things she hadn't done. The places she hadn't visited. The things that were missing from her life. Things like sex and love. Messy things which she was getting along quite well without, thank you very much.

Or was she? Was she really doing fine without these things? Sometimes she felt so...

Sometimes she felt like an idiot. Most of the time actually. A big, awkward, bumbling fool. Soon she would be a big awkward, bumbling, dead fool.

Well at least, if she was going to die, she wouldn't be dying a virgin.

Nyoman. Their brief romance probably meant very little to him. She knew that. Yet she felt such gratitude and tenderness towards him. He had taken her virginity. For that she would always be thankful.

Virgin. How she had hated that label. Not that she'd gone around with it pinned to her forehead or anything, but being a virgin, she had felt excluded from any conversation remotely connected with sex. The taint of virginity gone; she had thought that her life would be different somehow. It hadn't changed in any appreciable way. Yet, she had the memory of Nyoman, of the time they spent together. That was something, something she could take with her to the grave, because it looked like that was the place she was heading to, and soon, so much sooner than she had ever expected. She didn't drink. She didn't smoke. She ate her greens. She had thought she would live to be ninety at least.

But wait, the ground was no longer moving. The people on the traffic island looked around, assessed the situation and reassured themselves that the earth was indeed still.

Everyone started to move. Everybody knew what to do. They had been drilled in earthquake safety procedures since kindergarten. Charlotte knew what to do too. She had lived there long enough. She had an emergency survival kit waiting in her closet at home. She was prepared.

There would be no going back to the office. She could go home. She heard someone say that the trains would not be running. She would have to walk. That wasn't a problem. She knew the route, had cycled it often. It took an hour by bicycle. It would take two or more on foot.

No buildings had collapsed on-route, no trees fallen, no holes had opened up in the ground, not in this neighbourhood at least. Nothing out of place at all, except for the office workers huddled outside their places of business, reluctant to return to their desks; the troops of school children, padded hoods or helmets over their heads to protect them from falling debris; policemen cycling around calling out to the walkers, urging them to hurry home, and inquiring if anyone was hurt.

She was passing a park when the earth started to rumble again. The aftershock felt almost as powerful as the original quake, and this park, according to a sign near the entrance, was a designated evacuation zone, so she went in. She stood next to a group of old ladies; their wizened faces turned towards a row of narrow houses opposite the park entrance. Charlotte nodded at the old ladies. They nodded back.

'Sugoi desu ne,' the obaa chan nearest Charlotte said. *"Terrible, isn't it?"*. She looked worriedly across at her trembling home.

'Sou desu ne,' Charlotte agreed. *It is.*

A stooped grandmother of ninety years or more said that she had never seen anything like it in all her years. Charlotte knew then that what they were experiencing must be titanic. What lay ahead of them? Would they survive?

She thought again of Nyoman. She remembered snorkelling with him at the Japanese wreck. He'd taken her hand to guide her and had encouraged her to dive deeper into the water, right down, to touch the coral. She usually felt so clumsy and self-conscious around men. With him she had just felt alive, very much alive.

The touch of his hand on the small of her back or on her hip.

'You don't mind my hand here?' he'd asked.

Charlotte hadn't minded. In fact, she had liked it. Yet she wasn't sure if she should allow his hand there. Perhaps it was inappropriate. She had not foreseen then what was to happen between them. She was not the sort of person to have a holiday romance. Not the sort of person to have any kind of romance, really.

To be in Amed now, instead of trembling, crumbling Tokyo.

NEWS OF THE TSUNAMI REACHES BALI

Nyoman spotted tourists, a couple strolling along the beach together. They were young or young enough, on their honeymoon perhaps.

He slowed his pace. He listened. They weren't speaking English. High pitched and sing song, he recognised their language as French. Many French tourists came to Amed. They liked it very much.

'Bonjour,' Nyoman said when they came abreast of him.

'Bonjour,' they replied.

'Où allez-vous?'

'Pour une promenade sur la plage. C'est tout.'

For a stroll along the beach, he thought they meant. Nyoman liked French. He liked the way you pursed your lips to make the sounds. But he knew only a little of the language. He needed to switch to English to communicate properly.

'Maybe you like to snorkelling tomorrow? I take you to the Japanese wreck. It very nice, very good for snorkelling.'

'Ah, tomorrow, we go to that temple, what is it called? The Temple of a mille, a million steps.'

Nyoman smiled. They meant The Temple of a Thousand Steps, but he didn't correct them. It could feel like a million steps, especially on a hot day. 'After tomorrow then,' he said. 'I take you to the Japanese wreck. You like very much, many fishes.'

'Maybe.'

They were already walking away from him. The day after tomorrow, they might well want to go to the Japanese wreck, but they would have forgotten him. They would find someone else to take them. He needed a mobile phone and a business card. Then he could do good business.

He joined Ketut and Wayan Joe at the bamboo shelter. He needed a nap. He had been up early to go out fishing. He hadn't caught anything. The people of Amed had depended on the ocean's bounty forever. Nowadays too many fishermen fished in those waters. Everyone taking, taking, taking. The ocean could not replenish herself. But what to do? He loved the sea. Alone on his little boat, over near Gilli Tarawan, he felt at one with the world and happy, very happy. He wanted never to leave.

Ketut snored. Nyoman poked him with his toe. Ketut rolled over. Nyoman dozed and dreamt of a catch big enough to allow him to buy a mobile phone and to print business cards to distribute to tourists.

The ringing of Wayan's phone woke him from his slumber.

At first Wayan didn't understand who the caller was. Then he remembered, 'Ah Haruto, my friend. You good? You in Bali now?'

Nyoman listened eagerly to Haruto's answer. Haruto had visited Amed several months before. Nyoman had taken him fishing and Haruto had paid Nyoman handsomely. The Japanese man liked Bali very much. He said he would return. If he had returned already, Nyoman could take him fishing again, and snorkelling too, and soon he would have enough money to buy a mobile phone.

Wayan. Joe concentrated on Haruto's words. He jumped down from the shelter and walked towards the sea. He then quickly returned, but walking backwards, his eyes fixed on the ocean.

'Thank you, Haruto. Thank you, my friend. I pray for you. I pray for Japan.' Wayan put his phone back in his pocket.

'An earthquake hit Japan,' Wayan told him. 'They had a tsunami, very big, many people died. Haruto says the tsunami could be coming here.'

Nyoman sat up and looked at the sea. It didn't look any different. 'Wake up.' He shook Ketut's ankle.

Wayan did not take his eyes off the waves. 'Haruto said to run,' he said.

'Run?' Nyoman kicked Ketut. 'Wake up, Fathead,' he said.

Ketut shook his ugly head and looked around him.

They hurried along the beach, keeping an eye on the ocean. Ketut's son, still in his school uniform, came strolling towards them.

'Run,' Ketut told him. 'Warn everyone.'

A crowd gathered around the Dive shop's television screen. Together they watched the black water surge onwards taking buses, cars, homes, lives. Nyoman touched the pearls around his neck, a keepsake from Charlotte.

Charlotte lived in Japan. He did not think she lived by the sea. The wave would not take her. But the earthquake that had triggered the wave was powerful, powerful enough to knock houses, rip holes in the earth, ignite fires. Though safe from the tsunami, the earthquake might have got her. He closed his eyes and prayed for her safety.

Her hair was a light shade of brown. It was not as exquisite as the luxuriant black hair of the Balinese beauties, nor was it as long. It came only to beneath her chin. But when the sun shone on it, it sparkled like gold. He liked her hair, its waves and curls. She stuck pins in it to keep it back from her face. And he liked her soft white skin with those little brown speckles on it, and the way she laughed when she felt shy or embarrassed. He didn't mind that she was taller than him and sturdily built. He liked it. Indeed, he felt proud, potent to have attracted such a strong and powerful woman. She was different from other tourists. She was humble. And she was clever. She spoke Japanese and French. She studied Chinese. He hoped she would come again to Amed. He hoped she had come to no harm.

He looked out on the Lombok Strait. It remained calm.

The Gods of the Ocean had spared them. They had spent all their fury on Japan.

As the light began to fade, he trudged uphill through the dry scrub, to his humble home, where he told his mother about the treacherous black wave he had seen on the television screen, and the terrible fate that had been visited upon Japan.

SINÉAD SPENDS THE NIGHT

Charlotte registered the broken crockery and glass on the kitchen floor: the toaster oven and microwave toppled from their perch; the books more on the floor than on the shelves. Keeping her shoes on, she walked through to her living room. The television was still in its place, as was her laptop. She turned both on, sent emails to her family in the UK to let them know that she was safe, and remained glued to the screens into the night.

The earthquake was the largest ever recorded to have hit Japan. It had triggered huge tsunami waves in Iwate, Sendai, Miyagi, Fukushima and Ibaraki, with smaller tsunamis reported in Chiba, Kanagawa, Tokyo Bay and as far away as Okinawa. Tokyo had come to a standstill. A fire was raging at an oil refinery in Ichihara. But damage to the capital was minimal when compared with the destruction in Tohoku. There, whole villages had been vanquished. Cars, buses and lorries had been dragged out to sea. A train was missing. An entire train, full of passengers. Gone.

Charlotte's chin wobbled as she watched the wave invade Higashimatsushima, hurling a forty-five-metre ship over a pier and leaving it aground in the middle of the city; inundating houses, hospitals, schools and collapsing them; taking some inhabitants, sparing others. Charlotte knew Higashimatsushima. She had been based in that city when, fresh from Cambridge, she first came to Japan, on the JET programme. There was a wall near the harbour, built to save the city from tsunamis. They hadn't been built it high enough.

Saturday too was spent in front of the television. Cereal and chocolate biscuits keeping hunger at bay. The gas supply had been turned off. There could be no cooking, no baths or showers either. It was cold, but Charlotte had blankets.

There were reports about a possible leakage at a nuclear reactor in Fukushima. Later, a nuclear emergency was declared, nearby residents evacuated. Then at 15:36 there was an explosion at the Fukukshima Dai-Ichi nuclear plant. Later that evening the evacuation zone was extended to a twenty-kilometre radius of the plant. Experts said not to worry. They claimed that this would not be another Chernobyl. Even in the worst-case scenario, the effects would be felt only in the immediate local area.

There were emails to be replied to. Her parents, her aunt Eleanor, various friends and even her brother had sent enquiries as to her wellbeing and the wellbeing of the city she called home. She did her best to answer all the questions that they asked.

Her screensaver was a photo of herself and her aunt Eleanor on a little fishing boat heading off on a snorkelling trip off Bali's East Coast. Eleanor in the foreground, glamorous in her shades and looking much younger than her sixty-five years. The lifejacket she'd insisted on, covering her halter neck swimsuit.

Charlotte's face is half hidden by her aunt's broad rimmed sunhat. Her thick wavy hair blown out like a saucer around her head. Her shades are not as large or fashionable as her aunt's. Her swimsuit is the very practical one-piece that she bought in Debenhams some years earlier. She too looks well, healthy and happy.

Nyoman is in the photo too, perched on the outrigger of his boat. His jet-black hair cropped short, his smooth brown skin, those high cheekbones. Slender but quite muscular. Not as tall as Charlotte, but tall all the same for a Balinese man.

Sailing in the Lombok Strait, morning breeze in their face, Nyoman at the rudder. It had been wonderful.

On Sunday morning, Charlotte's phone rang. It was Sinéad. She wondered if she could spend the night at Charlotte's. She was scared to be alone. Of course, she could stay. Charlotte was scared too. There was much to be frightened about. A meltdown was now suspected at Fukushima.

Charlotte started to sweep up the broken glass and spilled soil and to return books to their shelves. She examined her toaster oven. Its door had come off, and one of the heating elements had cracked and was hanging loose. Irreparable, she thought.

The side of the microwave was dented, but otherwise it looked all right. She plugged it in and turned it on. It seemed to be working. Her gas had been reconnected. She could shower.

'Katherine is in the affected area,' Sinéad said.

Charlotte placed the tea tray on the coffee table and made herself comfortable opposite her guest. 'In Tohoku?' she asked.

'Yeah, Sendai, I think. Ichiro's from Sendai or Iwate or somewhere up north. She's alright though. She posted on Facebook. You should be on Facebook.'

'I don't see the point,' Charlotte started to explain her views on Facebook.

'The point is that you can connect with people and share information, important information, like whether you're alive or whether a television fell on your head and killed you.'

'You can email that information.'

'Who uses emails nowadays?'

Charlotte thought that quite a lot of people still used email. She used email at work all the time. But she said nothing.

Sinéad seemed quite tetchy. It had been a stressful weekend. Sinéad took a sip from the cup of tea Charlotte had made for her and wrapped her blanket more tightly around her shoulders. 'You know what I was thinking when it was happening?' she asked.

'No?'

'I was thinking I should get married,' Sinéad said. 'And I spoke to Fumiko this morning and she told me she was thinking the exact same thing. Were you thinking that?'

'Erm, no.'

'No? I thought maybe all the single women in Tokyo were having the exact same thought at the exact same time. Hmm. Apparently not.'

'Marriage isn't something I can really see in my future at all,' Charlotte said.

'No?'

Charlotte shook her head. Quite early in life, she had come to the conclusion that romance was not for her. In her teens, she had frequented youth discos with her school friends. They would all get dressed up, but only one or two of them ever got asked to dance. She had surmised then that romance was not for everybody. Not that it was reserved for the pretty girls, no. Boys sometimes wanted to dance with girls who were not particularly good-looking. But, they conscientiously avoided girls who were odd or who stood out it some way. Being so very tall and so terribly brainy, Charlotte had always stood out.

Sinéad seemed to expect further elucidation.

'I feel kind of awkward around men,' Charlotte said. 'I mean, I'm fine around them in normal situations. With friends and colleagues who are male there's no problem. I like them. I get on well with them. But if there's even a hint of anything other than camaraderie, I just get so uncomfortable.'

'But I think everyone feels uncomfortable around guys they fancy.'

'I suppose so, but in any case, I think men don't usually think of me in a romantic or sexual way. They see me as a friend. Which is fine. I really don't have a problem with that.'

'I'm sure there are lots of men who would find you very attractive. You have so much going for you. You're multi-lingual, extremely intelligent, involved and concerned about different global issues. And you're cute.'

Charlotte laughed. 'You can't really call someone my size cute,' she said.

'You're not that big. You just feel big because you're in Asia. Anyway, big can be cute. Look at Saint Bernard. They're cute.'

'Saint Bernard. Dogs?'

'Yes,' Sinéad giggled. 'I'm sorry. I didn't mean to compare you to a dog. But you know, it's hard for us Western women in Japan. I read an article recently in the "Japan times". It called Japan a sexual desert for western woman...'

'I don't think Japan is to blame. I wasn't exactly popular in the UK,' Charlotte said,

Once, at one of those youth discos, Charlotte had chatted with a boy. They had chatted for some time actually. They had chosen the same subjects for their A-levels, so they had plenty to talk about. He asked her to dance and they had kissed on the dance floor. First with their mouths closed, then with his tongue gently probing between her lips. She had secretly practiced kissing with her pillow. Now she was kissing an actual boy. She felt so excited. She and this boy might become boyfriend and girlfriend. Maybe romance was for her after all. But on her way back from the toilets, she heard his friends teasing him about kissing a fat girl. 'Fletcher is kissing Fatty,' they taunted. She wasn't so terribly fat back then, just a little chubby.

29

'You know what I'm going to do? I'm going to go home to Tipperary, find myself a nice farmer, settle down with him and bear his children.'

'Really? You think you might go back to Ireland?'

'Maybe.' Cups started to rattle. 'Fuck. Is that another one?' Sinéad rushed to open the door. It was important to secure the exits. 'This is horrible. I just don't feel safe.'

'Tomorrow everything will go back to normal,' Charlotte said. 'We'll go back to work. The supermarket shelves will be restocked.'

'You're probably right. This is Tokyo, the safest city in the world. Everything will be grand.'

They decided to leave the door ajar and settled down to sleep for the night, Charlotte in her bedroom and Sinéad just yards away, behind the washi door on the spare futon in the living room. Not that sleep came, to either of them.

'Charlotte, are you still awake?' Sinéad called.

'Yes.'

'I was just thinking' Sinéad said. 'I know you have a full life and are fine just the way you are. But maybe you shouldn't close yourself off to the possibility of romance.'

Charlotte's throat seized up. She nodded in the darkness, and mumbled agreement. Not that she saw anything wrong with eschewing romance. It was a perfectly legitimate choice. Many exemplary people chose celibacy. The Dalai Lama for example, and Mother Teresa. Not that Charlotte could compare her life to theirs. Yet, in her way she did what she could to make the world a better place. She baked bread and cakes for her friends and colleagues. Cake did wonders to lighten the mood in the 'Study in the UK department. She volunteered for "Second Harvest" and "Fair Trade Japan". She wrote letters weekly for Amnesty International. She lived a worthwhile life. She cycled, hiked, wrote sonnets, learned languages, travelled and expanded her horizons.

And yet, in that moment, in her chest she felt a yearning, a yearning for warmth and love and human touch. Maybe Sinéad was right. Romance, love and all that kind of stuff. Perhaps it wasn't just for other people. Maybe it could be for her too.

Or maybe not. Romantic relationships made people miserable as often as not. Sinéad had been terribly distraught after her break-up with Kotaro and for such a long time. Charlotte felt she would be as well off without all of that. And Katherine's marriage didn't seem to make her very happy. In any case it wasn't as if Charlotte had ever had many suitors.

Of course, there was Nyoman. She smiled under the blankets at the memory of him, of his cheekbones and those strong hands.

But why was she allowing herself to think of Nyoman? Nyoman hadn't been serious about her. Lonely Planet had forewarned her about the gigolos and Lotharios of Bali. They hung around the beaches and tourist areas flirting with female visitors, especially the older ones, becoming their lovers in return for gifts: t-shirts, jeans, mobile phones, I-pods. Charlotte had expected she might have to protect her aunt Eleanor from some potential toy boy. She had never imagined she would fall for the charms of one herself.

Not that he'd been her toy boy. Nyoman was younger than Charlotte, but only by six or seven years. He hadn't expected gifts and had insisted on paying for dinner, when he took her to the local warung. The food was cheap, a fraction of what it cost at Charlotte's hotel. If it had been otherwise, Charlotte would have felt terribly guilty about letting him pay. There was such a great disparity in their financial circumstances.

Was that another tremor? Or was she imagining it? The cups and plates began to rattle. It was real.

'Charlotte?' Sinéad called.

'Yes?'

They were not sleeping in their shoes, but they had kept them right beside their futons, just in case. The rattling stopped. Just a small tremor.

'Thank God,' Sinéad said. And they both returned to their silent sleeplessness.

THE PREVIOUS SEPTEMBER

The holiday had been Aunt Eleanor's idea. She had booked a month-long vacation in Bali to mark her retirement and had persuaded Charlotte to fly from Tokyo to join her for her final week. Charlotte met her Aunt in Ubud, where Eleanor did so much shopping that she had to buy an extra suitcase to cart all her purchases home. Charlotte shopped too, albeit in a more modest fashion. She loved the Indonesian textiles and bought some scarves, a summer skirt and a traditional sarong.

Eleanor wanted to spend some time soaking up the sun before heading back to damp and gloomy England. Charlotte was keen to avoid the overcrowded beaches to the South, so they headed Eastwards to the black sand beaches of Amed.

After checking into their hotel, Charlotte and Eleanor went for a walk on the beach. They were returning as daylight was turning into dusk, when Nyoman approached them.

'Hello, how are you? Where you come from?' he said.

'England,' Eleanor replied.

'Oh, England.' He nodded thoughtfully. Charlotte wondered if he knew where England was. Most of the tourists in Bali were Australian or Japanese. She hadn't met another Brit.

'When you come to Amed?'

'We've just arrived' Eleanor said.

'Where you staying?'

'There.' Charlotte pointed towards the fence.

'Oh, Coral Garden, very nice. What can I do for you?' he said.

'Well, I don't know,' Eleanor replied, 'quite a lot I would imagine.' Charlotte threw her Aunt a reproachful glance.

'Maybe you want to go snorkelling tomorrow? Japanese wreck, really nice for snorkelling.'

'Well, young man, we've had a long drive. I think tomorrow will be a day for relaxing on the beach. Besides, I've never been snorkelling. I don't know how.'

'No problem. I teach you.'

'Is that what you do here?' Charlotte asked. 'Teach snorkelling?'

'I'm a fisherman here. But sometimes I take tourists snorkelling.'

Charlotte quite liked the idea of going snorkelling. Lounging on the beach all day was not her thing. She thought she might be able to persuade her Aunt over dinner.

He told them his name and asked theirs, shaking hands first with Eleanor and then with Charlotte.

'Are you the mother?' he asked Eleanor.

'Yes,' Eleanor said with a laugh. 'I'm her mother.'

'If you want to go to Japanese wreck, remember my name - Nyoman. There's a lot of people working on this beach.'

'Okay Nyoman, we won't forget.'

'Wasn't he handsome?' Eleanor said to her niece as soon as Nyoman was out of earshot.

Charlotte hadn't really noticed that he was handsome. She'd found him pleasant though.

She consulted her guidebook for information on the Japanese Wreck that the fisherman had mentioned. Apparently, it was an old Japanese patrol boat that had sunk during the war and was now covered with soft corals and home to a large variety of colourful fish. Over dinner, Charlotte convinced Eleanor that a trip to the Japanese wreck would be just the thing for the following morning. She remembered the fisherman's name, as he had instructed them to do, and was adamant that they bring their business to Nyoman.

'It looks a bit flimsy,' Eleanor said at the sight of Nyoman's brightly painted jukung. 'What about lifejackets? We need lifejackets.'

Nyoman looked perplexed. He called out to Wayan Joe, the pony tailed man who had rented them their snorkelling equipment. Wayan strode off in the direction of their hotel and returned with a lifejacket for Eleanor.

'Thank you so much. But is there only one? What about Charlotte?'

'I don't need one,' Charlotte said. During her travels around the Philippines several years before, she had journeyed in boats flimsier than this one.

'What will I tell your mother if you drown in the Lombok Strait and I was the one wearing the only life jacket?'

'I won't drown, Aunt Eleanor. Really, I won't.'

Eleanor insisted on keeping her life jacket on even in the water. She wouldn't listen when Charlotte explained that its buoyancy would make snorkelling very difficult.

Nyoman showed Eleanor how to use her snorkel. Her Aunt in capable hands, Charlotte swam off to the wreck. Divers swam several feet below her. She spotted what she thought was a clownfish, then a shoal of flat fish, white with black stripes and a hint of yellow. Zebra fish, perhaps?

Once Eleanor was snorkeling with more confidence, Nyoman swam to join Charlotte. He pointed out a large yellow and blue fish to her, its body the shape of a hot water bottle. He was patient when her eyes had trouble finding what he pointed at.

Back on the boat, Eleanor praised Nyoman's teaching skills, said he inspired confidence and enthused about what a wonderful young man he was.

Charlotte asked him about the islands they could see in the distance. Nyoman told her they were the Gilli islands.

'The Gillis!' Eleanor exclaimed. 'Could you take us there?'

'My boat too slow,' Nyoman said.

Eleanor sighed in disappointment. The Gilli islands were famous for their pristine white sand beaches and the ponies they used for transport in lieu of Bali's scooters. They were on Eleanor's list of places to visit.

Nyoman told them that there was a fast boat from Amed to Gilli Tarawan and that he could organize the trip for them. Eleanor insisted that he come with them as their guide. Charlotte couldn't see why they would need a guide but had no objection to spending more time with Nyoman.

They reached Lipah beach. He helped them out of the boat, and they trudged back through the black sand up to the hotel.

Eleanor nudged Charlotte. 'I think he likes you,' she said.

'Don't be silly,' Charlotte said. Although, come to think of it, he had touched her back when they were swimming together, and he had taken her hand to guide her as they dived. But it didn't necessarily mean anything. She was not the sort of woman that men fancied.

There were twenty or thirty other tourists on the fast boat to the Gillis. All of them carrying rucksacks or suitcases, clearly planning to spend a night or two there. Eleanor and Charlotte carried only the baskets they'd bought at the Ubud market. Nyoman carried their rented snorkelling equipment and took a seat directly behind the skipper. Charlotte and Eleanor sat behind him. He turned to face them and make conversation. He asked Eleanor how many children she had.

'I don't have any children,' Eleanor replied.

'But' Nyoman said, pointing at Charlotte.

'Oh, Charlotte's not my daughter. She's my niece.'

'You're not married?'

'Divorced,' Eleanor replied.

'And you, you married?' Nyoman asked Charlotte.

'Me? Married? No, I'm not married.'

'Not yet,' Eleanor said.

'Maybe you marry me,' he said with a grin.

'Wouldn't that be lovely?' Eleanor said. 'Imagine the beautiful children the two of you would have.'

Charlotte blushed and laughed, then, as sometimes happened when she laughed, she snorted.

Eleanor asked Nyoman about his own family. He had four brothers, all living in and around Amed, and two half-sisters, both living in Denpasar. His father had had three wives.

'My goodness.' Eleanor raised her eyebrows.

'Is it common in Bali,' Charlotte asked, 'to have more than one wife?'

'Not really,' Nyoman said, 'too expensive.'

On Gilli Tarawan, the tourists outnumbered the locals by about twenty to one. Trendy young Australians and Europeans milling about sipping beers and cocktails long before noon. It was not Charlotte's kind of place. She preferred Amed's relative quiet, its relaxed local flavour.

She and Nyoman went swimming, leaving Eleanor to soak up the sun. Charlotte started to think that Eleanor might be right, Nyoman might like her. He often touched her arm or her back or took her hand in his. And she had an inkling that she might like him too.

Back on the boat, Nyoman suggested that they go up top.

'You go ahead,' Eleanor told Charlotte. 'I'm going inside.'

Charlotte didn't know if she would be able to climb onto the roof, but she tried, and it actually wasn't that difficult.

The return trip started off choppy and got progressively choppier. As the boat tore through the waves, she and Nyoman were tossed about violently. Nyoman squealed, whether in fear or delight, Charlotte was not sure. She was terrified that she would be tossed into the ocean. She wanted to go back inside, but if she tried to climb down now, she would surely land in the waves.

Nyoman told her it would be better if she lay down. It wasn't better. It was worse. Her body was thrown almost a foot into the air. She landed hard on her back. It hurt.

'Move closer,' Nyoman said.

For safety, she did move closer. She was thrown into the air again. Nyoman put his arm around her shoulder and pulled her closer still. That was better. If they went overboard, they would go overboard together. Nyoman was a strong swimmer. He wouldn't let her drown.

Nyoman turned Charlotte's face towards his and kissed her on the mouth. Charlotte was amazed that he could think about kissing when they were likely to be thrown to their deaths at any moment. He moved his hand and placed it on Charlotte's breast. He asked if it was ok. She said that she wasn't sure. He took his hand away. Then he asked if he could come to her room later. No, he couldn't come to her room. Charlotte's Aunt was in the room just across the way.

Charlotte's body was bruised and sore after the boat ride; her hair so matted that it took almost half a bottle of conditioner to detangle it. Yet she felt somehow exhilarated.

That evening he took her for a ride on his scooter. From the crest of a hill, they watched the sunset. He kissed her as the sun went down. It felt nice. Nyoman smoothed her hair away from her face and kissed her again, ever so gently. Her heart beat hard and fast. The kisses thrilled her. A tingling sensation spread from between her thighs to her stomach. That she identified as arousal.

He dropped her back to Coral Garden Villas and asked again if he could come to her room.

Charlotte shook her head. 'My Aunt,' she said.

He grinned, 'I see you tomorrow,' he said. 'I take you some place.'

Charlotte tiptoed to her room so as not to wake her Aunt. She put on her light cotton, polka-dot pyjamas and got into bed.

Eleanor was flying back to London the next day, Charlotte's flight to Tokyo wasn't until the day after that. Tomorrow night she would have the villa all to herself. If he asked to come to her room tomorrow, she could say 'yes.'

Not that she would. What was the point? It could only be for one night. Probably best not to. In any case, she wouldn't know what to do. It could all be horribly embarrassing. She suspected sometimes that there might be something wrong with her, something lacking in the sexual department.

Some ten years before, she had sort of, kind of, dated a slightly older man. An anglophile, he accompanied her to the Tokyo International Players productions of 'Othello' and 'My Fair Lady.' One evening, in a lift after dinner, Fujimori san had kissed her, then grabbed her hand and placed it on his crotch. She had felt more horrified than aroused and had pulled her hand hastily away.

He had stopped calling her after that, which was a shame, because she had enjoyed doing things with him. She wondered about the fact that she had not been physically attracted to him. Shouldn't she have been? She was inclined to think that she was wired differently from the bulk of humanity. She so rarely thought about men in a romantic or sexual way.

Mind you, there had once been somebody whom she'd had feelings for, a fellow linguist at Cambridge. She and Thomas had spent quite a bit of time together. When her friends had asked her if there was anything going on between them, she had insisted that they were just friends. Which of course was true, but she omitted to mention that she was crazy about him. She couldn't stop thinking about him. She was completely besotted. She didn't think he felt the same way, which accounted somewhat for why she didn't tell her friends. But she had hope in her heart, hope that his feelings would change and morph into love. Because he did seem to enjoy her company. He did like her. It didn't seem impossible that someday her passion would be requited.

They had studied together for their finals. These study sessions had been his idea. Charlotte concentrated better studying alone, but she was glad to study with him, and she thought maybe Thomas did like her in a romantic way and that was why he wanted them to study together. She thought about telling him how she felt, but, whether walking from the library with him or having lunch together in the refectory or revising side by side at the desk in his room, the words would not come from her mouth.

One evening, sitting next to him on his single bed, books strewn over a coffee table, his lips distracted her from the text they were studying, so full and soft and inviting. Their finals began in two days. This would be one of their last times studying together. She worked up the courage to kiss those lips. Thomas kissed her back, ran his hand along the length of her arm and, just when she thought he was about to ease her back onto his lumpy bed, he pulled away from her. He explained that he had a girlfriend, someone he'd met at home over the Easter break.

The embarrassment. How foolish she felt. Of course, he had a girlfriend. He would do, wouldn't he?

She mumbled an apology. Hot tears pricked her eyes and, in her rush to leave his room before they began to trickle down her cheeks, she collided with his bookcase. Thomas called after her, said something kind. He was so very nice.

Other people got over their disappointments in love and

went on to meet new people and love again. Charlotte stuck to herself. Not that there was anything wrong with that. She was quite happy by herself. Nonetheless, she hoped Nyoman would come by tomorrow. She'd like to spend more time with him. And she had to admit that she'd like him to kiss her again, to hold her in his arms.

Shortly after breakfast, the car the hotel had arranged for Eleanor arrived to take her to Denpasar airport.

'Be good,' Eleanor winked and gave a regal wave as the car pulled away.

Worried that she would miss him, Charlotte did not stray far from Coral Garden Villas all morning. It was afternoon before Nyoman arrived on the beach. He took her to Jemeluk to see the traditional salt making there.

Charlotte bought a bag of salt from a little old lady. Nyoman bought some papaya for them to share and then took her to see rice terraces. Charlotte didn't mention that she had already seen many rice terraces near Ubud and in Sideman nor that she thought she had passed these same rice terraces on the drive to Amed. They were beautiful and she enjoyed seeing them again in any case.

It started to rain. Nyoman parked the scooter and they ran to shelter under the roof of a raised platform. Charlotte had seen lots of these platforms across the island. They seemed to exist for just this type of occasion. Nyoman took her hand and helped her up. They sat together side by side, looking out at the rain. This was romance. This was what she had read about, what she had seen in films. She thought she liked it.

MONDAY, MARCH 14TH
(THREE DAYS AFTER THE EARTHQUAKE)

Though the trains were not running at full capacity, Charlotte managed to make it to work on time on Monday. The office was quieter than usual. Hayashi san was stranded in New York. There for a business trip, he could not return as scheduled. All the flights to Tokyo had been cancelled. Jen had fled to Singapore, Mayuko to Kyoto. Charlotte thought Mayuko and Jen were overreacting. But you couldn't be certain. Her father had rung before she left for work, telling her about a banker son of a friend of his who had left Tokyo for Hong Kong at the weekend. 'Embassy advice apparently,' her father had said. Charlotte had received an email from the embassy, presumably the same email this banker had received. It had not suggested that long term residents of Tokyo should pack their bags and catch the next flight out of the city. It had simply advised against unnecessary travel to Tohoku and Tokyo. She and the international banker had clearly interpreted the embassy's advice differently.

The deputy director convened a meeting. 'The past couple of days have been very trying for everyone,' their boss began. 'Our thoughts are with all of those in the affected area. Over the next few days, we could begin to think about ways in which we could assist the relief effort. Of course, I'm not suggesting that we go to Tohoku. We would only be making a nuisance of ourselves. But we could perhaps collect donations, not just of money, but of blankets and non-perishable foodstuffs.'

Charlotte had blankets and futons to spare. What else

might the survivors need? Toiletries possibly. To get the supplies to the stricken areas, that would be the difficult part.

'Now the first order of business is to tell you that our spring conference in Yokohama is cancelled. Under the circumstances and considering the projected energy shortages, it would be impossible. I'm sure I can trust you Charlotte to draw up notices to that effect and make sure they are sent to the relevant parties.'

Charlotte nodded her assent.

Nyoman had been kind, sensitive to her feelings. They had lay together on her bed at Coral Villas. For a while all they did was lie there, their hands and shoulders touching. Then Nyoman began to stroke her hair, her neck, her shoulders, and to plant kisses on her forehead, throat and mouth. She had returned his kisses and caresses quite freely.

She had been so nervous about the whole sex thing. Would it be very painful? Would there be a lot of blood? Would she be able to do it right? Would she be capable of giving pleasure? Or would it all just be horribly uncomfortable?

'The conference in Beijing in May will go ahead as planned,' Griffiths was saying. 'We can start working towards that. We are quite short staffed here today as you may have noticed. Now, I understand people's worries and fears. But I feel… and I spoke to Jones at the embassy only this morning, and Jones assured me that Tokyo is perfectly safe.'

When she had agreed to let Nyoman come to her room, she had fully intended to have sex with him. But when he produced a condom from his pocket, the sight of it reminded her of her lack of experience. In theory, she knew what to do with a condom, but not in practice. She blurted out that she'd never done this before.

'Me neither,' he'd said.

Charlotte hadn't believed him. She suspected she was one of a long line of foreign women Nyoman had seduced. She didn't want to believe him either. At least one of them should have some experience. At least one of them should know what they were doing. When pressed, he told her there had been one woman before her. A local girl.

'Long time ago,' he said.

'I firmly believe,' Griffiths continued, 'that the best that we can do is to go about business as usual, keep the wheels turning, so to speak. In order to do that, it is very important to have a core staff here to hold the fort. Any questions? Right. The meeting is adjourned. I will let you get on with your work. I will speak to Jones at the embassy again this afternoon. I will keep you all posted on any further developments.'

Charlotte returned to her computer, where she tried to compose notices about the cancellation in both English and Japanese. She couldn't concentrate.

Nyoman putting on the condom, then slowly entering her. Charlotte closed her eyes, and winced, expecting pain. It did hurt, but not too much. He'd asked her if she was okay. She nodded and said yes, then opened her eyes to see him looking at her. She breathed out. He started to move inside her. There was an uncomfortable stretching sensation. It made her catch her breath. Nyoman noticed. He slowed. Charlotte knew if she tensed, it would hurt more, so she tried to relax. That seemed to work. She relaxed some more. Soon she was moving with him. He shuddered when he came.

He asked her if she had come. She didn't know. She had felt some pleasant sensations, but she wasn't sure if she had reached orgasm, exactly. She didn't care. She'd done it. She'd had sex. And it had been fine. Nyoman seemed satisfied. That was enough. More than enough, it was wonderful. Wonderful, and unexpected, and amazing, really.

From the corner of her eye, Charlotte saw her boss emerge from his office, adjust his overcoat and leave the premises. During the meeting, when he'd said that bit about holding the fort, she thought he had looked pointedly in her direction. She would not be at all surprised if he planned to leave the department in her charge and flee home to Yorkshire. He would use his wife and children to justify his action. And the world would accept his excuse. The life of one who had accumulated offspring and a spouse was deemed more precious than that of one who had remained single. It wasn't fair. Charlotte's life was precious too. But if she believed her life was precious, then why was she spending so much of that life in front of this computer screen? She would much prefer to be in Bali.

Nyoman had left her room before sunrise. She'd wondered if she would ever see him again.

She did. He came back after breakfast to say good-bye. He helped her pack. Then pulled the shutters closed so they could have sex again. And although it still felt strange, this time Charlotte quite liked it.

He asked her for a keepsake, something to remember her by. She fished a pearl necklace from her suitcase. She had bought it at the Ubud market days before. Together they put it around his neck. Then they embraced one last time. She couldn't delay; a car was waiting to take her to the airport.

He'd claimed that he wasn't a playboy. He'd told her that he really liked her. Maybe, just maybe, those words were true. He didn't have an email address or a phone number to give her, but he'd said that he hoped she would return to Bali one day, return to see him. Charlotte was beginning to think that maybe she should. She picked up the phone on her desk. It was against the rules to use the company phones for personal calls, but Charlotte was tired of keeping rules. She called HIS travel agency. There were no direct flights available to Denpasar. They could offer her a flight via Singapore. It was expensive flying at such short notice. But Charlotte had rainy day savings, and if this crisis – an earthquake, a tsunami and a nuclear meltdown – didn't qualify as a rainy day, she didn't know what did.

Her parents were pleased about her decision to temporarily vacate Tokyo. They thought it wise.

Her Aunt Eleanor was all agog about her trip to Bali. 'Are you going to meet that lovely young man?' she asked.

'I don't know,' Charlotte replied.

'What was his name?'

'Nyoman.'

'Nyoman, that's right. Have you and Nyoman stayed in touch?'

'Erm no. He didn't have an email address.'

'Didn't he? I suppose lots of people over there don't have internet access. But shall you go to Amed?'

'Probably.' The Skype connection started to get fuzzy. Charlotte felt relieved. She didn't want to talk to her Aunt about Nyoman and her hopes to meet him again. She had never told her Aunt about what had happened with Nyoman, although her Aunt had been dying to find out.

'Why do you have to be so coy?' Eleanor had demanded shortly after their Bali holiday.

Charlotte couldn't answer the question. Her Aunt loved hearing tales of romance. Why should Charlotte deny her? But the very thought of discussing what had transpired between she and Nyoman filled her with embarrassment.

She had never been able to talk about these kinds of things, not in relation to herself at any rate. There had been so little

of it in her life anyway, there wasn't usually anything to report. She listened to Katherine complain about her husband;
to Fumiko going into raptures about Takeshi, to Sinéad's accounts of the dates she occasionally went on. But she had
not told any of them about Nyoman. It wasn't so much that
she feared they would think her gullible for succumbing to
the charms of a Balinese gigolo, or sleazy for having a fling
with the beach boy, they were open minded sorts. It was
simply that reticence was a habit she couldn't seem to break.

THE QUEST

During her stopover at the airport in Singapore, Charlotte went to the pharmacy and stocked up on condoms. If she was going to have a sex life, it was going to be a responsible sex life. The pharmacy shelves displayed a perplexing variety: ribbed, extra fine, super safe, skin sensation. Which was best? What would Nyoman prefer? Which would she prefer? Would it make any difference? Eventually she decided on one large box of what seemed to be normal or regular condoms and one small box each of every other available type.

Before boarding her flight, Charlotte tucked her purchases away in her carry-on bag. She might never use them. She might not be able to find Nyoman. She had no phone number for him. He didn't have a phone. No email address either. And if he had a postal address, he hadn't told her what it was.

Nyoman's boat was moored on Lipah beach, one of the longer and busier beaches on the Amed coast. Not a big place. It was not difficult to imagine bumping into Nyoman there. But it was not so terribly small that they might not miss each other.

In mid-air, she could not turn back. She might as well continue with her quest. She hadn't booked anywhere to stay. She didn't think it would be necessary to make a reservation in advance, not in March. In any case, prices negotiated in person were often better than those offered online. She didn't plan to stay in Coral Villas again. She would prefer something more modest. She'd had the entire villa to herself on the last night, after Eleanor had left. Nyoman had walked from her bedroom to Eleanor's, taking in the size, the solidity, the luxury.

'It's bigger than my apartment in Tokyo,' she'd told him. She didn't think he'd registered that information.

She picked up her Lonely Planet and looked through the accommodations listed for the Amed area. Hidden Paradise sounded nice. Right on the beach, it was locally owned and only $10 a night.

Charlotte woke when the taxi turned down the bumpy lane which led to Hidden Paradise. It was dark and quiet. And for a moment, she worried that she had made a mistake coming there so late in the evening. Then a smiling young man came out to greet them. He said his name was Koming and that they had a vacancy. He escorted her down a little path to the edge of the sands where he turned left. They walked past a row of small huts, stopping at the last one.

Three steps up to a narrow veranda. A wicker chair at one side of the central door, a hammock hanging on the other. Koming unlocked the door and turned on the light. The bare bulb flickered uncertainly and gave out a dim glow. The hut had a timber frame, and walls made of bamboo matting. There was a bed and a bedside locker. Several hooks and clothes hangers were attached to the wooden beam on one wall. A door at the back led to the bathroom. A toilet, a shower, a barrel of water. Open to the sky, but with high bamboo walls to protect the modesty of whoever was using the facilities.

'Good?' Koming asked.

'Perfect,' Charlotte said. Basic, somewhat spartan, it was exactly what she desired.

In bed, she could hear the waves. They reminded her of the tsunami, the lives it had taken. It occurred to her that it may have been a mistake to choose to stay so close to the sea. There were hotels on the hillside of the road. They would be safer. She wondered if the Balinese traditionally built right on the shore like this. She doubted it. She suspected that they lived in the hills, as Nyoman did.

There was a pot of tea waiting for her on her veranda when she awoke in the morning. She poured herself a cup and sipped it, sitting on the wicker chair, looking out to sea. The sea might be capable of terrible destruction, but it could soothe and calm also. It was lovely here.

She would have breakfast and then walk down to Lipah beach. That was where she was most likely to find Nyoman. She had met him there by chance the first time around. Perhaps chance would allow her to meet him there again.

Perhaps not. This was a fool's errand. Crazy to come all the way to try to find a man she barely knew. A man who might not want to be found, not by her. But he had said he hoped she would come back. He may have meant it. And she had flown three thousand miles to be here, she should at least try to find him.

She could ask about him. The Balinese were so friendly. But she only knew his first name. That wouldn't help much. Depending on their birth order, everyone in Bali's largest caste was named either Wayan, Madé, Nyoman or Ketut. Nyoman was therefore a very common name. Not quite so commonplace as Wayan or Madé, but still very, very common.

If only she had a photo... She did have a photo on her laptop. But what was she going to do? Produce the photo and ask, do you know this man? Where can I find him? Ridiculous! She was not a detective. She would have to rely on chance. And if chance favoured her, what then? Nyoman might have moved on to the next tourist.

The windy road that led downhill from Hidden Paradise was, for several hundred metres, void of any sign of human habitation. Then came a restaurant on the left, further along a hotel. After a sharp bend, a stream flowed over the road and into the sea. Charlotte got her feet wet crossing it.

She had thought it would be a twenty-minute walk, but after thirty minutes on the road she had not caught sight of Lipah beach yet. The only familiar landmark so far was the lookout post where Nyoman had taken her to see the sunset.

A woman walked by, wearing a sarong carrying a basket on her head, so intent on her own business, she didn't seem to see the gawky foreigner. Next came an old lady. She smiled at Charlotte, a toothless grin. Some houses and warungs now. No cars, but there were scooters aplenty. Children as young as ten commandeered them, swerving to avoid the chickens that wandered freely along the road. There were other chickens in wicker cages. Or were they cockerels? Perhaps these caged fowl were for cockfighting. Cockfighting was popular in Bali, she knew.

Eventually, after about an hour, she arrived at the Divers Rest, at the south end of Lipah Beach. A path at the side of the hotel led down to the strand. A small stall there advertised snorkelling equipment to rent. Several young men hung out next to it.

'You want to snorkel?' one young man asked.

'It's a good day. Water very clear,' said another.

'No, thank you,' Charlotte said and walked on. It occurred to her that she should ask them about Nyoman. They might know him. Yes, they would surely know him. This was his beach. But she felt shy. They would be curious. They would laugh. She kept walking.

Should she turn back and ask them? No, the moment had passed. To walk all the way back, all of them looking at her, speculating. That would be excruciating.

She passed many boats. Unless he was out fishing, or had taken some tourists snorkelling, one of those boats was

Nyoman's. If she could find his jukung, she could leave a note there for him. But there were so many boats. His was white, with brightly coloured red, yellow and blue stripes, but so were most of the others. If it had a name, she couldn't remember it. If she studied her holiday photos, maybe she would be able to make out some distinguishing feature on Nyoman's jukung that would help her identify it. She could come down again later this evening or tomorrow morning.

She passed the beach entrance to Coral Villas, where she and Eleanor had stayed. It was at the little wooden gate, where she had first met Nyoman, at dusk, on her first evening in Amed, and where he had met them to take them snorkelling the next day.

She longed for him to appear here on this beach now, as he had done in September. No difficulties, no embarrassments, just Nyoman standing there. Probably too much to hope for.

Charlotte came to the end of the beach. To re-join the road, she scrambled up a rocky outcrop, she had come this way with Nyoman. He had helped her, pointing out places for her to put her feet, and taking her hand to help her up. She had appreciated his care and attention. But it was not steep, nor difficult to climb.

It was uphill, most of the way back to Hidden Paradise. And it was getting hot. Thirsty, she bought a bottle of water at a roadside stall and resumed her walk. If she never found Nyoman, it was not the end of the world. She could travel around Bali. She had seen so little of it, having spent only six days here in September. Yet it would be such a shame, not to see him again, not to know. She would go back and ask those guys renting the snorkelling equipment. Surely one of them would know him.

They might think her a crazy, lovelorn Western woman. They might laugh at her expense. She didn't care. She had to find him.

She turned around to make her way back to the beach. A scooter passed by, carrying an entire family of five. She heard another and looked up in the hope that the rider might be Nyoman. The scooter slowed as it passed, her eyes met the rider's. They weren't Nyoman's eyes, but there was recognition in them, nonetheless. The scooter came to a stop just behind Charlotte. It was the guy who had rented them their snorkels and fins. Wayan Joe, she thought his name was. He had fetched the lifejacket that Eleanor had insisted on.

Wayan Joe held out his hand for Charlotte to shake. 'You came back,' he said.

'Yes.' Charlotte nodded.

'You see Nyoman?'

'Not yet. Do you know where he is?'

Wayan's forehead creased in thought. 'No. But I tell him you came.'

'Thank you.' Charlotte sighed in relief.

'Where are you going?'

'To Hidden Paradise. That's where I'm staying.'

'Ah, Paradise. I take you,' he said.

Charlotte said she'd rather walk.

'Too far,' Wayan insisted.

In the heat, she thought it probably was too far to walk. She hopped on behind him. She enjoyed the cooling breeze as they whizzed along.

Wayan dropped her at the entrance. 'I tell Nyoman. Hidden Paradise,' he said.

She thanked him.

'No problem,' he said, and sped away.

Charlotte smiled broadly. How easy it had been in the end. She had not seen Nyoman yet. But, she would. Wayan would tell him. He would come.

She managed only a couple of mouthfuls of her nasi campur at lunchtime. It was not like her. She normally had such a good appetite.

'Too spicy?' the waiter asked when he came to take away her plate. 'Balinese food too spicy for you?'

'No. It's delicious.' Charlotte tried to reassure her host. 'I seem to have lost my appetite. Maybe because of the long journey.'

'Ah, time lag' he said.

Charlotte smiled. Fumiko always called jet lag, time lag too.

After her failed attempt at lunch, Charlotte sat on the sand with her novel, Middlemarch. Her book club would have been meeting this evening to discuss this book, if it hadn't been for the earthquake. She wondered where her friends were now. Had Sinéad left Tokyo? Was Katherine still stuck in Sendai? What about Lauren and the kids? She opened the book, but instead of reading the words, she stared at the pages.

A fast boat passed. She wondered if it was the Gilli Star, the boat that had taken herself and Eleanor to Gilli Tarawan. It was on the roof of the Gilli Star that Nyoman had first kissed her six months before. He had made her feel wanted, desired and desirable. But had it meant anything to him?

By sunset, Nyoman had not come. Charlotte returned to her hut. The light inside was not strong enough to read by, and she was tired too. She would sleep. In Tokyo, since the earthquake, she had lain awake at night. She had a lot of sleep to catch up on.

A gentle knock woke her sometime later. There it was again. Could it be Nyoman? She got out of bed. She looked down at herself and smoothed her pyjamas. She thought she looked respectable. She unlocked the door.

Nyoman had walked a few steps away, but on hearing the

door open, he turned around. Their eyes met. He smiled. His smiled washed away her doubts and anxieties. She knew now that she was welcome, that he was glad she'd come. Around his neck he still wore the pearls she had given him last September.

He took her hand and they walked together along the beach, away from the huts. Most were in darkness now, but there were lights coming from the restaurant. He told her he had been worried about her. He had heard news of the earthquake, had seen images of the tsunami. He wanted to know if she was all right.

She assured him that she was fine.

And her family? Her home? Her friends?

Her home had not been washed away, nor had it suffered any structural damage. Her family was in England, so they were fine. She had not lost any friends, not that she knew of.

'Your eyes,' he said. 'Tired, sad.' He reached out and with the utmost gentleness touched the skin under her eyes. 'Here,' he said. 'Black.'

But despite her tired, baggy eyes, she had not been affected. Not really. It was more than a decade since she had worked in Higashimatsushima. She was no longer in touch with anyone from that town. It had been completely inundated by the tsunami, so it seemed likely that some of the people Charlotte had known there had died. And the idea of once familiar faces now gone forever made her sad. She looked down at the sand and concentrated on digging her big toe into the sand. Nyoman squeezed her hand. Charlotte thought that she might start to blubber if he showed any more sympathy or understanding. She was not worthy.

'And Eleno. She is fine?' Nyoman asked.

'Yes, Eleanor is fine.'

She come to Bali too?'

'No,' Charlotte said. 'I came alone this time.'

Nyoman was rubbing her middle finger gently between his thumb and forefinger. It felt nice. Soothing.

'I prayed for you to come,' he said.

'You did?'

He nodded. 'That is why you come,' he said.

My goodness. She was the answer to his prayers. Imagine that.

It was late. Nyoman needed to be getting home. He told her he would come again tomorrow. 'Dream of me,' he said, as he bade her goodnight.

BEACH LIFE

She was sitting on the beach, looking out to sea, when he came the next day. He sat down beside her. Close beside her. Whenever either of them made the slightest movement, their shoulders and upper arms brushed against each other. She reached for his fingers in the sand. Playfully, he pulled them away. When her hand was once again at rest, he walked his fingers across the sand and wrapped them around her thumb. She laughed. And when he let go, she made a move again to capture his fingers. It was a childish game. A game of the kind she had seen couples play at restaurant tables or while waiting for a train. She had wondered what enjoyment these people could possibly derive from such silliness. And now here she was, taking delight in snatching at his hand. The sea, the sand, the sunshine, Nyoman by her side. Bliss.

She felt extremely grateful for her good fortune. A toaster, some glasses, plates and cups were all she had lost in the earthquake. Tokyo had been spared the destruction that had laid waste to Tohoku. She really should be there now, helping those less fortunate than she. But no, aid agencies had warned against lay people traveling to the affected area. Well-meaning do-gooders could, they said, prove more of a nuisance than a help at this point in time. Maybe the best thing she could do for now was to try to cherish each moment of the life she had to live, thereby honouring all those victims of the tsunami for whom moments were no more. She bit her lip and clasped Nyoman's hand tightly.

On his scooter, they zipped along, her hands on his waist, the breeze making a halo of her bushy hair. When they had rounded several bends, the volcano Mount Agung rose before them to the west, to the east, the sun glinted on the sea.

On Lipah Beach, Nyoman's friends were sheltering from the midday sun under the thatched roof of a raised wooden platform. He introduced Nnengah, a wide eyed, skinny youth, and Ketut, a stocky, swarthy man, missing most of his front teeth. Ketut looked old enough to be Nnengah's father. But they seemed just to be friends. They made room for Nyoman and Charlotte. She felt conscious of her long legs and the bulk of her body. The Balinese were so small and neat, even smaller, she thought, than the Japanese. Nyoman and his friends chatted and joked in Balinese, but with smiles, friendly nods, and occasional asides in English, they managed to make Charlotte feel welcome.

A boy of about ten was floating a miniature jukung on the waves. He made these miniatures himself and tried to sell them to the tourists. Nyoman had done the same thing in his youth, he told Charlotte.

They went for a swim in the tepid water. Nyoman didn't stay in long. He found it cold. Charlotte floated on her back and squinted up at the sun. When she returned from her swim, Wayan Joe had joined the group. 'Welcome to our paradise,' he said.

In the cool of the evening, Charlotte and Nyoman walked to the end of the beach. They clambered up the rocky outcrop, Nyoman offering her his hand whenever necessary. They walked along the road awhile, before scrambling down and over another rocky bluff to a beach that Charlotte hadn't known was there.

They sat there as the sun went down behind them, holding hands and kissing. The stars were coming out when Nyoman eased Charlotte back onto the sand. She sensed he wanted to make love. She did too, but she would prefer to return to her room.

'Let's go back to Hidden Paradise,' she said.

'Is good here,' he said.

'But what if somebody comes?' Charlotte said.

'No-one is coming here. It is secret. Secret beach.'

It couldn't be entirely secret. Some jukungs were moored there. But there was no sign of any fishermen. And the beach was not so easy to get to, so it was unlikely that they would be spotted by holiday makers enjoying a moonlit stroll. Still she hesitated.

Nyoman explained that he didn't know the owners of Hidden Paradise, and that they would probably object if he came to her room there. She had never had sex outside before. Of course, she had hardly had sex anywhere before. All the more reason to try it now perhaps. She relaxed back on the sand and pulled Nyoman down to her.

They lay together afterwards, looking at the stars. She thought she could look at this night sky for years and not be bored by it. The stars were not visible in the Tokyo sky.

When the time came to leave, Nyoman helped her up and brushed the sand from her clothes and from her skin. He pushed her hair behind her ears and playfully pinched her nose. He took her back to Hidden Paradise and dropped her at the gate.

Charlotte felt pleased as she readied herself for sleep, glad to have made love in the outdoors, on the beach. It made her feel so much more sexually experienced than she had been just the day before.

By sunset the next day, she had had sex outdoors a second time. On this occasion in daylight, though well hidden by trees and scrub. Thank goodness for Bali's dense foliage.

Nyoman dropped her at Barong café and hung around

outside, chatting with other locals, while Charlotte found a table, opened her laptop and made use of the café's free Wi-Fi.

The survivors in Ishinomaki held placards, names of loved ones they were hoping to find, printed on them. The reporter spoke of the cold weather, the risks it posed for the frail and elderly survivors. Charlotte felt guilt gnawing at the inside of her stomach. All the blankets and duvets in her Tokyo apartment, and no-one using them. But Fumiko had a key. She emailed Fumiko and asked her if she wouldn't mind taking all the spare bedding to the nearest donation centre.

The death toll had reached nineteen thousand. The figure made Charlotte's eyes water.

There were rolling blackouts in Tokyo. Charlotte's freezer compartment was small, but its thawing would make a puddle on her floor. And its contents would be ruined. She hated the thought of the food going to waste. Perhaps Fumiko wouldn't mind emptying her fridge, and unplugging it

Nineteen thousand people dead, and she was worried about the contents of her fridge. But then, what could she do about the nineteen thousand dead?

She scanned the reports about the Fukushima Dai-Ichi Nuclear power plant. There was much discussion about what constituted safe levels of radiation. The terms mili-sieverts and micro-sieverts were bandied about. These systems of measurement were something Charlotte would have to grapple with when she returned to Tokyo.

An email from Tanaka san reported that all but one of the British Council's British staff had fled Tokyo. Good news for Charlotte. She was unlikely to get into trouble for her absence when so many of her colleagues had gone AWOL.

Tanaka san wrote too of rumours that Tokyo would be evacuated. Scaremongering, Charlotte presumed.

Nyoman chatted with a friend outside while Charlotte

was online. When she was almost ready to go, he came in and sat down next to her.

'Maybe you show me how to use one day,' he said.

'Of course,' she said.

He was not computer literate. His home on the hill was accessible only on foot. A steep forty-minute walk away, it had no electricity, and in the dry months water had to be carried up to it. Their lives were so different. She had graduated from Cambridge with a first-class honour's degree. He had left school at twelve, his family no longer able to pay for his uniform. Was it crazy, this attempt at a relationship?

There was a Japanese woman living in Jemeluk. She was married to a Balinese man. They ran a small hotel together. Nyoman had pointed it out to her. And there was a French woman living with her Balinese partner in Aas. It was not impossible. And Nyoman was smart, if uneducated. He had learned his English on the beach and had picked up a little French too. Charlotte could never have learned Japanese without the help of textbooks and teachers.

Her mother would be appalled. Charlotte had already disappointed the woman by remaining single into her late thirties. But an unsuitable husband would for Mrs. Henderson be worse than no husband at all. And Nyoman would most definitely be deemed unsuitable.

THE TEMPLE OF A THOUSAND STEPS

'There is snow in Japan?' Nyoman asked.

'Yes, in the mountains there's lots of snow.'

They were sitting at the wooden platform which served as a restaurant at Hillside Villas, where Charlotte was now staying. Her new abode was closer to Lipah Beach where Nyoman's boat was moored. Moving had been his idea. Putu, the owner, was a friend of Nyoman's and he had offered Charlotte the room at a very reasonable price. There were five two-story villas here, only three of which were complete. The only other guest was Kate, a Canadian woman in her early forties, who was at present floating on her back in the pool.

'I like to go Japan, stick my head in snow,' Nyoman said.

Charlotte smiled. Maybe he could come to Tokyo, once things had got back to norma there. He could get a job in manufacturing, possibly, or in the hospitality sector.

She flipped through the pages of the *Lonely Planet*. According to her guidebook, one of Bali's most important and most beautiful temples, Puru Lempuyang Luhur, the temple of one thousand steps, was just half an hour drive from here. She thought maybe she and Nyoman could go there one day on his scooter.

'The road dangerous,' he said. 'For bike, no good.'

When he saw the disappointment in her face, he said, 'Putu take you. Car, no problem.'

Putu was willing and the price he charged seemed reasonable.

'You should come too,' Charlotte said.

'I fishing,' he said.

Couldn't he take a day off from fishing? He'd told her fishing wasn't good at this time of year. But perhaps it was wrong to expect him to drop everything for her. She had shown up there unannounced after all and he had already brought her to see temple ruins at the edge of a cliff and to a waterfall where a crowd of small boys was splashing midstream, their brown skin shining in the sun as they leapt from rock to rock. He had taken her to a local primary school where children in white shirts, maroon skirts and shorts smiled and waved for her camera.

It seemed wasteful to hire a car just for herself. She would ask Kate if she would like to come. She liked the friendly Canadian woman. They had chatted over breakfast that morning and the previous day too. They had exchanged books (Middlemarch for *Room* by Emma Donoghue) and advice about where to go for free Wi-Fi.

The road winded its way upwards through rice terraces and jungle. It was steep, its bends precarious. Charlotte understood now Nyoman's reluctance to take her here by bike.

On the slopes of Mount Lempuyang were seven temples connected by not one thousand, but one thousand seven hundred steps. Putu advised them to hire a guide lest they get lost on the jungle trails. They asked how much a guide cost. Maybe 200,000 rupiah, he told them, or if they bargained well, 150,000. The women agreed that hiring a guide was a good way to contribute to the local economy and between the two of them it was affordable.

Their guide was a lanky, long limbed middle-aged fellow with a wide goofy grin. Brim full of fidgety nervous energy, he told them his name was Gusti. According to Kate's whispered aside, 'Gusti' meant Prince. Charlotte wondered if he really was a prince, if his branch of the Balinese royal family could have descended so far in the world that this prince had to hire himself out as a guide. He did look smart in his batik sarong, white jacket and matching headdress, but not quite princely.

Charlotte and Kate were also wearing sarongs. Sarongs were obligatory when entering temples. Kate's was indigo; with it she wore a simple brown t-shirt. Charlotte wore an orange batik; she had bought in Ubud last September. Wanting to be respectful for this temple visit, she had matched it with a white blouse. For a sash she had tied a cotton scarf around her waist. She would have loved one of the ornate, lacy blouses that the Balinese women wore with their temple sarongs, but sadly they didn't come in her size.

'You look good, very nice,' Gusti said to Charlotte. 'This sarong good.'

Charlotte was delighted by the compliment. She didn't often receive compliments on her outfits. She quite liked her clothes herself. But because she wasn't interested in trends, they weren't always fashionable. And because she was too tall, and didn't have much of a waist, they didn't look as good on her as they might on others.

'What about me?' Kate demanded, feigning anger. 'Don't I look good?'

'Yes, yes,' Gusti said. 'Very good. Two beautiful ladies.'

Kate, Charlotte thought, was one of those people who always looked good. Even that morning, in her pyjamas, her hair tousled, begging Jalan for her first morning coffee, Kate had looked quite presentable. Small in stature, with dark, shoulder length hair and olive toned skin, she blended in so much better than Charlotte did.

A German couple, in shorts and trainers, hired sarongs at the information booth and wrapped them clumsily around their waists. Gusti shook his head in smiling disapproval, pleased that the tourists in his charge were better turned out.

The Germans took a photo of the map at the entrance to the temple complex and marched off in a business-like manner. Gusti launched into his tour guide spiel. He told them that temples were the meeting places for humans and Gods, and also the resting places for Gods during their time on earth. He said that Puru Lempuyang Lehur was one of the island's nine directional temples. It protected Bali from evil spirits.

The first temple was a mere five-minute walk from the car park. At the wide staircase leading up to its entrance Gusti put his arm around Charlotte's shoulder to pose for Kate's photograph.

Kate raised her eyebrows. 'Wait 'til I tell Nyoman!'

Charlotte giggled. Gusti seemed to have taken quite a shine to her.

The temple was large and impressive, with an outer courtyard, a middle courtyard and an inner courtyard. The central stairs leading from the middle courtyard to the inner courtyard, Gusti explained, could only be used by the priests. Everyone else must take the stairway to the left or the right. Inside were stone pavilions and multi-tiered shrines, statues of Hindu Gods and Goddesses.

The clouds remained low over the forest and the air was cool, refreshing after the heat of the coast. The Balinese made the pilgrimage in family groups, the women carrying baskets on their heads, some laden with offerings for the Gods, others with snacks for themselves. Besides the German couple they had met in the car park, they didn't see any other foreigners, presumably the temple was too remote to attract many tourists.

Gusti told them that holy water was the reason the Balinese came here. He spoke animatedly about the holy water. He told them that it came from inside the bamboo at the uppermost temple. Charlotte didn't quite understand.

'The water is inside the bamboo?' she asked.

'Yes, yes. Water grows inside bamboo. Holy, very, holy,' Gusti said.

There were stalls selling snacks and beverages here and there along the way. At one, Kate bought a bag of banana chips and Charlotte a slice of watermelon. Kate had just opened her chips, when a monkey, who had been watching from behind a tree, ran up and grabbed it from her hands. Gusti and Kate chased the naughty monkey. Charlotte would have joined them, but she was laughing too hard. In any case she needed both her hands to hold her watermelon. The monkey escaped up a tree. Kate bought herself another bag of chips. Gusti stood guard while she ate them.

'It's a scam,' she joked. 'The monkey's in league with the stallholder.'

The temples decreased in size as they ascended, and the path grew increasingly uneven and slippery. Enchanted by the mist amongst the trees, they took their time, in typical Balinese fashion.

At one of the temples a family was receiving a blessing from a priest. Gusti said that they could receive a blessing too. He procured offerings for them. These They placed at a shrine. Then they knelt behind the family. In a whisper, Gusti told them that they should meditate. The priest offered prayers and incantations, before sprinkling the entire group with holy water. Whether or not this was the water which 'grew' inside the bamboo, Charlotte didn't know. The priest went in turn to each individual pilgrim and stuck several grains of coloured rice to their forehead. Charlotte didn't consider herself to be particularly spiritual, but the ceremony made her feel blessed indeed.

The fog lifted as they neared the summit. Through the ornately carved stone temple gates built on each side of the path, the Volcano Mount Augung loomed. All three stood awestruck for a moment. From Amed they had seen Mount

Augung in the distance. Seen through these stone gates, however, the volcano looked particularly majestic. Clouds obscured the crater unfortunately. Hoping the wind would disperse the clouds, Kate and Charlotte stood poised, cameras at the ready. They didn't have to wait long. As soon as they'd taken their shots though, more cloud drifted in and again obscured the view.

The descent was almost as slow as the ascent. The path was wet in places and there were no handrails. They had to take care not to slip. They arrived back at the car park, their legs tired and shaky, four and a half hours after they had left. A Balinese group boarded the back of a truck which was waiting for them. Putu appeared and started up the car. Charlotte had enjoyed the touristy day with a fellow westerner.

Later they had dinner together at Warung Ayu on Lipah beach. They noticed Wayan Joe sitting at a table with some friends. He came over to say hello to them.

'You get blessing,' he said, referring to the grains of rice still stuck to their foreheads.

'Yes,' Charlotte said. 'We went to Lempuyang Temple.'

He grimaced. 'Many, many steps. You like?'

'It was nice, but it could do with an escalator,' Kate said.

'Escalator?'

'You know, moving stairs.'

'Moving stairs...' Wayan laughed. 'Yes, moving stairs is good for Puru Lempuyang.'

He went back to the table where he had been playing the bongos. The waiter, when not busy serving customers, sang and played guitar.

'This place reminds me of my ex's place,' Kate said.

'In Canada?'

'No, in Lovinia, in North Bali.'

'A Balinese ex?

'Yes.'

Kate proceeded to tell Charlotte about the Balinese boy she had met the previous summer. She had come on holiday to Indonesia, and in Lovinia, in the North of Bali, she had met a man named Gedé. Gedé owned a little warung on a headland, with a great ocean view. A lively little place. In the evening, his friends would come and sing and play the guitar and the bongos. Gedé was charming and very good looking, with shoulder length hair, which he usually wore in a ponytail. His body was slender, yet strong and muscular. Kate had really fallen for him. He seemed to feel the same way about her. She'd had plans to visit Java, but she scrapped them and decided to spend the remaining days of her holiday with Gedé.

Back in Vancouver, she'd worked hard all year, taking whatever overtime was offered to her, in order to be able to come back to Bali to see Gedé. She had come back several weeks ago before. But Gedé was not the man she'd thought he was. From the moment of her return, Gedé hassled and harangued Kate, demanding she buy him a new motorbike. Kate was not in the habit of buying extravagant gifts for her lovers. In any case Gedé had a perfectly good bike already. He owned his own small business and was, by Balinese standards, quite well off. And even if she wanted to buy him a bike, she couldn't afford to. She had scrimped and saved all year just for her airfare.

'You know what he would say to me?' Kate asked.

Charlotte shook her head.

'How many men did you have sex with, in Canada? And, did you keep yourself fresh for me?' 'Fresh! As if I was a fish.'

Charlotte blushed. Nyoman had said almost the exact same thing to Charlotte. One day, when they were lying on her bed, he'd said, 'I hope you keep yourself fresh for me in Japan.' Meaning, she assumed, that he hoped she would stay true to him in the six months between her first trip to

Bali and her return visit. She hadn't been in the least offended. For so long, her lack of sexual experience had made her feel odd and undesirable. Nowadays, in much of the world, people were made feel aberrant if they weren't having sex. It was unjust and, for Charlotte, quite upsetting. But to Nyoman she seemed to be all the more appealing for her lack of sexual experience. It was such a relief.

'So, I left him,' Kate was saying. 'I came down to Amed and decided to hang out here until it's time to catch my flight back to Canada.'

'Well, it is a nice place to hang out,' Charlotte said, but then she immediately worried that it was an inappropriate comment, and that she had not been sufficiently sympathetic about that nasty Gedé, and the horrible way he had treated Kate.

'It is,' Kate said. 'But you know, you have to be careful with these Balinese guys... Nyoman seems nice though.'

Charlotte nodded. Nyoman wasn't at all like Gedé. He had never asked her to buy anything for him. In fact, she suspected that part of the reason for his reluctance to come with her to Puru Lempuyang Lehur was because he wouldn't have been able to pay his way.

'He goes out in his fishing boat every morning,' Kate said. 'Then he comes to see you, and then back up the hill to take care of his mother. He seems to have his act together.'

It was true. Her boyfriend was a good, kind, and sensible man.

Lying together in her bed, the curtains drawn, (he came to her bed now that she was staying at Hillside Villas) he guided her head towards his penis. She paused; her mouth poised over its head. She had never done this before. She was willing, but she wasn't sure she would be able to do it right. He nodded encouragement. She took the shaft of his penis in her hand. She thought maybe she should lick it first, so she did, imagining it was a lollypop or an ice cream. Then she took the head of his penis in her mouth and moved her mouth down and back up. She wished she had a manual. There were sure to be instructions on how to do this properly online. She could search the next time she went to the internet café. Mind you, it was a bit public. The staff always chatted with her and looked at her screen. Not the best place perhaps to look up oral sex techniques.

She glanced at his face. He was lying back, relaxed, and presumably enjoying what she was doing. How long was she meant to continue? Was she expected to bring him to climax in this manner, or was this just foreplay? Her jaw was getting tired. She took a break. He reached down and pulled her up towards him. He stroked her hair and her face. He seemed pleased. He reached for a condom. They were slowly making their way through her supply.

He came to her room now, but he never spent the night. He couldn't leave his mother all alone, he said, although, from what Charlotte had understood, his brothers lived in the same compound with their wives and children, so she wouldn't be completely alone. He said too that in Bali couples didn't sleep together before marriage. He was happy to have sex with her but drew the line at their sleeping together. Charlotte found this quite funny, but sweet also. She was touched that he chose to respect her honour.

She walked him to the gate and waved him goodbye.

The evening would be long and dull all alone. All the free time that she had there, had felt luxurious at first, but was now beginning to feel burdensome. During her normal life, when she wasn't too exhausted from hours of overtime, she would bake in the evenings, or sketch, or study mandarin. Recently she had taken up felting. Here the only thing she could do in the evening was read. She and Kate had done a book swap, but once she had finished Kate's book, she wasn't sure what she would do for reading matter. So frustrating, when she thought of all the books that were sitting unread in her Tokyo apartment. All the books she had bought, but not had time to read. Perhaps it was time to return to Tokyo. Unable to relax, Charlotte wandered downstairs.

Kate was sitting by the pool. 'You know there's live music at Wawa Wewe tonight?' She said. 'It's my last night. We should go.'

'Okay' Charlotte said. 'Let's do it.'

The band was playing 'No Woman, No Cry.' The lead singer had long dreadlocks and was clearly modelling himself on Bob Marley. Charlotte felt a little nervous. She didn't usually frequent bars. Kate ordered a Bintang, Charlotte a mango juice. They found a table near the door. A couple in their sixties were swaying together on the dance floor. Some local youths and younger tourists were out dancing too. Charlotte liked reggae. And when Kate suggested they get up and dance, she agreed. She liked dancing, but usually danced only with little Emi chan around Lauren's living room.

On the few occasions Charlotte had been to nightclubs, she got the impression that most of the dancers were more concerned about looking good on the dance floor than they were about enjoying moving to the music. But here at Wawa Wewe it was all about fun. The Bob Marley look alike was singing about waiting in vain. She closed her eyes and let the music seep through her as she moved her body in time. She bumped into someone. Perhaps closing her eyes hadn't been such a good idea. She wasn't sure whom she'd bumped into. It didn't seem to matter. Charlotte sang along with *A Message to you Rudi*, Kate leaned towards her singing 'ah-ah-ah' up at her. Charlotte leaned down singing back at her friend. Kate grabbed her hands, and they jigged around together. Charlotte twirled Kate around under her arm, and then spun her on the spot. They didn't sit down until the band took a break.

Two men joined them at their table. One was called Keysur. The other introduced himself as Madé. She recognised Madé. He had smiled at her on the dance floor. She thought he might be the person she'd bumped against. He was not as muscular or as tall as Nyoman, but he had a kind face and wavy bob-length hair

'You stay in Paradise?' he asked.

'I did,' Charlotte said. 'But I moved to Hillside Villas.'

'Madé told her that he wanted to build accommodation for tourists on his family's land. He was hoping the bank would lend him money. He was thinking about simple wood framed cabins with bamboo mat walls, similar to those at Hidden Paradise. They would be cheaper to build than brick bungalows. He asked Charlotte if she thought tourists would be happy to stay in such simple quarters. Charlotte promised him that they would. She had been very happy with her little room at Hidden Paradise. He invited her to visit the proposed site in the morning. Charlotte accepted his invitation. It would be nice to have something to do. Nyoman rarely came around until the afternoon. She briefly wondered if Nyoman might object to her making plans with another man. But what was there to object to? She was only going to look at a site after all.

Near the roadside there was a grove of trees, palm and breadfruit and others Charlotte could not identify. It was there Madé hoped to build two or three cabins. He showed her the precise spots he imagined they would go. Charlotte thought the location was charming.

Madé's home stood on a rise beyond the trees. His mother was outside, down on her haunches, washing spinach in a bowl. His father was sitting on the front step, surveying his surroundings.

His parents greeted Charlotte with smiles and nods. A teenage girl, Madé's sister or possibly his niece, came and stood in the doorway. Madé's mother said something to her. She went inside and returned minutes later bearing a tray laden with glasses of tea, for which Charlotte was very grateful. She had forgotten her water bottle and her throat was dry.

The house was a small but sturdy structure of bricks and mortar. It was not painted, and Charlotte could not see any furniture through the open door. There were a couple of other similar dwellings behind it. From what Charlotte understood, in Bali the extended family lived in one compound, but each smaller family unit had its own dwelling within it. A sensible, practical way to live, so long as you liked your family. Charlotte never spent more than a couple of days at a time with her own parents, and that was quite enough.

She wondered if Nyoman's home was similar to Madé's. Of course, it would be more isolated, way up on the hill. But otherwise it was probably much the same, several small structures of bricks and mortar.

The mother issued some more instructions to the girl, and this time she came out with a large bowl of popcorn. Charlotte took a handful. Madé, his mother, his father and the girl all watched her closely as she ate. They were all curious to know if she liked the popcorn. They appeared to be under the impression that the snack was unique to Indonesia.

Madé's father asked him some questions. Charlotte thought she was the subject. She heard the word 'England' and they were looking at her when they spoke. She didn't really mind that she couldn't join in the conversation. It felt good, just sitting here with those kind people, sipping her tea and eating her popcorn. Nyoman might someday invite her to his house for tea. She wondered that he hadn't already, but there was time. And perhaps it was better not to rush things.

Through the trees the sun was glittering on the waves. Madé was lucky that his home was close to the sea and he could, with minimal investment, make some money from tourists. Nyoman's home was so far up the hills and, with only a rocky footpath leading to it, no tourist would ever find it.

Poor Nyoman. It was not easy for him to make a living. He hadn't taken many tourists out snorkelling recently, there weren't many around. And he often came back from his fishing trips without having caught a single fish. 'Too many fishermen,' he said. Recently he had been talking about selling his mother's cow in order to make the payment on his motorbike. Charlotte hoped it wouldn't come to that.

When she had finished her tea, Charlotte returned the glass to the tray and nodded a thank you at Madé's mother and at the girl. Madé suggested taking a spin further along the coast. Charlotte was tempted, Madé was pleasant and easy to talk to, but she thought it better to return to Hillside Villas in case Nyoman was waiting for her.

On the pillion on Madé's scooter, she was careful to keep her hands by her side, lest her hands around his waist be misconstrued. He drove more slowly than Nyoman, so she felt safe enough with her hands by her side.

A QUARREL

Two mackerel were all he had caught. Well, at least they would have something for dinner. Still, it was hardly worth his while taking his jukung out at this time of the year.

Ketut strolled down to the waves and helped him heft the outrigger up past the tide line, where they put the boat down. 'Charlotte has another man,' Ketut said gleefully. 'They ride on his bike. She holds him so tight.' He mimicked a woman snuggling up close to her lover.

Nyoman paid no attention to him. Charlotte wouldn't go with other men. Charlotte was shy. Ketut liked to joke. He was jealous. Ketut would never have a European girlfriend. He was too ugly.

Wayan and Komang joined them to help lift the boat back to its mooring space high up on the beach. As soon as they had set it down, Ketut started off again about Charlotte.

'She dancing at Wawa Wewe.' He danced on the sand, pretending to hold a lover close. 'She drinking Bintang, too much Bintang.'

Nonsense. Charlotte didn't like beer. 'Shut up, fool,' he said.

'It's true. Wayan Joe saw her.'

Nyoman turned to Wayan Joe.

Wayan nodded. 'She was there. She danced.'

'Look his face,' Nnengah said. 'Shock.'

'She go with other men?' Nyoman asked Wayan Joe.

Wayan shrugged.

'She was with Madé Suwitera,' Nnengah said, 'on his bike.'

'Madé Suwitera? From Selang?

They all started teasing him now.

'Boo hoo. Poor Nyoman.'

'Madé steal Nyoman's girlfriend.'

'Suwitera make sex with Charlotte.'

'Nyoman crying.'

Nyoman strode away from them. He walked to the end of the beach, clambered up the rocks and onto the road and kept walking until he reached Hillside Villas.

He saw Charlotte sitting on her balcony, brushing her bushy brown hair. She looked so innocent. She had fooled him.

He strode past the restaurant, not stopping to say hello to Putu or Jalan. He rounded the pool and took the steps to her room two at a time. When he burst through the door, Charlotte tried to smile a welcome at him, but her smile could not defuse his anger.

'You go with other men,' he said.

'No, no, I just...'

'Everybody say me you go with other men. You dance with other men.'

'I went to Wawa Wewe with Kate. It was fun. We should go together sometime.'

What was she saying? Acting as if she didn't know what he was talking about. Did she think she could fool him forever? 'You dancing, drinking with other men.'

'I drank mango juice. I was dancing with Kate mostly.'

'You go on a bike with Madé Suwitera. No lie me.'

'He just wanted to show me the site where he plans to build cabins for tourists. That's all. It was nothing.'

'Nothing? I go some place with another girl, it's okay? It's nothing?'

'I don't know. It depends.'

Depends? He didn't understand this word 'depends.' He didn't understand anything. How could she seem so innocent, so trustworthy, and be so deceiving? He couldn't stand this. He couldn't be with her if she was running around with other men, making everybody laugh at him.

'Okay. Go with other men. You are free. It is finished with us. Better for me to be alone.' He turned to move towards the door.

'I don't want other men.' She reached for his arm, to hold him, to make him stay.

He shoved her off. 'I no trust you,' he said.

'I made a mistake. I'm sorry. I shouldn't have gone with Madé Suwitera,' she said, her chest heaving. 'I see that now. I was stupid. I'm sorry.'

Nyoman was pacing the room now. He was so angry. Charlotte, devious woman, was trying to touch him to hold him. He didn't want her hands on him.

'I'm so used to being alone,' she said, 'so used to being single, I don't usually have to think about another person.'

Now she was trying to explain, to make excuses. It was no good. She was no good.

'I'm so sorry,' she said.

Sorry, sorry, what good was sorry? On the beach everyone was laughing at him.

But then she started to cry, messy sticky tears. She blubbered and snuffled. The tears confused him. They made a pain in his chest. He stopped pacing.

'No cry. No cry,' he said.

He sat down on the bed, flummoxed. He thought maybe it was his fault. Yesterday he made her take him in her mouth. She didn't like it.

'It's because what I made you do?' he said, gesturing towards where the sheets were, where they had lain just the other day.

'No, no, it's not that,' she said. 'I wanted to do that.'

But he didn't believe she had wanted to do it. She had been hesitant. He had pressured her. The European girls, they liked to give oral sex, everyone said so. But Charlotte was not like other European girls. Charlotte was modest.

'It's just... I am here every evening on my own,' Charlotte said. 'It's lonely. I have nothing to do. I get bored'

Nyoman nodded. He saw that it was hard for her here all alone, with no family. Nyoman couldn't be with her in the evening. Then, her books were all she had. And Kate was leaving today. Charlotte would be even more alone. He had to try to think of something, a solution to this problem. He frowned. He was still not sure if he should trust her. He rubbed the back of his neck.

Charlotte got some toilet paper from the bathroom. She blew her nose and tried to dry the tears.

'No more cry,' he said.

THE COCKFIGHT

'This is awesome, dude,' Rob said. He turned to Nyoman and showed him the images he had caught on his camera; dolphins cavorting in the distance.

The American had checked into Hillside villas the previous day. Nyoman was taking him to the Japanese wreck and had suggested that Charlotte come along. Things were all right between them again. He seemed to have forgiven her.

Rob wore a baseball cap, shorts and a singlet. He looked large and flabby, next to Nyoman, so lean and muscular.

Charlotte hadn't been on Nyoman's boat since that snorkelling trip with her Aunt Eleanor back in September. She would have liked to go out on the jukung more often. She had imagined the two of them sailing the waves together. She had asked if she could join him when he went fishing. 'Some day,' he had said. She was still waiting. She wondered if the Balinese were superstitious about having women on fishing boats. Many cultures had such beliefs.

Nyoman stayed in the boat while Charlotte and Rob went snorkelling. He said he was tired and that the water was cold. It didn't feel cold to Charlotte, but she was English and had swum in much colder water.

Rob had a good yawn and a stretch and then flopped down on the chair opposite Charlotte. 'This is the life,' he said.

Rob was staying in the room Kate had vacated. Charlotte wondered if Hillside Villas ever had more than two guests at a time. Apparently, July and August were the two busiest months, so maybe then.

Though not especially big for an American, Rob was considerably taller and broader than Charlotte. She wondered what her life might have been, had she gone to America after graduation instead of Japan. In America, she would not be plus size, she would be normal size. Her whole-body image would be different, possibly. Mind you, she'd not been at all body confident when she'd lived in the UK, and English people weren't that much smaller than Americans. Anyway, Japan had appealed to her. It still did; the culture, the society, the way humility was valued. Leaving at a time of crisis, she felt like a traitor. She hoped Japan would be all right. Tanaka san was convinced that Tokyo would soon be evacuated. Charlotte did not believe the evacuation rumours, but if they were true, at least, being here in Bali, she would be one less person to evacuate.

Jalan appeared to take their breakfast orders. 'Banana pancake?' he asked Charlotte.

Charlotte nodded. The breakfast menu was not extensive. Jalan was able to fry eggs and to make banana pancakes. That was it.

'Three of those for me,' Rob said. 'I'm starving. God, I had the best time last night.'

'What did you do?' Charlotte asked.

'Jalan here took me to see the cockfight.'

Charlotte glanced up at Jalan as he placed a cup of tea on the table for her. He was studying English at the university in Amalpura. She had helped him with his homework. He seemed so gentle, so civilized. Not at all the type she had imagined would be a cockfighting fan. But then perhaps cockfighting was so prevalent there that it precluded types. She seemed to remember reading something about Balinese cockfighting in her uni days. A couple of Anthropologists, the Meads possibly, had attended a cockfight, and in doing so they had found a way in to Balinese society.

'Such a privilege to be invited to something so far off the tourist track, you know what I'm saying?'

Charlotte did see what he was saying. Still, it was a blood sport. 'Wasn't it gruesome?' she asked.

'A lot less gruesome than I'd expected. I've been thinking that maybe the cockfight is a means for the men of Bali to channel all their primitive feelings, violent urges and what have you, 'cos Bali sure is one helluva peaceful place."

It certainly was peaceful. Each morning Jalan laid offerings of a woven tray of petals and grains of rice at the foot of the statue of Ganesh. He replaced the offering in the evening. Devotion formed part of the rhythm of life here.

'Seems a bit hard on the rooster though, don't you think?'

'I don't know. I try not to judge.' Jalan was telling me that last year some American tourists protested at the arena. 'That's wrong, man. This is Bali, we're just visitors. We can't be telling the people how to live.'

Charlotte agreed.

'I saw your friend Nyoman there,' Rob said.

'At the cockfight?' Before leaving the previous evening, Nyoman had told her that he was going to see a friend. Well, he probably met his friend at the cockfight. Bit strange that he hadn't mentioned it though.

'Yeah. You should get him to take you, see for yourself.'

Perhaps she should go with him someday, see for herself what cockfighting was about.

They stopped for gado gado at Nyoman's favourite warung. A small child peeped at Charlotte from behind a large water barrel. Charlotte smiled at him. He ducked shyly away, only to peep at her again a moment later. This continued for a while, until the boy was distracted by a passing chicken to which he gave chase.

There were cockerels in wicker cages in front of the house across the road.

'Are they for cockfighting?' she asked.

'Yes. You want to see cockfight? Rob see cockfight. He like.'

He had read her mind. 'Okay. When is it on?

Nyoman looked at his watch. It was a nice watch, a waterproof one. A tourist had given it to him, someone he had taken out on his boat. 'Now,' he said. 'We go now.'

He started his bike. 'Let's go,' he said.

At the end of a dirt lane, at the edge of a pebble beach, the cockfights took place in a covered bamboo arena. Tiered wooden benches surrounded the ring. There were men sitting on the benches, men milling around talking to other men, men arriving on scooters, others on foot. Men, men everywhere men. Some greeted Nyoman. They shook his hand or slapped his shoulder.

Apart from the women selling fish satay outside the arena, Charlotte was the only woman there. Some men gaped, others glanced, some smiled and said hello, while others still were too busy petting their roosters to pay Charlotte any attention. They caressed their cockerels so tenderly that it was hard to imagine them putting the birds into the ring to fight to the death. Charlotte spotted one other westerner, tall and thin, German possibly, or Dutch. She glanced in his direction and would have smiled, but he looked at the ground, not wanting to acknowledge their common foreignness.

Two cockerels were selected for the first fight. Charlotte winced when she saw the handlers lash small blades onto the fighters' talons. Then they ruffled their feathers, and bounced them on the ground, in order, Nyoman explained, to make them angry so they would fight. There were men taking bets. Betters shouted and waved rupiah at them. The shouting grew frenzied as the fight began. The cocks ran at each other in a flurry of squawks and feathers. It was over within seconds, as soon as blood was drawn.

Wayan Joe arrived. He shook Charlotte's hand.

'You like?' he asked, gesturing towards the fight.

Charlotte shrugged, not ready to admit that she was kind of enjoying being an onlooker here. 'What happens to the roosters now?'

'This one,' Wayan said, pointing at the winning rooster, 'he rest, he fight next week, maybe.'

'And the losing one?'

'He... Ayam goreng' Wayan called to Nyoman to help him with his explanation.

'In the pot.' Nyoman laughed. 'Fried chicken.'

The second bout took longer to resolve. The roosters lost interest in the fight. Their handlers took them aside and ruffled their feathers once more. Nyoman had money on this one. He was tense and anxious. Charlotte's eyes were on him and she didn't see the final blow. She only saw Nyoman jump in the air and squeal in delight.

'Now you get fried chicken,' Wayan grinned.

Charlotte wasn't sure if she wanted fried chicken. The idea made her squeamish just now, but her squeamishness was silly really. She couldn't really object. She had no moral high ground to stand on. She wasn't a vegetarian. And it was surely better to eat a recently slaughtered fighting cockerel that had been treated like royalty all his life than to eat battery farmed chicken. These fighting cocks, despite their violent end, had probably led a far better life than the chickens she usually ate. Because, whether she liked it or not, the yakitori she often picked up on her way home from work came from battery farmed chicken.

The rooster had always been destined for the cooking pot. Was it really so awful then to put a rooster into the ring to fight before he was slaughtered? Animal rights activists would say so. Perhaps they were right. Having seen the cockfight for herself, it didn't seem so very terrible, but

Charlotte realised that her thinking on the subject might be completely off.

She had always been far more interested in human rights than animal rights. Having never had a pet as a child, or at any point in her life, she had little first-hand experience of animals really.

The next evening, Charlotte went again with Nyoman to the cockfight.

'You put money,' Ketut suggested.

'How?' Charlotte asked. There were men in the ring, walking around and taking bets. Spectators were shouting, holding up rupiah. It was all a great confusion to her.

Nyoman took over. 'Which cock you like?' He asked.

The white rooster was bigger, but his opponent, black with the rust coloured wings, looked like he had more pluck. Charlotte chose the black one. Nyoman attracted the bookie's attention and helped Charlotte make the transaction. The crowd got louder as the fight got under way. The neck feathers of both roosters stood up. They looked sinister. They flapped their wings and appeared to float around each other, until suddenly the white bird launched an attack on Charlotte's bird. The men on the bench in front stood to get a better view. Charlotte stood too; her bird fought back. Suddenly both roosters were on the ground. The white one stayed down, hers stood up.

'He won! My rooster won!' Charlotte jumped in the air.

Nyoman laughed and clapped his hands in delight.

'I won! I won!' She squeezed Nyoman's shoulder. So distracted was she, she missed her chance to place a bet in the next bout, but in the one after that, she placed another bet and won again. Nyoman high-fived her. She had a good eye for rooster. Who'd have thought?

'Fish satay is on me,' she told Nyoman.

'Okay,' he grinned.

Charlotte was pleased to be allowed to buy something for Nyoman at last. And winning felt fantastic. Yet she was not sure if she was entirely comfortable with this new betting, cockfighting version of herself.

After finishing their fish satay, they strolled back to Nyoman's bike. Ketut and Wayan were standing next to it. They spoke in Balinese first, and switched to English to include Charlotte.

'Charlotte, what do you think this face?' Wayan asked grabbing hold of Ketut's chin.

'I don't know,' Charlotte said. 'It looks fine to me.'

'No fine,' Wayan said, pushing Ketut away from him. 'Ketut ugly.'

Nyoman and Wayan laughed heartily. It was true, Ketut was not handsome, but as one who had suffered teasing about her looks in the past, Charlotte thought their teasing was cruel.

The men switched back to Balinese for a few minutes and then back to English again.

'I go back up the mountain now,' Nyoman told her. 'You go with Ketut.'

'With Ketut?'

'Yes, he live near. He stay with you when I go home.'

'All right,' Charlotte said, feeling uncertain.

'See you tomorrow,' Nyoman said before revving up and speeding off. Wayan waved at them from the pillion seat.

Ketut's bike looked as if it might fall apart at any minute. Hopefully it would stay in one piece for the short journey to Hillside Villas.

Charlotte had expected Ketut to take her straight home, but he stopped at a warung and bought a packet of cigarettes.

'Have something,' he suggested.

Charlotte asked for a coke, although she didn't really

want anything and didn't usually drink fizzy drinks. They sat at a plastic table at the side of the road. The owner came and sat with them.

'This Wayan,' Ketut said.

Another Wayan. So many Wayans on the island. This new Wayan shook Charlotte's hand. He and Ketut shared a cigarette and chatted. Charlotte longed all the while to be back in her room.

A child peeped out at her from behind the counter. Charlotte smiled at him. He ducked away and peeped again. Charlotte winked. He tried to wink back but couldn't quite manage it. Another child appeared, a girl, older and braver than the boy. She beckoned to Charlotte to follow her.

'Go,' Wayan said, smiling.

Charlotte got up and followed the children. They led her around the back of the warung, where in an old cardboard box lay a skinny cat and her litter of three kittens. The girl picked one up and handed it to Charlotte. It was tiny, its eyes still closed.

'It's beautiful,' she said.

The girl beamed proudly and insisted that Charlotte hold each kitten in turn. Charlotte was glad to do so. She was in no rush to return to Ketut. But then, from the little house behind the warung, a voice called for the little girl, and she ran off pulling her little brother behind her.

As Charlotte walked back to join the adults, she saw Ketut looking at her legs and rubbing his hands together. She felt wary of this man. She didn't trust him.

She assumed that Nyoman had asked Ketut to keep her company because he was concerned about her spending too much time alone. After all she had used the complaint of loneliness to explain that business with Madé Suwitera.

But why Ketut of all people? Why not Wayan Joe? She liked Wayan Joe. Or Nnengah. He seemed nice too. Maybe it was simply that Nyoman trusted that she would not be tempted by Ketut because of his famed ugliness. He still didn't trust her after the whole Madé Suwitera thing. Well, it was certainly true that she wouldn't be tempted by Ketut. Nyoman had got that right. But that didn't stop Ketut wanting her. She knew she was not the most alluring woman on the planet, but Ketut seemed to be attracted to her, nonetheless. And she didn't believe she was being vain or silly in thinking so. The man was practically salivating, for God sake. It was horrible.

Nyoman called up to her room before noon the following day. He had been out fishing all morning. He said he couldn't stay long. He was tired, but Ketut would call around later.

'Why is Ketut coming around?'

'You lonely, here by yourself.'

Loneliness was not the real problem. She was used to her own company, and she would rather spend the evening alone than with Ketut. Boredom was the thing that was getting to her.

'I'm okay. I can read my book.'

'You go with Ketut,'Nyoman said. 'Is better.'

'I don't like the way Ketut looks at me,' she said

'He looks?' Nyoman laughed nodded his head in agreement. 'Ketut ugly.'

'That's not what I meant... I don't trust him.'

'Ketut good. He my friend.'

Well, Charlotte presumed Nyoman knew the man better than she did. And Ketut had got her home safely last night, eventually.

Ketut called round at dusk with a bottle of arak that he wanted to drink on the beach. Charlotte was not a drinker. The very occasional glass of wine was her only indulgence. She had sipped arak before, and the local brew tasted foul to her. She told Ketut she was tired and would rather rest. But he was insistent. She thought the best way to get rid of him would be to accompany him for a while. Most likely, he was a perfectly decent human being, her misgivings unfounded. He had a wife, several children. Anyway, if he tried anything, she was bigger than he was, and could probably run faster. But, though short, Ketut was broad, and she wasn't at all certain that he couldn't overpower her.

They joined a couple of other guys on the beach. Some of their faces were familiar to Charlotte, but she couldn't remember their names. They smiled and nodded at her, but Ketut seemed to be the only one who spoke English. When they reached the end of the bottle of arak, Ketut said they should get another.

'Maybe you should be getting home to your wife,' Charlotte suggested. 'She might be angry with you for staying out so late.'

'My wife no angry,' Ketut said. 'If I with a Balinese woman – angry. With a tourist – no angry. Same with the wife of Nyoman.'

'Nyoman doesn't have a wife,' Charlotte said.

'Yes. Nyoman has a wife.'

'What?'

'Is normal. In Bali, at twenty-five, thirty, everybody get married.' Ketut said.

It couldn't be true. Nyoman had told her that she was his first real girlfriend, that he was shy and a bit slow in getting around to that whole business. It was something they had in common, Charlotte had thought. He couldn't have been lying to her. He had been so upset after she had spent a morning with Madé Suwitera.

And yet, Nyoman had never spent the night with her. Not once.

'I'm tired. I think I'll go home now,' Charlotte said.

'I go with you.'

'No, it's fine. I have my torch. I can go by myself.'

'I come,' he said.

'No, really,' she insisted. 'Stay here. Drink with your friends.'

'I come. I come,' he said.

She hurried away. He followed. He tried to put his arm around her shoulder. She quickened her pace. He probably hoped she would seek comfort in his arms. That was why he had told her Nyoman's secret. Contemptible fool. He didn't know Charlotte. She had managed just fine without men her whole life. She would manage without one now.

He walked her to her door, but she was quick to close it on him.

'See you tomorrow, yeah?' he said through the barrier.

'See you tomorrow.' Charlotte replied, but she wouldn't see him tomorrow or the day after that. She pulled her suitcase out from under her bed, opened her wardrobe and started transferring its contents to her case.

It was a wife Nyoman had been rushing back up the hill towards every evening. God, she was such an idiot. So gullible, so stupid, so blind.

In the bedside locker was the supply of condoms she had bought at the airport in Singapore, less than half of it used. Sometimes, when he came to see her, he was too tired to make love. It all made sense now. He had a wife to satisfy as well as Charlotte. She left the condoms where they were. She wouldn't be needing them anytime soon. Perhaps Putu or Jalan would make use of them.

She would leave Amed in the morning, go straight to the airport and get the first available flight back to Tokyo. There was no point in confronting Nyoman. What could he say? What could he do to make it better? And she would be bound to blubber and snivel. Better to avoid that.

She should never have left Japan. It was criminal really, leaving her adopted homeland in its hour of greatest need. Such a selfish thing to do. She could have been packing boxes with blankets and foodstuffs for the tsunami survivors. Instead she had been hanging out in Bali like some spoiled dilettante. It wasn't like her. She would make up for her failings. When she got back to home to Japan, she would spend every free hour she had helping the Tsunami relief effort.

NYOMAN'S PROMISE

Rob had paid Nyoman well, which was lucky. If the American had not come, Nyoman would have had to sell the cow to make his next motorcycle payment. And the cow wasn't his to sell. The cow was his mother's. His father, on his deathbed, had charged Nyoman with looking after his mother. He had promised he would care for her and always protect her. Selling her cow would upset his mother. It was good he didn't need to sell her cow.

He missed his father. Dead two years now.

When he'd told his mother that he had a girlfriend and that this girlfriend was a tourist, his mother nodded slowly. She didn't say whether she minded that his girlfriend was a foreigner. All she said was, 'Do not sleep in her bed until you are married.' Nyoman had heeded his mother's words. even though Charlotte would have liked him to sleep in her bed and felt lonely at night in her hotel room without him. And he would have liked to have stayed there himself. It would have saved him the long walk back up the hill to his home every evening. Yet he would not defy the woman who gave him birth.

Nyoman took a jug of water from the barrel and poured it over his head and shoulders. He splashed water into his armpits. Today was the day. Today he would bring Charlotte to meet his mother.

He still had doubts about Charlotte. He knew she was kind. He knew she was good. But she always insisted on condoms when they had sex. He thought, if she loved him, she wouldn't worry about getting pregnant. If she got pregnant, they could get married directly. There was no problem.

Charlotte might not want to live in his hillside home. She had her job in Tokyo, but she did not like her job. She worked too hard. All the tourists they work too hard. The French, the American, all say the same. They want to stay in Bali, in Bali they relax.

It was beautiful up here, calm, quiet. Charlotte liked calm and quiet places. And she liked to walk. She didn't mind the hills. She could walk fast. She could walk far. But up here, in the dry months, there was no water. Nyoman had to carry water from down below. Hard going, carrying water up the hill. He thought Charlotte was the kind of woman who would be willing to help with this type of work. She was strong. But it was not easy. The hill was steep.

He put the string of pearls around his neck, the pearls she had given him last September. He had put it on every morning since she gifted it to him. The pearls had cast a spell joining them together and bringing Charlotte back to Bali, to Nyoman.

He said goodbye to his mother and began his descent.

In front of him on the path were a couple of women from his banjar. They were on their way to Lipah beach to offer massages to the tourists. He greeted them as he passed them on the path. 'Nyoman, in a hurry to see his girlfriend,' they teased. He laughed, but he didn't delay. The women were right. He was in a hurry to see Charlotte.

If she had money, they could buy land somewhere, near the road, somewhere that had water all year round. Someplace nearby, it was not good to go far from your banjar, better to stay close to the place where you were born.

Jalan was sweeping the yard when Nyoman arrived at Hillside Villas. Putu looked on, smoking a clove cigarette. Nyoman greeted them. They returned his greeting. Their faces wore strange quizzical expressions, expressions he couldn't read. He didn't waste time puzzling over it. He went straight up to Charlotte's room.

The door was open. The bed had been stripped, her back-pack, her clothes, her books, everything gone. Nyoman stared around him for a moment, then turned and went back downstairs.

'What happened?' he asked Jalan.

'She left early this morning,' Jalan said. 'Putu drove her to the airport.'

Nyoman ran his fingers through his hair. He understood Jalan's words, but he couldn't make sense of them. Why would she leave? Why didn't she tell him? Had someone told her a lie about him? But who would do that? He had no enemies, not that he knew of.

He felt a pain in his chest, his face began to crumple. He didn't want Jalan to see his reaction. He walked away, along the road and up the path that led to his home on the hill and the mother whom he had pledged to care for until death.

PART TWO
DEATH AT LIPAH BEACH

Those on the twenty-ninth floor had to wait forty minutes before they could begin their descent. The stairs were thronged with people from the floors above.

Fumiko's legs were wobbly, her stomach queasy. Motion sickness. She needed the support of the banister as she made her way down. Sometimes she thought the building had begun to sway again, but it hadn't. The swaying came from inside herself.

'Ichi, ni, san, shi,' *One, two, three, four.* The voice was young and male.

'Go, roku, shichi, hachi,' *Five, six, seven, eight.* A chorus of office ladies sang in response.

'Ichi, ni, san, shi,' the young man.

'Go, roku, shichi, hachi,' the OLs.

'Ichi, ni, san, shi.'

'Go, roku, shichi, hachi.'

'Cut it out,' roared a man a few steps behind Fumiko.

The OLs giggled but quit their chanting. Fumiko kept up the singsong silently. It carried her along on the way down.

Outside it was cold. Fumiko was glad of her woollen coat. Those on the lower floors, those who had evacuated earliest, were in their shirtsleeves, shivering. Fumiko wondered if Takeshi was among them. He worked on the third floor. She roamed around the edge of the crowd, looking for him. She imagined he might be looking for her too.

She spotted him. He was chatting to a couple of OLs, everyone as young and pretty as he was. He turned and saw her.

'Fumiko san, are you alright?'

In his voice she detected only friendly concern. There was

none of the deep yearning that she felt. He was not yet thirty. Fumiko was forty-five, an old lady to him.

'I'm fine,' she told him, before re-joining her co-workers.

Lauren said that Fumiko was not really in love with Takeshi. She was merely infatuated with him. Fumiko did not understand the distinction. At night, she bid Takeshi enter her dreams. The fantasy she had built around him was better than any reality she had ever known.

Still, maybe Lauren had a point, because when Fumiko was cowering under her desk, praying for the world to stop shaking, it was not Takeshi who had come into her mind, but Morioka san. That must mean something.

Morioka san, with his receding hairline, hooded eyes and heavy jowls. She would marry him if he was still interested.

THE ROAD TO AMED

The rates offered for the Japanese yen were the same as those at all the other travel agencies on Monkey Forest Road. This place looked cleaner and brighter than most. A rack on one wall held brochures and fliers offering white water rafting, temple tours, day trips to coffee plantations and rice terraces, car hire, scooter hire and shuttles. On the other wall hung a map of Bali. A long counter faced the road. Another customer, a woman in a short denim skirt and tank top stood at the counter. Nice legs.

Greg approached the desk, stood next to the woman and waited for another member of staff to assist him.

'So, you don't have a shuttle to Amed,' the other customer said.

She had an accent. Italian or Spanish perhaps. Greg had been dating exclusively Asian women for the past two decades. A Mediterranean lady would make a refreshing change. She was in her early thirties, he thought. Thirty-two, thirty-three, a perfect age, it was when women were at their best.

Haruko was in her early thirties when they wed. The women he had dated after the divorce had all been in their early thirties too. He got older, but the women he dated remained the same age. Well, it stood to reason, men aged better than women did. Feminine beauty faded with the years. Men grew distinguished with age. It was a fact, pure and simple. Japanese ladies tended to age better than their Western counterparts, but once they hit fifty, they grew squat and dumpy. Haruko was still stunning, but she was an exception.

'We have car to Amed,' the travel agent told the woman.

'You have a shuttle to somewhere close to Amed?' she

asked. Long dark hair, with a couple of golden streaks here and there, very attractive.

'The shuttle go to Padang Bai.'

Greg handed his yen over to the assistant, who unlocked a safety deposit box with a key that dangled from a chain around his neck, counted out the required amount of rupiah and handed it to Greg who recounted it.

The young woman stepped toward the map to check the distance between Padang Bai and Amed. She turned back towards the counter and frowned in indecision.

'I'm going to Amed myself tomorrow,' Greg said. 'Perhaps we could share a car.'

It was a spontaneous decision, but a good one, he thought. He had been in Ubud for almost a week now. He was growing weary of the town. True, there were some wonderful restaurants and fine galleries here, but the potholed pavements, the noise. It was too much. He had heard East Bali was unspoiled. It could be fun to check it out. And the company of this lady would make it all the more interesting.

She looked at him sharply.

'I'm sorry. I couldn't help but overhear. I'm Greg, by the way.'

She shook the hand he proffered. 'Francesca,' she said.

'How about it? It would save us both some money.'

'Okay.' She shrugged, throwing her palms up, dramatically. Italian, definitely.

'Perhaps this place will sort out a car for us.'

'It's okay. I know a guy. I'll call him.'

They arranged that the car would pick Greg up at his hotel in the morning.

'Fancy getting something to drink, a coffee or maybe a beer?'

'I can't,' Francesca said. 'I have a yoga class.'

Yoga. All the important women in his life had been into yoga. A good omen.

Francesca and the driver were old pals. Apparently, she had stayed in his sister's home stay accommodation. She sat up front chatting with him, while Greg was stuck in the back looking out at the scenery. He would have preferred to have been getting to know Francesca, but, there would be time enough for that in Amed. A quiet, backward spot, from what he'd heard. Not much to see or do. A handful of hotels and restaurants, no nightlife to speak of. Himself and the lovely Francesca would be thrown together. He couldn't think of a better situation for romance to bloom.

The driver didn't shut up for the entire journey. It didn't even occur to the man that what he had to say might not interest Francesca. The Balinese tendency towards over-familiarity really bugged Greg.

Busy two-way traffic for most of the two-and-a-half-hour journey, then at a junction they turned down a road that gradually grew narrower and more rustic. The driver had to slow down for the occasional cow or chicken that strayed across their path. Dry scrub covered the parched hills in the background. Palm trees and flowering plants, the usual lush Balinese vegetation grew by the roadside.

He smelled the salt in the air before he saw the sea. The beaches were crowded with brightly painted outrigger fishing boats, and the sand was black. It looked dirty as if from an oil spill. The driver reassured them that the colour was natural. He said it was because of the volcano. When they rounded the next bend, the aforementioned volcano came into view. Mount Augung.

Neither Greg nor Francesca had booked anywhere to stay. The driver didn't think this would be a problem.

The first place the driver stopped at was still under construction. That didn't seem to put Francesca off. Nor did the fact that there was no reception and no sign of any staff.

'A pool,' she said. 'Fantastico!'

'It's miniscule. My hot tub in Auckland is as big.' They were standing on a platform that had a couple of tables and several rickety chairs scattered about. No sign of a menu. 'Do you think this is the restaurant?' Greg asked.

Francesca shrugged, apparently unconcerned.

The driver hollered and alerted the attention of a young man who appeared to be the only staff. He introduced himself as Jalan, got a key and showed Francesca a room. Greg had already decided he wasn't staying at this dump, but he followed them upstairs to the room, nonetheless. It was surprisingly decent: a big bed, tiled floors, gleaming bathroom. There was a balcony too, looking down at the pool and across to a grassy headland where a couple of brown cows were grazing. Beyond lay the ocean.

'I like it,' Francesca said.

She started negotiating a price. Greg left them to it and went down to look at some of the plants by the pool, enormous red blossoms as big as his hands.

'He's offering me a great rate,' Francesca said when she joined him there.

.'You'll never get a moment's peace.'

She frowned a puzzled frown.

'The construction,' he explained.

'He said they're not building right now. They won't start up again until next month.'

'You should at least see another place,' Greg said.

Coral View Villas was much more to Greg's taste. The entrance featured a moat with slabs of rock to step across, a staffed reception and porters ready to take his bag. A large landscaped garden dotted with two-bedroom bungalows, a decent size pool at the centre. It backed onto the beach. Its restaurant faced the ocean.

'We could share one of these,' Greg said. They were standing on the patio of a vacant bungalow.

'I need my privacy.'

She would have her privacy. There were two bedrooms. He wasn't suggesting they share a bed. He would at the very least buy a woman dinner before making such a suggestion. He supposed she wanted her own bathroom, women usually did. These bungalows must have been designed with families in mind, or friends travelling together.

'I'm going to take the room at Hillside Villas,' she said.

'But here you're right on the beach.' As the words came out of Greg's mouth, images of the tsunami surging over walls and highways flashed upon his inward eye and he wondered if he might not be better off at a safer distance from the sea. He pushed the thought aside. All the better hotels would be on the beachfront, and there was no way he would demean himself by staying in a dump like Hillside.

Greg's mind flitted to his financial troubles. The disaster had hit him hard. The stocks he had invested company funds in had fallen sharply. He wasn't at all sure if his firm could survive this setback. He steered his mind back from the brink. After all, he had come to Bali to take his mind off his troubles. He concentrated on the pretty young thing in front of him.

'Why don't you join me here for dinner this evening?' he asked.

'Si, that would be nice.'

Yes. Even if they were not staying at the same hotel, they could still have meals together.

HONEYMOONERS

Fumiko woke from her nap and went to sit on the balcony, leaving Morioka snoring gently.

Known as the Island of Love, Bali was the obvious choice for their honeymoon. Before booking the trip, Fumiko had contacted Charlotte for travel advice. Her friend had visited Bali a couple of times. But Charlotte hadn't had time to meet up to talk about Bali. These days Charlotte san spent all her free time on the Tohoku relief effort. She put Fumiko to shame. At first the Englishwoman had spent her weekends packing boxes to send to Tohoku. More recently she actually drove to the stricken province to deliver relief supplies and to dig mud from buildings that were once homes. Fumiko was Japanese, but apart from making donations and organizing a fundraiser, she had done nothing for her fellow countrymen and women in neighbouring Tohoku. After the earthquake, she had been more concerned, with getting her own life on track, getting married, securing her future. Perhaps after the honeymoon she would join her friend in Tohoku one weekend. Morioka san might be interested in coming too.

In an email, Charlotte san had recommended Amed as a nice quiet beach resort and reviewed briefly several of its hotels. Fumiko chose Hillside because Charlotte mentioned that it was locally owned, and Fumiko was trying these days to be a more ethical consumer and citizen of the world, to be more like Charlotte, in fact.

Until now, all of Fumiko's holidays abroad had been highly organized package tours. This honeymoon trip was a real departure for her and, although she had been a bit shocked to see that Hillside Villas was still under construction, Fumiko was enjoying herself.

Fumiko's book was on the table. She hadn't been able to concentrate on reading for several months after the earthquake. She hoped, on this holiday, to get back to it. Middlemarch was very challenging. Dorothea was too serious, but she liked Celia, and would like to know what happened to the sisters. She would persevere with the book even though, at the rate she was going, it would take a year to complete.

Fumiko noticed a woman gliding through the water of the small pool below. A new guest perhaps. Fumiko and Morioka had been the only guests for the first couple of nights and had enjoyed Putu and Jalan's undivided attention. The woman raised herself out of the pool. Slender tanned body in a skimpy blue bikini. Fumiko wished she could wear such a skimpy bikini, but she was too plump.

Fumiko and Morioka san had been introduced originally through omiai. Her parents had contacted the matchmaker because they were worried that their only child would be too much alone when they were gone. Although Fumiko had desperately longed for love, she had not been too keen on the idea of meeting someone through omiai. It just didn't seem very romantic.

She and Morioka had spent a pleasant evening together. Morioka san told corny jokes and made her laugh. He was kind, but he wasn't very good looking. Afterwards her father had asked her what she thought of Morioka san.

'He seems nice,' she had said. 'But he's no oil painting.'

'Well, neither are you,' her father had said.

And her father was right. Fumiko was plain. Still, she was stubborn and had declined a second date with Morioka san when he called several days later. She didn't speak to him again until after the earthquake.

Through her marriage, Fumiko had acquired two stepdaughters. She had worried that they would have trouble accepting her. They had welcomed her warmly. Just as Fumiko's parents had worried that she would be too alone when they were gone, Hitoe and Natsue chan had worried that their father would be all by himself when they went abroad for study and adventure as they planned to do when Natsue graduated from high school and Hitoe completed her course at the two-year college.

Hitoe and Natsue were fun and friendly and Fumiko enjoyed hanging out with them. In fact, sometimes she thought she liked her stepdaughters more than she liked her husband. But she liked her husband too.

The elegantly dressed waiting staff in their sarongs and lacy blouses outnumbered the diners. An elderly German couple were the only other customers at the restaurant at Coral View Villas.

Over dinner Greg revealed that he lived and worked in Tokyo.

'Tokyo, wow. I've always wanted to visit Japan.'

'Why don't you?'

'I will someday. I was going to go now, on this trip. But because of the earthquake and Fukushima, I thought maybe it wasn't such a good idea.'

'It's now that Japan could do with visitors,' Greg said.

'Sì. I suppose so.'

'And so long as you avoid the affected area, you wouldn't even know there had been a disaster.'

'Yes, this is what I like about Japan. It's fantastico,' Francesca said. 'After the earthquake – no looting. And I saw these pictures someone posted on Facebook. This road immediately after the tsunami – completely destroyed, just, how do you say, just rubble. Then the same road just one week later – perfetto. Completely restored. In Italy it would take years, no millennia.'

'Hmmh,' Greg mused. 'Actually, I think that Japan's ability to cope with disaster has been grossly exaggerated. Tohoku is still a no-go area. Tsunami survivors are living in these temporary shelters, totally inadequate. And even in Tokyo, though it was business as normal shortly after the earthquake, supermarket shelves were bare for weeks afterwards. You couldn't find bottled water for love nor money.

And this when we had been warned against drinking the tap water. When you consider that Tokyo port was operational again the day after the quake and all of the harbours to the south of Tokyo were fine, it really was a baffling state of affairs.' Greg cast his eyes heavenwards and shook his head. 'People have this image of the Japanese being extremely efficient but speaking as someone who has lived for two decades in the country, I can tell you that Japanese incompetence can be staggering.'

'No! Really?'

'Look at how they're botching the containment of the nuclear disaster.'

'Sì, sì, but I wonder if any other country could handle it any better. It's not easy, no?'

'Of course, it's not easy, but the Japanese, they lack that creative flair. And no-one will take initiative. The group is more important than the individual, you see. No-one will risk sticking his neck out.'

Francesca wondered what the man was doing in a country he seemed to have so little regard for. 'What took you to Japan?' she asked.

'A woman, actually. Haruko, my ex-wife. I met her in Auckland. She was there for a year to improve her English. I followed her back to Tokyo. With my background in finance, I had no trouble finding a job in investment banking. I stayed on after Haruko and I split up because, well, we had a son. And Tokyo was good for me business wise. I set up my own recruitment firm, recruiting for the banking sector mostly. Started it ten years ago and it's gone from strength to strength.'

He told her about his luxury apartment in Azabu Juban, one of Tokyo's most desirable neighbourhoods, his house in Auckland, his beach house in the Bay of islands.

Poor Greg. Francesca thought he must be quite insecure if

he needed to boast so much, his sense of self all bound up in his achievements and his property. Good thing her own self-worth was not connected to her possessions. The most expensive thing she owned was the MacBook Air she'd treated herself to at Christmas.

Greg ordered a fish curry. Apparently, his ex-girlfriend couldn't eat spicy food, but he liked hot dishes himself. He had mentioned the ex-girlfriend, Midori, in the car on the way down as well. Francesca surmised that the break-up was recent, the wound still raw. Underneath the swagger, he was fragile.

They were having dessert before he got around to asking Francesca about herself.

'So, what is it that you do in Milano?' he asked.

'I don't do anything now,' she said. 'I worked for a marketing company, but they made me redundant recently and so I decided to travel for several months before I look for a new job.'

'Good for you.' He raised his glass to her.

After dinner, Greg and Francesca moved on to a bar that Francesca had spotted while exploring Lipah earlier in the evening. The only bar in the neighbourhood, it opened onto the roadside. A high, exposed thatched roof gave the place an airy feel. The billboard outside advertised live music tonight. The band were just setting up, but quite a crowd had gathered already.

They sat at the bar. And because Greg had insisted on putting their dinner on his tab, Francesca insisted on getting the beers.

There was a lull in their conversation. Francesca tried to think of something to say. She remembered something she'd read about Japan. 'I heard that pay rises and promotions in Japanese companies depended not on, how can I say ... merit, not on merit, but on the age of the employee, and how long he has been with the company and whether or not he is married.'

'Yes, that's right. It's ridiculous really. The reason the country has been in a slump for the past thirty years.'

'There are advantages to the Japanese way, no? I read an article about it and it was quite positive. What did it say? Ah, sì. Less friction between colleagues, less office politics than in Western companies.'

'If the Japanese economy is ever to recover, it really needs to shake itself up and shake off these ridiculous policies. Companies need to reward merit. Otherwise...'

Francesca excused herself and went to look for a toilet. Greg was such a know-it-all and so negative about the country which he'd chosen to make his home.

Just one cubicle towards the back of the building. An Asian woman was waiting at the door. Pleasantly plump, in her mid-forties, a neat bob framed her face. She nodded and smiled at Francesca. Francesca smiled back.

'Aren't you staying at Hillside Villas?' the woman asked.

'Sì,' Francesca said. 'Yes, I am. You too?'

'Yes. I noticed you by the pool earlier. I am Fumiko by the way.'

'Francesca,' said Francesca.' Nice to meet you. Is it a Japanese name – Fumiko?'

'Yes, it is. I am Japanese.'

'The guy I am drinking with, he lives in Japan.'

'Really? Does he speak Japanese?' Fumiko asked.

'I think so. He has lived there a long time.'

'So, in that case, why don't the two of you join me and my husband? We're sitting over there.' Fumiko pointed to a table in the middle of the room.

'Sure. I'd love to.'

Francesca led Greg to the Morioka's table and introduced him to Fumiko. The Moriokas bowed low and exchanged some pleasantries in Japanese with Greg before switching back to English, for Francesca's sake. Fumiko spoke near perfect English. Her husband struggled, but he smiled and laughed a lot which more than made up for his lack of English.

The music started up.

'You like dancing?' Fumiko asked.

'I do,' Francesca said.

'Me too, but my husband, his knees get sore. He is too old... '

'You go,' her husband said. 'Dance, dance together.'

Fumiko pulled Francesca to the dance floor. Greg joined them there, leaving Morioka san sipping his beer at their table.

A handsome Balinese boy began dancing opposite Francesca. Dark glossy hair; strong, broad shoulders; his body muscular, yet slender. He smiled and revealed a set of even white teeth. He moved closer to Francesca. He spoke some words in her ear. She didn't catch them. She mouthed 'what?' and lent towards him. He was bending his head to repeat the words when suddenly Greg stuck his body between them. The boy raised his hands as if in surrender and backed away.

'Oh, Greg.' Francesca slapped her forehead. 'You scared him away.' She fell against his shoulder in mock despair.

'I thought he was bothering you,' Greg said.

'Bothering me?' She reached her hand out in the direction the Adonis had vanished. 'He's beautiful.'

'You weren't interested in him?'

'No, Greg, no. I have a boyfriend.' She shouted to be heard over the music.

'You have a boyfriend? In Italy?'

'Si, Si. Ale is in Milano.'

Francesca thought she saw disappointment flitter across Greg's face. Yet, he could hardly have thought she would be interested in him. He was twenty years her senior. And his spindly legs sticking out from under his shorts, his paunch and his thinning hair did nothing to excite her desire.

Back at their table, Morioka san chatted to a local man. Wavy shoulder length hair and a well-toned body, he was almost as good looking as the Adonis on the dance floor.

'Wayan Joe san, how are you?' Fumiko said.

'Wayan san, let me introduce you,' Morioka san said. 'This is Francesca san. She is from Italy.'

'Welcome to Amed.' Wayan shook her hand. 'You need anything, I help you.'

'And this is...' Morioka san couldn't remember Greg's name.

Greg introduced himself and shook Wayan's hand.

'Let's dance,' Wayan said when the band started up again. Both Fumiko and Francesca accompanied him to the dance floor. He danced well and he was gorgeous. Francesca found it hard to take her eyes off him.

When the night came to an end. Wayan organised lifts for the Moriokas and took Francesca home himself. Coral View Villas was close by. They left Greg to walk home alone.

Francesca woke to the sound of rain pelting the roof of her villa. Not much of a day for the beach. She met Fumiko at breakfast. There was no sign of her husband. Apparently, he was not feeling well.

'Do you know of any cafés with Wi-Fi?' Francesca asked.

'I think I saw one near the bar we went to last night. By walking it takes maybe ten minutes.'

'Okay. I'll check it out. I need to Skype my boyfriend. I haven't spoken to him for days.'

'Have you been going out with your boyfriend for long?' Fumiko asked.

'Sì. Forever, ten years almost.'

'Wow, that is a long time. Do you think you will marry him?'

'Actually, recently Ale started talking about marriage, but I didn't feel ready. But probably I will marry him. We have been together for so long I can't imagine my life without him. How long have you been married?'

'Just three weeks. This is our honeymoon.'

'No! I thought you had been married for years.'

'Actually, we are one of the earthquake marriages.'

'Earthquake marriages?'

'Yes, you know Japan had a big earthquake in March.'

'Sì, sì. I saw it on the news. Terrible. No?'

'Yes, the biggest quake in Japan's history. In Tokyo, we were not so much harmed by the earthquake, but it had a strange effect, because there was a spike in marriages. And divorces too.'

'How interesting,' Francesca said. 'But had you and Morioka been thinking about marriage?'

'Not really. Actually, we only started dating after the earthquake. Well, we had been out for dinner once before the earthquake, but then we didn't see each other for several months. Somehow during the earthquake, I thought of him, and a couple of weeks later I called him and that was that.'

'Wow,' Francesca said. 'And you are happy?'

'Yes. So far. Sometimes I still have the doubt, but I think I made the right decision. Morioka san is very kind.'

'Yes. And funny you know. He doesn't speak the English very well, but I can see he has a good sense of humour.'

'Sou desu ne. Sense of humour is important.'

'Very important.'

Fumiko went back to her room then, to see how her husband was feeling. Francesca was left alone, staring out at the rain.

Fumiko's spontaneity and quick decision making impressed her. All the years she had been with Alessandro and still she didn't feel certain. Although in truth it wasn't marriage that caused her to hesitate. Alessandro had suggested that, since she was out of work, now might be a good time to have a baby. She had flown into a rage. What did he think – that Francesca would become the typical Italian 'mamma', slaving over a stove all day long so her husband and children could have homemade pasta every single day? Alé protested that he hadn't meant that at all. She hadn't stuck around to listen to him. She had booked a flight and escaped to South East Asia, saying they could discuss it on her return.

Over the past two months, she had seen so many beautiful Asian babies that she had started to feel a little bit broody. Ale would make such a good papa. And she'd just love a little boy with floppy hair and dark eyes, a mini Ale. But she didn't feel quite ready for it all. Not yet, although at thirty-four, in a biological sense, she would probably never be as ready again. Perhaps she should just go for it. Start trying, she might not get pregnant straight away, in any case. And by the time she did, maybe she would feel ready.

At lunchtime, she answered a knock on her door. Greg stood there holding an enormous golf umbrella.

'Hungry?'

'Sì.'

He offered her his arm and escorted her to Barong Café, a restaurant situated between Hillside Villas and Coral Garden Villas. They were the only customers. But several geckos darted across the walls. Greg spoke of the enormous fruit bats he had seen in Ubud and told Francesca about waking up one morning in his beach house in the Bay of Islands, his New Zealand getaway, to find a baby bat on his bedroom floor. Neither he nor his son, then about ten years old, had any idea how it got there. Their neighbour's cat almost pounced on it, but they managed to keep it safe until nighttime, when they put it out on the roof. It had vanished by the following morning, and he and his son had assured each other that the baby had been found by its mother as they had hoped.

Greg was good company when he wasn't boasting.

FUMIKO AND FRANCESCA

Morioka san made a dash for the bathroom. Fumiko heard noises she would rather not have heard. Morioka san returned looking a little paler and flopped down into the wicker chair.

'Do you think you will be able to go out to dinner?' she asked him. The rain had finally cleared, and Fumiko felt hungry.

Her husband shook his head sadly. 'Why don't you ask Francesca to have dinner with you? She's a nice person.'

'Are you sure you will be okay here alone?'

'Yes, all I need is the toilet.'

'Arigato ne.' *Thank you.* She kissed him on the forehead.

The waiter sat with them while they perused the menu. He said that the food was even better than the view. Fumiko agreed. The food was fantastic. She and Morioka san had eaten there the previous evening. The view was wonderful too. Cafe Lipah opened right onto Lipah beach where the light was now fading over the ocean.

'I recommend the fish in banana leaves,' she told Francesca. 'That's what I had last night.'

'This is a really good dish,' the waiter said.

'Okay, I'll have that.'

Fumiko chose a chicken curry. She thought she would buy an Indonesian recipe book when she got home. She had taken a new interest in cooking since getting married.

Francesca told her that she'd always longed to visit Japan.

'Please come. You can stay with me and Morioka san.'

'I'd love to.'

'The Japanese government is trying to encourage tourism now, and flights are getting cheaper.'

'Ale is interested in Japan too. Maybe we will go there on our honeymoon.'

'Yes! Do it.' Fumiko clapped her hands together. 'I want to meet your boyfriend.'

The restaurant had begun to fill up. Several tables were pushed together in the centre to accommodate a large group of Europeans. Francesca started talking to them. They were from France and were on a cycling tour of Bali. Wayan Joe walked up from the beach. He sat and chatted with Fumiko and Francesca until their food arrived. Then he joined a couple of local guys who, with bongos and a guitar, began playing music. When the waiter wasn't too busy serving food, he joined them in singing. He had a powerful voice. As well as traditional Balinese songs, they sang rock anthems by Bruce Springsteen, U2 and the Beach Boys.

Some of the French cyclists got up and started dancing. They pushed back their table to give themselves more room. Nnengah, the boy who had given Fumiko a lift home the evening before, came and asked Francesca to dance. A pot-bellied French man pulled Fumiko to her feet. It was fun. Such a pity there weren't restaurants like this in Tokyo, Fumiko thought.

So pretty and lively, Francesca turned many heads. The French cyclists and the Balinese, they all admired her. Fumiko overheard a couple of Balinese boys ask her to come and look at the stars with them. Francesca laughed heartily in response but did not venture out to look at the stars.

When they sat down to catch their breath, Wayan Joe came over and shared some arak with them. The arak tasted like nihon shu but was even sharper. It was brewed locally, Wayan told them, from palm trees.

Fumiko wished for a moment that she was single again

and could enjoy the attentions of all these lovely men. Then she reminded herself that, even if she were single, the men would not be paying attention to her. She was not attractive like Francesca. She was very ordinary, and she was plump. Good-looking men didn't see her as a potential girlfriend. They hardly noticed her. Never mind, she didn't need a handsome man. She was getting used to Morioka san's face. She liked it more every day. His diarrhoea, and the noises and smells that came with it, were off-putting. But, she supposed, even handsome men got diarrhoea.

Wayan Joe took Francesca back to Hillside Villas on his scooter. Nnengah brought Fumiko. She thanked him and went straight to her room to see if her husband was okay. Francesca and Wayan stayed chatting by the gate.

By morning Morioka san was genki again. Jalan came to take their breakfast order.

'Let me see, I think I will have one of your delicious banana pancakes,' Morioka san said winking at Fumiko. They had had banana pancakes every morning since they came to Amed. Banana pancakes were all Jalan knew how to make.

Having spent an entire day in his room, Morioka san was eager to go somewhere. He consulted Jalan about interesting sights in the local area. Jalan recommended the Temple of One Thousand Steps.

'Are you sure you can handle one thousand steps? Have you completely recovered?' Fumiko asked.

Morioka san said that he was strong as an ox and flexed his muscles to prove it. Fumiko was not convinced. Her husband was a salary man. He had spent his life at a desk. He had plenty of padding around his middle, but his arms and legs were thin.

Jalan said that there were actually a thousand seven hundred steps at Puru Luhur Lempuyang.

'No problem,' Morioka san said. 'Your pancake will give me the strength. Where is Putu? Can Putu drive us?'

Jalan found Putu, who confirmed that he could take them.

'What about Francesca? Would Francesca like to come?' Morioka asked.

Fumiko climbed the steps to Francesca's door and knocked. No answer. She waited and knocked again. Francesca opened the door a crack and stuck her head out.

'Ohayo gozaimasu,' Fumiko said, then, remembering that Francesca didn't speak Japanese, she switched to English, 'Good morning.'

'Good morning,' Francesca replied in a weak and croaky voice.

'I'm sorry to bother you, but Putu is driving Morioka san and me to a temple. It's just half an hour drive and they say it's a very beautiful and sacred place.'

Francesca blinked wearily. Fumiko had disturbed her. 'We were wondering if you'd like to come.'

'Thank you, Fumiko san, but I have seen enough temples. I want to spend the day on the beach.'

It was suspicious the way Francesca opened the door only a crack and didn't let Fumiko see inside. Fumiko wondered if Wayan Joe was in the room with her.

Jalan told them that they needed to wear a sarong to enter the temple, so Fumiko went to her room and changed into a sarong she had bought in Sideman. Morioka san didn't have a sarong. Putu offered to lend him one. Fumiko waited at the dining area, while Putu kitted her husband out in a ceremonial sarong.

Francesca arrived down for breakfast. There was no sign of Wayan. Probably she had slept alone.

'You know, when you opened your door, I thought maybe you were hiding Wayan in there with you,' Fumiko said.

Francesca started laughing. 'Sì, it must look like that.'

Then laughter took her over completely. She laughed so hard, she had to lean on the chair for support. She looked really lovely when she laughed, Fumiko thought.

'You didn't bring him to your room?'

'No, Fumiko, no. He wanted to come, but no. When you knocked, I wasn't dressed. That's why I didn't open the door.'

'Weren't you tempted?'

'A little,' Francesca shrugged. 'But I have a boyfriend.'

Fumiko had a husband, but she would be very, very tempted, if a gorgeous young man like Wayan asked to share her bed. She thought she might not be very good at this business of being a wife. She would too easily give into temptation.

THE BEACH

Francesca scrambled down the rocks, a short cut to Lipah Beach. Except for the occasional spot where a hotel backed onto the strand, the dry sand was cluttered with fishermen's outrigger boats.

There was an empty stretch of beach in front of Coral Garden villas, she laid her towel there on the black sand. As she was doing so, she saw Wayan Joe coming towards her. Mamma mia. This could be awkward. He had been really keen to come to her room the night before.

He crouched down beside her on the sand. 'You good?'

'Sì. You?'

'Yes, good. Wayan always good. You want to snorkelling?' Wayan made his living renting snorkelling gear to tourists.

'Sì, why not,' she said.

'Okay,' Wayan said. 'I give you good price. You want fins? What size your feet?'

He returned with the equipment and joined her snorkelling. There were no hard feelings. Easy come and easy go for Wayan Joe.

Later, while she was sunbathing, Nnengah came and chatted with her. A skinny youth with big wide eyes, he looked about thirteen but was actually twenty, Francesca discovered. Nnengah was feeling glum because on his way home the previous evening, he had dropped his phone. He couldn't find it in the dark. He'd returned to the spot in the morning but couldn't find it then either. He didn't know when, if ever, he would be able to afford a new phone.

The loss of the phone wasn't the only thing that was bothering him. He had an opportunity to return to school. Nnengah told Francesca that he had left school at twelve because his family could not afford the uniform. Now an American charity that sponsored Balinese youths who had had to leave school early were offering him a chance to return to school. If he got a diploma, he should be able to get a job at a hotel. But the school was in the North of Bali, so he couldn't go. He couldn't leave his parents. They wouldn't be able to manage without him. In the dry summer months, there was no water on the hill. Water had to be carried up from the shore. His parents were too frail to carry water.

'Couldn't neighbours help? Just for a year or two, just while you were getting an education?'

'Is too much for neighbours,' he said.

Francesca advised him to take the opportunity to go back to school, if at all possible.

'No possible. No good. I wish I born in Europa,' he said. 'Next life, I will born in Europa. I come to Bali for relax.'

Francesca didn't tell him that there were problems in Europe too, that most Italians couldn't afford a holiday in Bali. It was only because of a redundancy package that she could afford it herself. And unemployment was high in Italy. She didn't have a job to return to. Finding one at the current time would be challenging to say the least. Her friend Gabriella had been unemployed for almost two years now. Francesca couldn't stand that. She would go crazy.

Enough sun for one day. Francesca pulled her dress on and strolled over to the bamboo shelter on stilts, where Wayan was hanging out with his mates. She wanted to ask if she could hang on to the snorkelling equipment for one more day. The day after tomorrow, she would fly to Singapore. She wanted to spend her last day, like she'd spent today: snorkelling, sunbathing and taking it easy.

'Francesca, my friend, come, sit, have papaya.'

Francesca heaved herself up onto the platform, sat cross-legged and accepted the slice of papaya that Wayan handed to her. He introduced his friends, Ketut and Nyoman. Nyoman had closely cropped hair, chiselled cheekbones and a string of pearls around his neck. Ketut had a broad, coarse face and was missing several teeth.

'You go to Café Lipah tonight?' Wayan asked.

'I might. You?'

'Wayan always go Café Lipah.' Ketut said. 'He play the bongos. He dancing.' Ketut mimicked Wayan's moves on the dance floor. He flicked imaginary hair and tried to look seductive. Wayan ignored him.

'I like your pearls,' Francesca told Nyoman.

'His girlfriend give he,' Ketut said, grabbing at the pearls. 'Then she love he. Now she no love he no more. Nyoman crying.'

Nyoman muttered something angrily at his friend, probably telling him to shut up.

Ketut was just warming up to the topic. 'His girlfriend go. Nyoman crying, crying, everyday crying.'

Nyoman jumped down from the shelter and walked away across the beach. Poor guy. Francesca wondered if his girlfriend was a foreigner. The pearls he wore looked like something a tourist would buy.

She spotted Greg on the beach, said goodbye to Wayan and his friends, hopped down from the platform and called out to him.

He had been for a dive earlier and planned to take it easy until dinner. He wondered if Francesca would join him then. Francesca said she would and suggested Café Lipah. They arranged to meet there later.

Though tired after their trip to the Temple of a Thousand

Steps. Fumiko and Morioka san joined them at Café Lipah. Greg addressed all conversation to Francesca and barely acknowledged the couple. Francesca thought him quite rude.

Wayan arrived at the café later. He and his friends played music as they had done the previous evening. The played and sang well but the atmosphere did not reach the vibration it had the day before. There were fewer customers, but no-one pushed the tables back to dance.

Greg was planning to rent a scooter and ride all the way to Padang Bai the next day. He invited Francesca to join him.

'Grazie, Greg, but no,' she said. 'Tomorrow is my last day. I just want to hang out on the beach.'

'I'll drop by Hillside Villas when I get back,' he said, 'and we can have one last drink together.'

'Okay,' she said, and promptly forgot the arrangement.

GREG HAS TOO MUCH TO DRINK

Swerving around chickens, breaking to avoid dogs, his long scooter ride to Padang Bai had worn him out. The port town, when he finally reached it, had provided interesting sights and several decent restaurants, but he'd felt lonesome. Had Midori agreed to marry him, they could now be enjoying this tropical paradise together. Or if Francesca had come along, her company would have been equally agreeable.

He stopped by Hillside Villas on his hired scooter to take Francesca out for a drink. She wasn't in. He waited for twenty minutes, then got back on the bike and looked for her at Barong Café and at Bar Wewe, before stopping at his hotel and returning the scooter to its owner.

Greg strolled out to the beach. He thought Francesca might be in Café Lipah, so he walked up there. The only other customers in the beachfront shack were the Japanese newlyweds. Dull as ditch water those two. He'd left the country to get away from the likes of them. He said hello and then took a table as far away as possible.

The bar was quiet, but he had a couple of drinks there anyway.

Francesca puzzled him. Standing him up like that, what was that about? And if she had a boyfriend, why was she holidaying alone?

Women. He couldn't understand them. He had flown Midori to Paris in order to pop the question. She'd turned him down. He couldn't fathom it. Paris in the springtime, a large diamond. They had been practically living together for the last two years. Love and marriage were on everyone's minds after the earthquake. Yet, she said no. Baffling.

That was six months ago now. He needed to stop thinking about Midori.

His business, his losses. Would he be able to turn things around? He had his deposits in Jersey and his properties in New Zealand. They were secure, he thought. If worse came to the worst, he could earn his living as an English teacher. He heard that those with business experience were highly sought after to teach business English. But to be reduced to that? The shame. Perhaps he should return to Auckland, invest in a bar or restaurant, start a new life. If he had anything left to invest. His son would start university soon. Christ, the expense. The boy had been raised to believe that his father could always provide, no matter the cost. What if his father couldn't provide? Could his son cope? And he the father? To win for all those years and then, because of events beyond his control, to appear a loser to the world. The indignity. Ignominy.

He ordered a beer. Whiskey was what he really wanted, but the only spirit available was arak, the locally brewed piss. It was vile tasting, but he ordered one anyway in a cocktail called Bali Breeze. He downed four before he wandered back to the beach.

The light from the stars was not sufficient to guide his path. He bumped into a jukung and then another. He fished his mobile phone from his shirt pocket. It fell in the sand. He bent down and felt for it, found it and used its light to guide his way. The beach was deserted at this hour. Francesca would surely be back in her hotel by now. He would call up and take her out for that farewell drink.

He heard voices. He wasn't alone on the beach after all. He waved the torch towards the speakers. Beach boys hanging out on one of those raised platforms. Didn't they have any homes?

He heard laughter, higher in pitch, female. He flashed his light again towards the platform. There in the middle of those layabouts sat Francesca. Cunt.

What the fuck did she see in them? What could they talk about?

Those bums had no education. They had never been anywhere. They hung around the beach all day in second-hand Speedos some tourist had forgotten to pack.

Greg stormed to the end of the beach. He stepped on a rock to climb up to the road. He slipped, cursed and began again.

He glanced down to the beach and saw a light coming towards him. Francesca, on her way back to her lodgings. They could yet have their farewell drink. He shone his torch on her as she scrambled up.

'Mio Dio,' she said. 'Greg, what are you doing here?'

'We were supposed to go for a drink.'

'It's late.' She was level with him now.

'Just one drink, to say goodbye.'

'Everyplace is shut.'

'I'm sure we can get a drink at my hotel.'

'Goodnight Greg, Ciao.'

She made to walk past. She had time for one last drink with those beach bums, but not with him. He took a step forward, blocking her way.

'Scusa,' she said.

Greg did not move. She pushed his chest lightly. Flicking him away as if he was a piece of dirt. Infuriated, Greg pushed back. Francesca slipped. She fell backwards. Greg smiled as she fell. That would show her.

It wasn't far down, five, six feet at most. He heard a soft thud as she hit the sand. Then nothing, not a curse, not a shriek, not a moan. He scrambled down to where she was lying, shone his torch in her face. Her mouth was open, her eyes too, staring. Something sticky in her hair. Oil? Blood. It was leaking out the side of her head.

THE HONEYMOON COMES TO AN END

Fumiko and Morioka san sat out on the beach and looked at the stars. They tried to find constellations, Orion and Ursa Major, but neither of them knew anything about astronomy. They didn't have much success. They helped each other up and strolled along the beach to return Hillside Villas. The New Zealander almost collided with them hurrying in the opposite direction.

'Help,' he said. 'There's been an accident.'

They hurried with him towards the rocky outcrop that led up to the road. Francesca lay there on the sand.

'She fell,' he said. 'Her foot slipped.'

Even Fumiko had climbed those rocks, Morioka san too. Francesca was lithe and sure-footed. How could it be? But there she lay. Fumiko went to her.

'Francesca chan, okite. *Francesca dear, wake up.*

Francesca's eyes stared into the night sky but didn't see the stars.

Morioka san held her hand as the plane took off. With the other hand, he wiped a tear from his eye. The sight of this tear made Fumiko cry again. Morioka squeezed her hand and placed his other hand on top of it.

Since the accident, Fumiko had gone over and over the events of that evening in her mind. Francesca had joined them for dinner that night. They had exchanged email addresses and promised to befriend each other on Facebook. Francesca had talked about coming to see them in Tokyo. And Fumiko and Morioka had thought aloud about a trip to Italy in a year or two.

Francesca hadn't stayed for dessert. She wanted to find Nnengah. He had lost his phone. She had brought a cheap old phone with her from Italy which she had bought an Indonesian sim card for at the start of the Indonesian leg of her trip. She was going to give it to Nnengah.

Fumiko shouldn't have let Francesca go alone. If they had gone together, Francesca might be alive today.

Soon they would be back in Tokyo. She found it hard to imagine how she would return to normal life.

'I have no souvenirs for Hitoe chan and Natsumi chan,' she said.

'They won't mind" Morioka said. 'They will understand.'

Fumiko planned to buy beautiful clothes and jewellery for her stepdaughters in Ubud. But after Francesca's death, she couldn't think about shopping, so they had stayed in Amed until the end.

Someone had contacted Francesca's boyfriend, Alessandro. He arrived in Amed late in the evening two days after the accident. Putu and Jalan took good care of him. Such young men, but somehow they knew exactly what to do in a crisis. They fed Alessandro, insisted he eat even when he said he wasn't hungry.

All of Amed was upset by Francesca's death. Local people laid wreathes on the beach and said prayers for her soul.

Something niggled at Fumiko's mind about the accident.

After Francesca left the restaurant, the New Zealander had come in and ordered a drink. He waved hello, but he didn't talk to them. He was only interested in Francesca. Stupid man, he couldn't see that Francesca was too young and too pretty for him. Greg san was old, even older than Morioka. Or maybe he wasn't quite as old as that. Westerners didn't age so well as Japanese. Greg san drank several drinks in quick succession and then left without even saying goodbye. He looked angry, angry and drunk. He bumped into a table on his way out.

When Greg san ran into them on the beach, he wasn't calling for help. That puzzled Fumiko. Nnengah and Wayan Joe were resting in their shelter further up the beach. Had he shouted, he could have alerted them. But maybe he didn't want to alert anyone. Maybe, when he collided with them, he hadn't been running for help, he had been running away.

She could contact Alessandro and tell him her suspicions, but that would only distress him further. Poor man. A police officer had interviewed Fumiko and Morioka san after the accident. He had given her his card. She could email him and tell him her misgivings.

'Do you think maybe Greg san pushed Francesca?' Fumiko asked her husband.

Morioka's mouth dropped open. He stared at her. 'Huh?' Then he shook his head. 'I don't know,' he said.

Morioka san blinked away tears. 'If he killed Francesca, I'll break his neck,' he said.

Fumiko couldn't imagine her husband breaking anyone's neck. But when she looked at him sitting next to her in his aisle seat, a tear of grief rolling down his cheek, she knew she loved him. She no longer had any doubts. He was a good man. She was lucky to be his bride.

She would try her best to be a good wife.

PART THREE
A CHERRY BLOSSOM AFFAIR

THE QUAKE

It took Katherine a moment to realise what the clattering was. When she did, she pushed the sliding glass doors right open. The ground shifting shape beneath her almost unbalanced her. She set her legs wide apart and bent her knees to steady herself. She reckoned the middle of the yard would be the safest place to be. She turned and scanned the room for her mother-in-law. The old woman sat crouched under the kitchen table.

'Okaa-san, kiitte,' she said. *Mother come.*

Her mother-in-law did not budge. She couldn't leave the old woman inside all alone. Tins of sweet corn toppled off the table and hit Katherine on her back as she dove under to join Ichiro's mum.

Okaa-san never ate at the kitchen table. Instead she used it as a place to store food supplies. Tins of tomatoes, packets of miso soup and pots of noodles tumbled to the floor. The table rattled so hard, they had to hold firmly to its legs to prevent it from deserting them.

Cups and glasses toppled from the dresser. A loud bang -– the microwave hit the floor. Katherine thought for sure her time was up. Of all the places she could be at the end, there she was, in Godforsaken Miyagi, stuck under a table with her bloody mother-in-law. Okaa-san's eyes were closed under the tight perm, no longer fashionable except among the obaa chan of Miyagi. She whispered something. The hairs on the wart over her lip bopped up and down as she repeated an incantation.

Ichiro's mother had always made it clear that she did not want a gaijin for a daughter-in-law. Katherine often wished that she had let the old bat scare her off, but she'd been in love. Or so she'd thought – more likely she'd been deluded. These days she and Ichiro led separate lives, slept in separate bedrooms. They were more like flatmates than husband and wife. It served her right getting stuck here with this woman. She should have left Ichiro years ago.

The house was creaking and groaning. Slates were falling off the roof and breaking on the ground outside. The old woman let go of one of the table legs, reached forward and placed her hand on top of Katherine's. Katherine moved her thumb and wrapped it around her mother-in-law's. A crash, loud as thunder. Some part of the house had collapsed.

Katherine glanced towards the sliding doors. Their exit was still clear.

They were outside surveying the damage when the first aftershock struck. They clung to each other in the yard.

They had no electricity. The phone lines were down, but Okaa-san kept a battery-operated radio tucked away in the back of a closet. They dug it out, switched it on, twiddled the dial and heard news of the tsunami. They listened in silence as the broadcasters told how it had travelled ten kilometres inland, just a few kilometres short of their home, and how it had flooded Sendai airport, the airport Katherine had flown into that morning.

'My son, my son.' Okaa-san cried. She worried that Ichiro might have been at Sendai airport when it was inundated by the tsunami.

'He would have called before boarding a flight,' Katherine told her. 'He's still in Tokyo. He probably never left his office.'

'But the phones aren't working,' her mother-in-law said.

'They would have been working when he took off, if he took off, which he didn't.'

She failed to reassure her mother-in-law and managed to confuse herself. She felt annoyed with her husband. He had been booked on the same early morning flight Katherine had taken. There were issues at work, surprise, surprise, and he stayed in the office all night Thursday. He never made it to the airport.

It was the first anniversary of his father's death. He should be there in Miyagi with his mother.

As the hours passed, Katherine began to wonder if maybe Ichiro had been in Sendai airport when the tsunami flooded it, and if she was now a widow. She felt bereft at the thought. She didn't want to be with Ichiro anymore, but she didn't want him dead. He was not a bad man.

Although it was March, there was little sign of spring. They pottered about in hanten, woollen hats and gloves to keep out the chill. At least they would not go hungry. Okaa-san kept a well-stocked kitchen. As well as fresh fruit and vegetables and sacks of rice, there were tins and pot noodles and dozens of bottles of drinking water and oolong tea stored away in the back of a cupboard. The freezer contained fish and some pork chops, now thawing but slowly.

Okaa-san kept candles, torches and even a gas cylinder in case the gas supply was cut off. She was so well equipped for emergencies, Katherine thought that on some level the old woman must be glad that disaster had struck and she was vindicated in her preparedness.

Katherine pushed a wheelbarrow loaded with empty barrels and old plastic bottles to the well to fetch water for washing and for flushing the toilet. The return journey with the heavily laden barrow wore her out. When Katherine stopped to rest, the old lady took over, and, to Katherine's dismay, made better headway. At five foot nine inches, Katherine stood a whole foot taller than her mother-in-law. But the old lady was wide set, as broad as she was tall.

They could have taken the car, but Okaa-san was canny. She knew to save the fuel.

The radio broadcast informed them that in Tokyo public transport had come to a standstill. No trains, no buses, no subways or trams were running.

'Poor Ichiro. How will he get home?' Okaa-san asked.

Katherine reckoned he would feel right at home sleeping in the office. He spent so much of his time there anyway.

It was Sunday before they finally made contact with Ichiro. He was fine. Tokyo had been less severely hit than Sendai. Electricity and gas had already been returned to the apartment in Kichijoji. Yet Okaa-san still worried about her only son. 'Ichiro kun,' she murmured to herself. 'All alone in Tokyo.'

Katherine thought about Ichiro too. Lying awake at night awaiting the next tremor, she relived their relationship in her head. They'd met at a party when she was still new to Tokyo. She'd noticed him across the room: tall, broad shouldered, his hair gelled back, geeky glasses and a square jaw. Exactly her type. A Japanese version of Ben, a guy on whom she'd had a major crush first year at uni.

They made eye contact. She boldly held his gaze. It did the trick. Ichiro came and sat on the sofa next to her. They watched the people dance to the salsa beat.

Ichiro asked her where she came from.

'Australia,' she told him.

'Which city?'

'Perth,' she said.

'No way! I lived in Perth for a year.'

'Really?' Katherine seldom met anyone who'd been to her hometown, let alone spent a whole year there; students and holidaymakers alike tended to choose Sydney, Brisbane or Melbourne.

He told her he had been there on a working holiday visa, improving his English and having some fun before returning to Japan to settle in to the life of a salary man. He liked to make day trips to Fremantle and Rottnest Island when he lived in Perth. These were some of Katherine's favourite haunts too.

Kevin pulled Katherine off the sofa to dance. She didn't speak to Ichiro again until she was leaving. He noticed her putting on her shoes in the genkan, strode over and handed her his card.

'Call me,' he said. 'I'll show you around Tokyo.'

She'd called him the next day.

The house trembled during the night. Not a tremor, just the wind. The cold air bit at her nose. She pulled the blanket over her head.

Had their child been born, their marriage might have survived. Normally, when thoughts about her unborn child surfaced, Katherine pushed them back down, but this night she let herself imagine what might have been.

She would be five now, their little girl, had Katherine not lost her halfway through her second trimester. The child would have captured Ichiro's heart in a way Katherine had never managed to do. The doting dad would have held his daughter's hand and walked her to her kindergarten, grinning all the while delighted at her childish babble. In the evening, he would have repeated to Katherine the funny things that Hana had said. Hana is what they would have called her. They would have been a happy little threesome.

Or maybe not. Maybe the fact that Katherine and Ichiro's relationship had not been able to survive a miscarriage indicated that they were never really meant to be. Miscarriages were commonplace after all. Between ten and twenty percent of all pregnancies ended in miscarriage. Still Katherine's had been a late miscarriage. Eighteen weeks. Two more weeks and it would have been labelled a still birth. There would have been something to mourn, a baby to grieve over. And all Katherine's weeping and wailing might not have seemed so disproportionate.

For a year or more, whenever she was alone, and sometimes when she was not, the tears would flow. Not just quiet tears either, but messy, snotty heaving and sobbing. Ichiro would come home from work to find her sitting in the dark bawling her eyes out. He would back out of the living room and go to his computer room. Soon he started sleeping there. It was where he slept still, even though Katherine had long since cried herself out.

They never fought, shouted or snapped at each other. It was worse than that. They were polite, each wary of offending the other. 'Are you finished in the bathroom?' 'Do you mind if I open a window?' That kind of thing. God, it was lonely. Quite similar to Dorothea's marriage to Causubon, now that she thought of it. Not that Ichiro was anywhere near as awful or as dreary as Causubon. Ichiro was basically a nice bloke. Nor was Katherine's plight as pathetic as Dorothea's. Katherine had a job, friends, a social life. And Katherine didn't live in 19th century Middlemarch. She lived in 21st century Tokyo. Katherine could get divorced, Dorothea couldn't.

Happily married with a decent job, that's what she liked people to think. By people, she meant her family and friends at home in Perth. Her friends in Japan knew that her marriage was a fraud. Time to let the rest of her world know too. Time to move on. As soon as she got back to Tokyo, she would tell him.

She had come to Japan originally with the idea of teaching English for a year and then, with the money she'd saved, to go to Europe, to South America and to the US. But one year had turned into two and then she met Ichiro and decided to stay. She had never been to America, unless you counted Guam. Apart from a trip to visit family in the UK in her teens, she had never been to Europe either. Imagine if she had landed in Sendai airport a few hours later, or if Okaa-san lived closer to the coast – she could have died without ever sipping coffee on a Parisian boulevard or ordering eggs over easy at an American diner.

It had taken an earthquake to shake her from her stupor. The shame of it. She would not wait for another disaster. She would start living now.

They planned to drive to Yamagata, to park the car at Okaa-san's sister's house, and from there to take a bus or a train to Tokyo.

'Before we leave, shouldn't we donate the tins and the pot noodles?' Katherine suggested.

Okaa-san hesitated. Perhaps she was thinking to take the food down to her darling boy in Tokyo. They had heard reports of empty supermarket shelves in the capital. Yet according to Ichiro, restaurants were open and serving food. The people of Tohoku needed the food more, Katherine argued. It would be wrong to take food out of the stricken province. The old woman relented. They piled the tins and the pot noodles into the wheelbarrow and rolled it to a neighbou''s house. The neighbour had a van and was using it to bring supplies to the relief centres. It occurred to Katherine that she should stay and help this man, but she quickly reconsidered. If she stayed, she would be one more mouth to feed. Instead she convinced Okaa-san to donate her many futons and blankets. She and the old woman had started to get along, so much so that she thought she might actually miss her mother-in-law. But the Great World beckoned.

She would definitely include Brazil in her itinerary. When she first left Australia all those years ago, it had been a toss-up between an ESL job in Brazil and one in Tokyo. She chose Japan because the money was better, and she thought it would be safer. What with tremors, tsunamis and a nuclear meltdown, Japan hadn't turned out to be so very safe after all. She wondered what her life might have been had she chosen Brazil.

MIGRAINE IN RIO

The hostel was situated in Rio's art district. Katherine lay on the bottom bunk in the four-person dorm, feeling like an axe had been lodged in her right temple. The pain radiated out into her cheekbone, her jaw, the back of her head, her neck, her right shoulder. She had felt the migraine coming on the previous evening but had hoped she would sleep it off.

Migraine had afflicted her forever, or, if not forever, then since puberty. The attacks came more frequently now than they had in her teens and twenties. She could blame the long journey, the delayed flight. There was always something to blame. The truth was that over the past three or four years, flight or no flight, migraine put her out of action several days every month.

A therapist had suggested making friends with the migraine, talking to it nicely, welcoming it.

'Hello Sweetie. How nice that you've come to visit again.'

This therapist believed that the migraine had a message for Katherine and said she should politely and lovingly enquire as to the purpose of its visit. Katherine had tried that tactic. The migraine had not responded.

She had thought that stress from an unhappy marriage might be the cause of the increased frequency of the attacks and had naively believed that as soon as she found the energy to leave her husband, the headaches would cease. She was wrong about that. Migraine had trailed her across Europe and had now turned up here in Rio de Janeiro. The bastard.

No, she mustn't call it that. Migraine was her friend.

She needed to pee. She eased herself out of bed, taking care not to bump her fragile head on the beams of the top

141

bunk. Her feet found their way into her sandals. She staggered across the tiled floor and pushed open the bathroom door. Thankfully the dorm room was en-suite. She remembered to put the toilet paper in the bin provided. Pipes were narrow in this country.

Back in the room, she flopped into the wicker chair by the window, and rested her head in her hands. God, it hurt. She started to cry. Luckily there was no one to hear her. Her roommates were, no doubt, sipping calpirinha on Ipanema or hiking through Tijuca forest all the way up to the statue of Christ the Redeemer, which is exactly what she would be doing too, if she weren't stuck here with her throbbing head. Totally unfair that she should suffer so. She sobbed self-pitying tears before making her way back to bed to wait it out.

Painkillers had no effect. Only time lessened the throbbing. Some migraines required more time than others. Some seemed to abate and then came roaring back before they had ever truly left.

The bedroom door creaked open, signalling the return of a roommate. The roommate rustled plastic bags. Katherine squirmed and let out an involuntary moan.

'Are you okay?' The roommate had an Eastern European accent. 'Can I do something to help?'

'No, no,' Katherine mumbled. Speech came only with great effort.

'Are you sure? I could ask Dona Maria to call a doctor.'

'Thank you. No. No need.'

Katherine felt a hand on her forehead.

'You don't seem to have a fever. Well, I hope you feel better soon.'

The door opened and closed. She was alone again.

As night fell, the migraine loosened its grip. The roommate returned. Oxana was her name. She was Ukrainian. Fortyish, Katherine reckoned.

'Was it a hangover?' Oxana asked.

'I wish.'

'Something you ate?'

'No, no it was just a migraine.'

'It wasn't *just* anything. You were in agony,' Oxana said.

'Yes, yes I was.' Katherine almost started to sob again. Sympathy often reduced her to tears.

Oxana told her that she had spent the last six weeks in São Francisco de Goiás, a small town in Brazil's interior, home to Arturo dos Milagres, and his meditation and healing centre. According to Oxana, Arturo of the Miracles was renowned all over the world.

'It's a wonderful place. It attracts opened minded travellers, seekers if you will. And of course, lots of sick people go there too. He has cured people that medical science had given up on. An amazing man. You should go see him. He could heal your migraines.'

Katherine was doubtful. Besides regular medical doctors, she had visited physical therapists, acupuncturists and Reiki healers. All had failed to cure her migraine. But perhaps all this time it had been a miracle worker she needed. It often felt like it would take a miracle to shift her migraine.

'How exactly does he perform these miracles?' she asked.

'He incorporates spirits of medical doctors and Catholic saints and they heal through him,' Oxana replied.

'He's a medium?'

'Exactly.'

Freaky. Katherine thought she should stay well away from all that weird stuff. Yet, there was a part of her which felt curious. This was her year of travel after all, a time to open her mind and let in different ideas, new approaches.

'So, is he Catholic? You said he incorporated Catholic saints.'

'Born Catholic, yes. But the Centro is not affiliated to any religion. It welcomes people of all faiths and those of no faith. Are you Catholic?'

'No, I am one of those of no faith.' Katherine had been baptised into the Anglican church, but her parents were not religious, and she had never felt drawn to religion in later life.

'I don't belong to any religion either. But I am a very spiritual person,' Oxana said. She went on to explain that purpose of her visit to São Francisco de Goiás was spiritual development. Oxana was, thankfully, in excellent physical health.

Katherine didn't consider herself to be a spiritual person. But funnily enough, for some time now, and even more so since the earthquake, she had been thinking that she should develop her spiritual side. Perhaps the Centro de Dom Arturo would be a good place to start, and if Arturo cured her migraine too, all the better.

'It's a truly beautiful place, with these crystal-clear waterfalls. It's situated quite high on a plateau, so there are no mosquitoes. Really, Dom Arturo was so wise in choosing this location.'

Oxana's description tempted Katherine. She would research São Francisco de Goiás and the Centro de Dom Arturo in the morning. Her head was not yet robust enough to face a computer screen.

Pousada Dona Irene was one of the cheaper inns listed on the Centro de Dom Arturo website. Katherine's bed was narrow, her room tiny, yet to have a room to herself felt luxurious after months of hostelling and couch surfing across Europe. The bedrooms opened onto a secluded courtyard, while the dining area opened onto the street. Residents could sit outside at the white plastic tables and watch the world saunter slowly by.

Dinner was buffet style. She helped herself to beans and rice, chicken wings, sautéed carrots and a stringy green vegetable she'd never seen before. She sat next to a man in his mid or late thirties, a man her own age. He had an Irish accent and sandy hair. Katherine had visited Ireland on the European leg of her world tour. She had stayed with Sinéad who, like Katherine, had fled Japan shortly after the earthquake.

'It's a beautiful country,' she said to the blue-eyed Irishman.

'Pity about the weather,' he replied.

'It wasn't too bad when I was there, actually. And anyway, I kind of liked the mist. It felt magical, mysterious.'

'The rain really affects me,' he said. You see, I have rheumatoid arthritis. It's a curse,' he went on. 'My life was perfect, you know. Self-employed, work going well, lovely girlfriend. I'd built my own house. Then I'm struck down with this thing.'

'It must be tough.'

'You don't know the half of it. The girlfriend left me for another man, a man in good health. Who could blame her really? I couldn't work, so I'm in danger now of losing the house.'

'That sucks. But are you getting better now that you're here?'

'Hard to say. The thing is, and this is my second time coming to this place, when I'm here the symptoms are gone more or less, but once I get back to the damp auld sod, they're back again.'

'So, is it the climate here? Or is it Dom Arturo's healing powers?'

'Well if I could tell you that –,' he said. 'What is it you're here for yourself? Spiritual growth, is it?'

'Kind of. I suppose I would like to develop that spiritual side, if you know what I mean.' She didn't really know what she meant herself. 'And I suffer from severe and fairly frequent migraine attacks. So, I'm hoping Arturo of the Miracles might be able to help with that.'

Irene, the owner, approached their table. A fellow Aussie, the middle-aged woman had shoulder length golden hair with half an inch of white roots and a deep tan. She asked Liam if he would take Katherine down to the Centro later and show her around. The pousada keepers in São Francisco de Goiás usually took it upon themselves to show their guests around the Centro and ensure that they knew its rules and guidelines, but Liam knew enough to show Katherine the ropes.

'No problem at all,' he said.

Little light shone from the widely spaced streetlamps. Several times Katherine almost tripped on the cracked and creviced pavement.

They passed a couple of restaurants and hotels, a juice bar, an ice cream parlour and a coffee shop, all empty of customers at this hour. The paved street led only as far as the Centro. Further along it turned into a dirt track leading off into the darkness. Liam told her, when Dom Arturo was in residence, as he would be the next day, the large car park would be overflowing.

They entered the main hall where several people sat in silent prayer. Pictures of Catholic saints lined the walls. Katherine noticed a photo of the Dalai Lama among them, and a depiction of Ganesh and other Hindu Gods as well as several images of the Buddha. A large crucifix dominated the front wall of the main hall. The hall was somewhat church-like, but unlike the great cathedrals she had visited in Europe, it was not awe-inspiring. It merely aroused her curiosity.

'Tomorrow morning you'll wait here,' Liam told her. 'When your line is called, you'll file through the two meditation chambers.'

'Won't that disturb the people meditating?'

'Well, you'll go quietly and the people meditating will have their eyes closed. The meditators are supposed to generate a kind of cleansing energy. The man himself sits at the far end of the second meditation chamber. You'll be in front of him for only a second. He'll tell you to meditate or he'll prescribe an operation.'

'An operation?'

'Well, that's what they call it, but don't worry, he won't open you up. It's a spiritual operation. I had one myself only last week. You won't feel a thing.'

It was too dark now to explore the gardens properly, but Liam insisted on showing her one feature; a large statue of Virgin Mary standing in a stony alcove. The Madonna was depicted with olive skin and dark hair and eyes. Her robes were white and edged in gold.

'Nossa Senhora de Goias,' Liam declared. 'Our Lady of Goias. Beautiful, isn't she?'

Katherine found the statue a bit creepy. It was lit from below and the lighting cast strange shadows.

Several large baskets filled with folded pieces of paper sat at the Virgin's feet. 'What's all this about?' Katherine asked.

'People write down prayers and petitions and drop them in the basket,' Liam explained. 'I put in a request for a soul mate when I was here last year. No luck yet. Lots of people claim to get what they wish for though. Great success rate.'

For breakfast there was a delicious array of coffee, tea, juice, slices of papaya, pineapple and mango, bread rolls, cold meats, cheese and marmalada. Marmalada was not marmalade, as Katherine knew it; it was quince jam, good with cheese in a bread roll. Her appetite surprised her. Normally, when she felt nervous, she couldn't eat, but here everything tasted so good. Soon she would present herself to Arturo of the Miracles. She wore a white dress. White was obligatory during the healing sessions at the Centro de Dom Arturo.

'Ready?' Liam stood at the doorway in a white shirt, and beige trousers. Presumably beige was acceptable. The Irishman had been here before. He would know.

On their way, other figures in white emerged from pousadas and hotels and side streets, some pale and gaunt and in obvious pain, some in wheelchairs. Others too, like Katherine and Liam, looked perfectly healthy.

Liam took a seat in the first meditation chamber, while in the main hall Katherine waited to see Arturo the Healer. If she understood correctly, Arturo would not be himself when she stood before him, he would have incorporated a spirit entity. So, really, she was waiting in line to see that entity whomever it might be. Too weird.

She looked around the packed hall and noticed that not everyone wore white. She reckoned that many of the Brazilian visitors wouldn't have the ready cash to buy a new outfit for the occasion. As well as Portuguese, Katherine heard French, German and English. Volunteers stood on a raised platform and led the congregation in prayer or in song. Sometimes someone who had received healing would stand on the platform and tell their story. A volunteer announced, first in Portuguese, then in English, that first time visitors to the Centro could now make their way through the meditation chambers to present themselves to Dom Arturo.

They filed through the first chamber. Katherine spotted Liam, his eyes closed, palms upward, his face concentrated. They proceeded into the second meditation chamber. She glimpsed Dom Arturo on his throne at the far end of room. It wasn't really a throne, just a comfy high-backed chair, but he did look like a king up there. The line progressed slowly past row after row of Arturo's devotees seated with their palms upturned, eyes closed. Some mumbled quiet prayers, others managed to remain silent. Katherine felt nervous as she drew closer to the great man. The woman in front of her knelt and kissed his hand. Should Katherine kneel and kiss him too? Or should she just hold his hand perhaps? In the end she just stood awkwardly, frozen to the spot. He glanced at her for just a second, his eyes a piercing blue, and issued an instruction in Portuguese, which the interpreter told her meant, 'sit in meditation.'

Those sitting in meditation arrived early at the Centre each day. They had to remain seated on hard benches, arms and legs uncrossed, eyes closed while entities incorporated, spiritual operations were performed, and all those who wished to see Dom Arturo passed through the meditation chambers to present themselves to him. Meditation sessions lasted between two and three hours each morning and another two to three hours in the afternoon, but if there were a lot of visitors to the centre, it could go on for four or five hours each session. Yikes. Apparently, all those people meditating helped the medium incorporate and cleansed the visitors going to see him. The meditators reaped advantages too. The volunteer guides at the Centro claimed that the meditation chambers were where the real healing occurred.

Meditation interested Katherine. Many articles she had read on health and happiness recommended it. She had tried to meditate at home by herself. She had taken Deepak Chopra's twenty-one-day meditation challenge and failed. Deepak's challenge was to meditate for just fifteen minutes every morning. If she couldn't manage that, how could she possibly manage five or six hours of meditation per day? What had she let herself in for?

A niggle in her shoulders caused Katherine some discomfort during the morning meditation the next day. And when she had thought the session almost over, it had dragged on for what seemed like another hour. And yet there she was, emerging from the meditation hall, having completed her first prolonged meditation session. She felt pleased with herself. Following the example set by those in front, she dipped her fingers into the holy water font at the doorway and made a sign of the cross, or a version of it, at least.

Liam was waiting for her in the main hall. 'Well? How did you find it?' he asked. 'Torturous?'

'Yeah, at times. But at other times it felt, you know, good.'

'Those benches, they're agony, what?'

'My bum started to go numb after the first hour. I noticed the seasoned meditators brought cushions. Very wise.'

'Oh, they have all the tricks.'

Katherine craved something sweet, so they stopped at Café Gigi's on their way back to the pousada. From the delectable array of desserts, she chose a sumptuous pineapple cake. Cake selected, she joined Liam out front. He was sitting with a striking woman whom he introduced as Fiona. With a thick mane of curly red hair and pale freckled skin, Fiona looked like a Celtic Goddess. Liam and Fiona gossiped about goings on in São Francisco de Goiás while Katherine tucked into her cake.

'What brought you here?' Fiona asked.

'Migraine, I guess, and curiosity.'

'You should drink more water,' Fiona said.

Katherine couldn't count the number of times people had advised water as a remedy for her headaches. She drank water. She drank gallons of the stuff. It did nothing to deter her migraine.

'And meat and green leafy vegetables,' Fiona continued. 'I sense an iron deficiency.'

Katherine didn't remember asking this woman for a diagnosis.

'There's a big knot in the area of your stomach,' she said.

'That could be something to do with the enormous slice of cake I just devoured.'

Fiona didn't laugh. She didn't even smile. 'It's something you've been carrying around for a while. Shame or remorse, possibly.'

The knot could be guilt about leaving her husband or about leaving Japan. It could be survivor's guilt. Fiona's eyes rested uneasily on Katherine's mid-section. The silence grew uncomfortable.

'Maybe it's survivor's guilt or deserter's guilt or something,' Katherine said.

Fiona frowned. She seemed to want detail.

'I live in Japan,' Katherine said. 'But I left a couple of months after the disaster –the earthquake and tsunami. You probably remember seeing it on the news?'

'Yes, when was that? A year ago? Eighteen months?'

'It happened in March,' Katherine said. 'Seven months ago, now.'

Fiona nodded slowly; her eyes still fixed on Katherine's torso.

The silence grew uncomfortable, Katherine filled it, babbled on about her recent history. 'I flew into Sendai airport that morning. That afternoon the tsunami inundated that airport. The earthquake damaged my mother-in-law's house, but the tsunami didn't reach it. So, we were fine really, unaffected relatively speaking. I mean, we didn't have electricity or gas, or running water, but we were okay. So many people lost their homes, their loved ones, their whole communities. And instead of sticking around to help, I fled.'

'Write it down,' Fiona instructed. 'All your feelings of remorse, put them on paper, then put that paper in the basket at the foot of Nossa Senhora de Goias. Ask her for forgiveness and release.'

Katherine thought she might do just that. It couldn't do any harm.

With Liam, she strolled back to the pousada. 'She's an amazing medium, that one,' he said.

Katherine didn't answer. Although she planned to follow Fiona's advice, the woman had made her uncomfortable. She didn't like these mediums looking into her soul uninvited, intruding into her inner world, invading her subconscious mind. There should be a law against it.

The hatchet struck her right temple this time, a sudden blow during the morning meditation session at the Centro. She focused on her breathing and willed the migraine to depart as swiftly as it had come. The bastard had other ideas. A wave of nausea overwhelmed her. She opened her eyes and raised her hand. The meditation guide came to her side.

'I feel sick,' Katherine whispered.

He led her to the sick room. From there the nurse took over. Making soothing noises in Portuguese, she let Katherine know she was in good hands. Katherine lay down on a trolley. The nurse stroked her forehead and her hair. Katherine longed for the her to take her in her arms and cradle her head in her bosom, but the woman bustled away to re-arrange the sick room.

Intense heat spread through her body. She was going to throw up. She looked around and started to panic. She didn't want to mess up the nice clean infirmary. She saw a sink next to the wall. She lowered herself off the trolley and tottered over to it. She reached it just in time. Thank God, she wore her hair short, and didn't have to worry about getting vomit stuck in it. She retched until her stomach was empty. The nurse came to her side and uttered words of comfort. She wiped Katherine's face with a cool cloth, gave her a glass of water and helped her back to the trolley. Katherine lay down and let the pain take her over. After some time, the nurse arranged for a taxi to take her home. Back at the hotel, she closed the shutters in her room and went to bed.

By morning the pain had gone, but she felt weak and disoriented as she often did after a severe migraine. She chose not to sit in meditation that morning. Instead she waited in line to see Arturo dos Milagres once more. She planned to ask for a spiritual operation.

No knives or sutures were involved in these operations. Recipients sat in a special chamber, a spiritual operating theatre, if you will. Those meditating in the meditation chambers, the spirits floating around the Centro and Dom Arturo himself, sent a blast of healing energy their way and boom – healing occurred. It was all far beyond Katherine's powers of comprehension. Nonetheless, it seemed worth a try. She wanted rid of these migraines.

Dom Arturo agreed to the surgery and that afternoon she sat in the spiritual operating chamber with all the other patients. The guides first led them in prayer and meditation and then instructed them to place their hands on whichever part of their body required surgery. Katherine placed both her hands on her head. The guides continued to pray and chant until they declared the surgeries complete. Dom Arturo advised against walking post-surgery, so taxis awaited to take them back to their hotels and pousadas.

Reading and watching TV were forbidden during the thirty-six-hour period of bed rest on which Dom Arturo insisted for post-op patients. A jug of water sat on her bedside locker. The toilet was twelve steps away. Irene brought her soup when she was hungry. What more could she want? The day and a half passed in a comfy haze.

She finally resurfaced and went to the dining room for a herbal tea.

'Well,' Liam said, looking up from the Portuguese phrasebook, he'd been studying, 'Do you think you'll be able to follow all those post-op rules?''

'Sure,' Katherine said.

'You're good at following rules, are you?'

'I'm too cautious to rebel,' she said.

Katherine didn't imagine the rules would pose much of a challenge. For forty days after a spiritual operation, patients were required to abstain from pork, alcohol and sex. Katherine ate no other meat besides chicken. And although during her travels she had sampled raspberry beer in Belgium, champagne in France, Drambuie in Scotland, Guinness in Ireland and port and muscatel in Portugal, she was not normally much of a drinker.

And sex? Well, who would she have sex with? Even if she did meet someone new, they could surely wait forty days. During the six long years of her marriage there had been many periods of forty days and more when she and her husband had not had sex. And in the six months since they'd separated, she hadn't had sex either. She had found companionship on her travels, but not romance or sex. It seemed unlikely that it would crop up in the next forty days.

AN ULTRASOUND

Katherine hadn't checked her email since before her operation. The pousada didn't have Wi-Fi, so she took her laptop to Café Gigi. There were many emails to open and many to discard without opening. A message from her sister came with an attachment. Curious, Katherine opened it before opening any of the others.

'A bun in the oven,' the message read. The attachment was an ultrasound of the baby growing in her little sister's womb.

Katherine felt sick, so sick she thought she might throw up. She zipped her laptop back into its case and left the café without taking a sip of the coffee she ordered. She returned to her room and lay in bed soaking in envy, confusion and self-pity.

Six years before, when Katherine had discovered she was pregnant, she hadn't shown the first ultrasound to her family. She had shared it only with Ichiro. She wasn't sure, you see, if she wanted the baby or not. She had grown more attached to the life growing inside her as the weeks went by, but it wasn't until she lost the child that she realised how much she wanted her. She thought sometimes that if she had welcomed the baby more openly initially, her womb might have felt cosier, warmer and the child might have stuck around.

Her rational mind knew this was nonsense. These things happened. No one was to blame. But …

Katherine returned to the s café the following day. She liked it there. It was spacious and bright. The walls were painted a warm golden yellow and decorated with tiles and tapestries. Books and magazines, left behind by travellers passing through, were stacked in shelves and on the window ledges. But she would not peruse the books, not yet. She had come there to write the requisite congratulatory email to her little sis.

She found a comfy sofa on the mezzanine level, deposited her laptop there and returned downstairs to order an acai smoothie. As she was taking it back upstairs, she saw that a man had sat down on the sofa right next to where she had left her laptop. Leather jacket, dark hair, olive skin: the stereotype of a Latin lover. He watched her through his Ray-Bans. He looked like the type who would chat up any woman who came within a six-mile radius. Katherine sighed. What to do? She supposed she could grab her laptop and take it back downstairs.

She approached the table and reached for her computer. The interloper took off his shades, admired his reflection in the lens and slipped them into the top pocket of his biker jacket. He looked at her with liquid brown eyes.

He swept his hand across the vast sofa alongside him and the armchairs opposite. 'It's okay,' he said. 'Sit.'

He had a laptop too. He might not bother her too much. Anyhow, it might not be such a bad thing, if he did chat her up. He was rather good looking. Why should she run from the attentions of an attractive man? She wasn't married any more.

She sat in the armchair. He turned his attention to his computer screen. She put on her glasses.

'Nice,' he said.

She smiled. Purple frames with a pale pink inlay, she thought of them as her sexy librarian glasses. His eyes lingered on her as she opened her computer and got online.

When their eyes next met, he asked her where she was from.

'Australia,' she told him.

'Australia.' He nodded his approval. 'Good country.'

She turned her attention to her emails and opened the one that had upset her so much the day before. Her chest tightened looking at the ultrasound. She took a deep breath, clenched and unclenched her hands and wrote an email to her little sister congratulating her on her pregnancy. She wrote that she was happy for her and Tom. She lied. She felt jealous. She felt resentful. Not that she wanted a baby herself, not now, not in the middle of her year of travel and adventure. But if not now, then when? Never probably, that's when. Newly single at thirty-nine, her chances of ever becoming a mother seemed slim.

People talked about choosing whether or not to have children. Surely, whether planned or unplanned, all pregnancies were a matter of chance. Katherine had lost one chance of becoming a mum. It seemed now that it might have been her only chance.

She looked at the thumbnail photo of Olivia, five years her junior, at that point a year older than Katherine was when Katherine had miscarried. Olivia looked healthy. She would carry the baby to term. And with her nice house in a nice neighbourhood, her sensible job and sensible husband, Olivia was well set up for parenthood. Good for her.

Olivia, a mother, Katherine, the maiden aunt.

Katherine forced herself to look at the bright side. It would be nice to have a little niece or nephew, an added interest in the next generation. She would be a good Auntie, travelling Auntie Katherine, bringing gifts from afar. Her parents would be delighted about becoming grandparents. Not that they had ever complained about the lack of grandchildren. They were too sensitive for that.

Katherine clicked on Facebook and sent a message to Marina to let her old friend know that she had arrived in Brazil. She and Marina had shared an apartment when Katherine was new to Tokyo. Marina had since married a fellow Brazilian and returned to São Paolo. Katherine then checked the ABC website for news from home, closed her laptop and sipped the remainder of her smoothie.

The leather-clad man opposite her slapped his thigh and convulsed into laughter. Something on his screen must be really funny. He turned his laptop around and passed it to her to let her see. A baby panda sneezed, startling his mother. Katherine had seen it before. She laughed anyway.

'Obrigada,' she said.

'De nada,' he replied.

She zipped her laptop case shut and got up to leave. 'Tchau,' she said, raising her free hand in an awkward and silly looking wave. Why was she getting self-conscious? He wasn't her type.

'Vai con Deus,' he said.

She thought that meant 'go with God.' She had spent two weeks in Portugal before coming to Brazil. She had picked up a little of the language.

She felt his eyes on her as she walked down the stairs.

Downstairs she heard Liam's voice: '... this tingling in my wrists and hands,' he was saying. 'The doctor diagnosed it as carpal tunnel syndrome. Misdiagnosed, as it turned out. I thought it strange you know, because carpal tunnel would usually affect people who spent a long time on the computer, and I don't really, you know.'

He sat at a table out front with Suzanne, a recently retired American woman whom Katherine had met a few days earlier at the Centro, and Fiona, the striking redhead. Katherine hoped the Irish woman wouldn't try to read her aura today. She stopped at their table to say hello. Katherine liked Suzanne. The American was spending several months there on retreat before embarking on the next phase of her life, a phase she hoped would be long and rich.

'Where were you?' Liam asked.

'Upstairs, sending emails.'

'Join us. Have a seat,' Suzanne said

'The next doctor diagnosed fibromyalgia,' Liam continued.

'Symptoms are similar, aren't they?' Suzanne said.

'They would be yeah. Fibromyalgia sufferers would have the joint pain and the tiredness, but with fibromyalgia it's not progressive.'

His listeners nodded and made sympathetic sounds.

'I thought I had sprained my ankle playing football, but it took ages to heal. I know now that that was the very first symptom. And that was two or three years before I got the diagnosis.'

Suzanne turned to Katherine. 'Are you okay?' she asked. 'You walked right by me on your way in. You seemed distracted.'

She told Suzanne about Olivia's pregnancy and the resentment it engendered in her.

'I'm afraid I'm turning into a bitter old hag, a nasty, horrible person. I can't even feel happy for my sister.'

'You're not a horrible person,' Suzanne said. 'Your response is perfectly normal.'

'It is,' Fiona agreed. 'And I'm sure in time you will feel genuinely happy for your sister.' Fiona didn't have children either but explained that she had lots of nieces and nephews and well understood the conflicting emotions news of a sister's pregnancy could give rise to.

Katherine didn't usually bare her soul to people she had just met, but São Francisco de Goiás seemed to have that effect on people. Or perhaps it was just that, when travelling, random strangers took the place of close friends. In any case, she felt better for having talked with Suzanne and Fiona.

She made her way back to her pousada. A horse meandered down the centre of the road. Boys played soccer on the hard dirt in front of lopsided looking homes that must have been constructed in haste. A motorbike pulled up beside her, the man from the café.

'Hop on,' he said.

'It's okay. I can walk.'

'Where you going?'

'Pousada Dona Irene.' It was a mere five minutes on foot.

'Hop on,' he insisted.

She obeyed. Seated behind him on his bike, she thought she could detect sandalwood in the scent of his cologne. Quite nice, whatever it was. He dropped her at her door. He told her he worked at the café and said she should drop by and say hello. She promised that she would.

Irene sat out front dragging on a cigarette. She hollered something at the man in Portuguese. He laughed and sped away.

'Where did you meet that Romeo?' Irene asked.

She saw him again a couple of days later. He was leaning into a stalled sedan, gabbing with its driver. His bum looked delectable in khaki combats. A horn tooted. The sedan was causing an obstruction. He straightened himself and slapped the roof of the car. 'Adios, amigo,' he shouted. He hollered a greeting at those in the car behind, turned and saw Katherine.

'Why you no come see me?' he asked.

She hadn't really meant it when she had promised to come see him. But she could drop in to say hello. Why not? 'I'll come,' she said. 'I'll come.'

'I come, I come,' he mimicked. 'But you no come.'

'I ...'

'Come *now*,' he said.

'Okay,' she said.

'Okay? Okay.' He led her into the café. They stood at the counter. 'You want coffee?' he asked. 'Juice?'

'I'll have a latté.' She reached for her purse.

'I pay,' he said. He joked with the barista while she prepared their drinks. 'Come,' he said, and led the way through to the garden at the rear. He pulled out a chair. 'Sit here,' he said.

She sat.

On the next table lay a pile of white tiles, oil paints, a palette and a rag. He squirted paints onto the palette and re-arranged the items on the table.

A group of American ladies in late middle age sat at a table in the centre of the coffee garden. He approached them.

'I ready,' he said.

They batted their eyelids and simpered at him until one

stood and declared that she would go first. He took her hand, kissed it and sat her down at the table with the paints. He picked up a tile, wiped it, focused his attention on the woman for a moment, then dipped his fingers first into yellow, then blue, and smeared the colours over the tile. He wiped some space clear with his rag and added more colour. At this point, it looked like something a child might produce. But gradually images appeared: cascades, trees with dangling vines, pink skies, a winding path leading into a yellow sunset. His fingers moved deftly across the tile. He used a piece of card to trace fine lines and finished by clearing a narrow border all around to frame his masterpiece. He showed it to his subject. She oohed and ached. He laid it on an empty table to dry.

The next lady took her turn. Again, he stared into her eyes, before he began. He seemed to pull some essential quality out of each customer and splash it in Technicolor onto the tableau.

Katherine studied the tiles drying in the sun. The paintings, his talent, filled her with awe. When he'd told her that he worked at Café Gigi, she had assumed he was a barista.

She glanced at her watch. It would soon be dinnertime at her pousada. During a breather between paintings, she touched him gently on the arm and said that she had to go.

Late Sunday afternoon Katherine strolled down to the Centro de Dom Arturo: her intention was to sit in silent contemplation in the gardens. It seemed a spirit nurturing kind of thing to do and she wanted to get serious about developing her spirituality.

She sat on a bench near the blue wooden fence that marked the garden's boundary and gazed across the *cerrado*. The beauty and the cooling breeze should have made silent contemplation easy, but Katherine felt fidgety. She wished she'd brought a book. Contemplation was all very well, but she preferred reading.

She bumped into him as she was leaving.

'Olá. You like to walking?' he asked.

'Yeah.' She nodded.

'Now?'

'Sure.' She might as well. She had no pressing engagements.

'Okay!' He fist pumped the air in delight.

They walked along an undulating path into the landscape she had been gazing at moments before. The earth red beneath their feet, they passed through low-lying scrub and yellowish-brown grass. Trees grew alone or in small clusters. He picked an odd-looking fruit from a tree. He showed her how to remove the prickly green skin and reach the succulent flesh inside.

His name was Fabio. He told her he had been married once and had a daughter, Clarissa. She was nine years old and lived with her Mama.

'You married?' he asked.

'Divorced,' she said.

He nodded, slowly taking her in with a sidelong gaze.

He pointed to the summit of a hill in the near distance. 'We go there,' he said.

He placed his foot on the lower thread of the barbed wire fence and held it down as she ducked through it. When they reached the summit, they sat on the grass and watched the sun set. He put his arm around her shoulder. She didn't object. He nuzzled her hair and her neck. She didn't think she wanted this.

'Let's just be friends,' she said.

'Okay,' he said.

He withdrew his arm. She missed the weight of it there.

'Look.' He pointed at something in the grass.

Yellowish green, like the grass, she didn't see the butterfly until he took it on a twig. Larger than her hand, its wings were dotted with glass-like specks.

The sky turned red as the golden sun sank out of view. He helped her to her feet, and they started back down the hill.

He mimicked the call of a bird. He waited, then did it again. A bird called back. She laughed. The path began to climb and suddenly she felt weak. Post-op instructions included a warning against strenuous physical activity in the first ten days after an operation. She supposed this hike might be considered strenuous. He saw her flagging and offered to carry her on his back.

'I'm okay. I just need to rest for a moment,' she said.

He insisted and gave her a piggyback ride as far as the town.

'You come to my place, I make you coffee.'

'Okay.'

'My coffee very good.'

She'd already agreed. 'Okay,' she repeated.

He grinned an enormous childlike grin.

His house was on a side street, not far from her pousada. They entered through his garage where his motorbike stood. A table, chairs and an orange settee occupied the living room. Through an open door she saw a king-sized bed and a large plasma TV on top of a chest of overflowing drawers. Several of the drawers were on the floor, their contents scattered all about. He opened another door to reveal his spare room: a single bed cluttered with clothes, CDs, a drawing pad and other miscellanea.

He guided her through the archway at the end of the small living room and into the kitchen. He spooned coffee grains into his cafetiere and lit the gas stove to brew the coffee. He searched for cups from the large pile of dishes on the draining board, found two and washed them.

She sat perched on the edge of the orange settee drinking the coffee. She noticed a framed photo of a golden-haired, brown-eyed child on the wall opposite.

'Is that your daughter?'

'Sim.' He planted a kiss on the child's image. 'Linda,' he said.

Katherine felt certain he'd said his child's name was Clarissa. He couldn't have forgotten his own daughter's name, could he?

Next to the picture of his daughter was one of him in the cockpit of a light aircraft.

'You fly?' she asked.

'Sim,' he said. 'My passion. My dream to be pilota.'

He explained that he took flying lessons in Brasilia whenever he had the spare cash. She found it endearing, this childlike dream of his.

The next day was Monday, but because Dom Arturo was in situ at the Centro only from Tuesday to Thursday, Monday was still the weekend in São Francisco de Goiás. There was little to do, so Katherine joined Suzanne volunteering at the soup kitchen that the Centro ran to serve the needy of the area. Katherine was scraping carrots when the apron-clad lady who ran the kitchen, came up to her and stroked her cheek. 'Que linda,' she said.

'She says you're beautiful,' Suzanne explained.

So that was what Fabio had meant when he kissed his daughter's photo and called her 'Linda.'

Dazed after a day of meditation, Katherine walked back to the pousada with Liam.

'Oi, Linda,' someone shouted as they passed Café Gigi. Katherine turned around. Fabio stood there, finger streaks of paint staining his shirt.

'I love you,' he yelled, reaching his arms out towards her. Katherine couldn't help but smile.

'I love she,' he shouted to a passer-by.

'He's gas, that lad,' Liam said. 'Loves the ladies.'

'I can tell,' Katherine said.

'Dom Arturo healed his girlfriend.'

'He has a girlfriend?' Katherine's heart sank a little.

'I'd say he could have more than one.'

A womanizer well, that shouldn't come as any surprise.

'What was wrong with his girlfriend?' she asked.

'What's that thing that affects one side of the face? Bell's Palsy, that's it. Nice girl too, a Paulistana.'

'A what?'

'A Paulistana, that's what they call the people from São Paolo. Smart too. She's a lawyer.'

A lawyer, no less.

Irene sat in front of her pousada, smoking a cigarette. Katherine pulled out a chair and joined her. They heard a motorbike and turned to look. He blew kisses at her as he passed.

'You know he has a girlfriend?' Irene said, taking a drag on her cigarette. 'She's a lawyer in São Paolo, very successful, very smart.'

Enough already, Katherine had no intention of trying to compete with this lawyer lady. Fabio was fun to hang out with, but nothing was going to happen between them, nothing. The attention he paid her flattered her, boosted her ego, but she wasn't interested in him, not really. He was not her type. And why did Irene have to comment on every single occurrence in São Francisco de Goiás? It drove Katherine nuts. In fact, the pousada was really getting on Katherine's nerves recently. So small and poky, it provided no privacy whatsoever. Liam had suggested that they rent a place together. He'd found a two-bedroom bungalow and reckoned it would work out cheaper than staying in Irene's pousada. Katherine decided she would take him up on the offer. The pousada was fine for short stays, but she had decided she wanted to hang out in São Francisco de Goiás for a few weeks; soaking up the spiritual vibes, practicing meditation and taking a breather from the constant motion that had been her life those past five months.

Fabio pulled up at the pousada on Saturday afternoon. 'Bom dia, meu amor. Tudo bem? he said.

Katherine blushed. She hoped no one noticed. She was doing her utmost to feign indifference to the attentions of this Don Juan.

'You want to go to festa?' Fabio asked.

'Now?'

'Yes, there is festa in Palméiropolis today.'

'That's the little town over that way?' Liam pointed towards the highway.

'Sim. You come too?'

'Will I fit?'

'Sim. No problema.'

Katherine sat sandwiched between Fabio and Liam on the bumpy unpaved road to Palméiropolis. She wore the spare helmet. Presumably Fabio deemed Liam's head harder and less precious. The smell of barbecued meat greeted them as they neared the town. The streets were lined with bunting, and thronged with men in check shirts, women in tank tops and skin-tight jeans. Both sexes favoured Stetsons and cowboy boots. A band played Brazilian country music on a stage in the plaza. Couples danced. Children chased each other between the plastic chairs and tables and the stalls selling food and drink.

They joined friends of his close to the stage. Fabio danced with Katherine but grew frustrated with her clumsiness and handed her to a female friend to be taught how to move her hips properly. The friend quickly gave up on her.

Katherine watched Fabio dance with another. She liked how he moved. The dance seemed simple enough. She thought she could figure it out if she watched closely.

They sat and ate skewers of barbecued beef. They washed it down with Guaraná. A woman with dark hair and dark eyes told Liam that his eyes were beautiful. He seemed chuffed. Later the dark- haired woman pulled Liam up to dance. Katherine's lack of Portuguese barred her from the conversation at the table, so she watched the dancers. Every so often Fabio clinked cans with her so she wouldn't feel too left out. Sometimes he caught her eye and asked, 'tudo bem?' If he were there with his lawyer girlfriend, she would be able to join in. She would be better company for him.

Later he gave her a second chance on the dancefloor. Their feet were in sync. His hand on her back made her feel secure. He agreed her dancing had improved.

'Katarina, minha gattinha,' he said.

'Gattinha?'

'My little cat,' he explained.

She smiled and glanced at his face. God, he was handsome. She hadn't noticed it so much at first, had told herself he wasn't her type. And he wasn't, not really. Anyway, he had a girlfriend. She should ask him about the girlfriend, find out what he was playing at.

'I hear your girlfriend is a lawyer,' she said.

His face grew stern. 'Who tell you I have girlfriend?'

'Irene mentioned something.'

'Selena no my girlfriend,' he said. '*Was* my girlfriend.' He pulled away from her.

She had ruined the moment. Why had she felt the need to pester him like that? He was flirting with her and she was enjoying it. Why couldn't she have left it at that?

When it came time to leave, they could not see Liam anywhere. Fabio took her hand and together they scoured the crowd for him. His anger had evaporated. Good spirits had returned. He thought Liam might not want to be found, that he might be happily lost with the dark-haired Brazilian. Katherine agreed that that was a possibility but didn't want to leave without Liam. Yet she yearned for her bed and couldn't stop yawning.

They found no sign of him anywhere and had to give up. They were pulling away when he ran towards them waving his hands.

'Would ye have left without me? Ye would. Ye bastards.'

A policeman stopped them. What did they think they were doing, three on a bike, and one with no helmet?

'What?' Fabio said. 'I no speak the Portuguese. I Americano.'

The policeman grumbled and waved them away, defeated.

Strolling through the Centro garden, she saw him chatting with one of the Centro guides. He observed her through his Ray-Bans. Katherine chose a bench that faced away from him and sat down.

He came and sat down next to her. 'You no come me. You want me find you?'

She thought about that and concluded that for him to pursue her was exactly what she wanted. She noticed dark stubble on his chin and over his lip. He looked unusually sombre.

'My girlfriend have baby now,' he said.

His girlfriend? Hadn't he told her just the other day Paulistana lawyer was an ex-girlfriend, not a current one?

'She have baby in her...' He placed his hand on his stomach.

'She's pregnant?'

He nodded.

So that was why he seemed so serious and why there were dark circles under his eyes.

He sighed a long weary sigh. He explained that his girlfriend had called him last night to tell him the news. She was very happy and expected Fabio to be happy too. She wanted him to go to São Paolo and live with her there. He told Katherine he would welcome any child God chose to send him. But he didn't want to live in São Paolo. He didn't like big cities and he didn't love this woman. 'Is difficult,' he said. 'Difficult situation.'

Poor guy. Katherine couldn't but feel for him. He seemed so burdened.

He looked at his watch. 'I go now,' he said. 'I go Goiania,

see my daughter.' He put on his helmet. She walked with him to his bike.

She felt ill at ease and not at all sure what she was doing in this strange Brazilian town. She traipsed back to the bungalow she and Liam were now sharing.

Katherine sat on the sofa in the bright and spacious living room in São Francisco de Goiás in Brazil's interior, but her mind was in Japan. She wondered how Okaa-san had reacted to the news of her departure. Did the old woman feel relieved that her darling son was at last free to find a Japanese bride? Or did the divorce upset her? They had made quite a pair, Katherine and her mother-in-law, united in fear and struggle in those days immediately following the disaster.

And what of Ichiro? What was he doing now? Did he miss her? Or was he glad that she had left? Though he'd looked sad when she'd told him she was leaving, he hadn't begged her to stay. He hadn't said anything much at all.

What would have happened if, instead of deciding to give up on the marriage, she had resolved to make it work? In the last few years of their marriage she had made attempts to turn it around. She'd arranged dinners in fancy restaurants and weekends away. They'd enjoyed many of those evenings and weekends, but afterwards they'd returned to being awkward and uncomfortable around each other. From the moment that things went wrong in their marriage, things never came right again.

Liam opened his bedroom door and ambled through to the kitchen. 'Penny for them,' he said.

'What?'

'A penny for your thoughts. You're lost in them, must be interesting.'

He could keep his penny. She wasn't going to share her thoughts on the wreck of her marriage with anyone.

'I'm heading out for something to eat. Want to come?' he said.

'I have fruit. That will do me for my tea.'

'Suit yourself.'

Delighted to have the house to herself, Katherine stretched out on the sofa with her kindle.

On his return, Liam handed her a polystyrene bowl. It felt warm and appeared to be filled with soup.

'What's this?'

'It's from Casanova. He was worried you might be hungry.'

'Fabio sent it?'

'Yeah, I went to that new place across the highway. You know, the one that serves twenty different kinds of soup? Himself was there. He really likes you. He asked me to help him win you over.'

'What did you say?'

'I said you'd be a hard one to catch.'

Katherine didn't think she would be hard to catch, not if Fabio continued to do sweet things like sending soup to her. In truth, she wasn't sure she hadn't already been caught.

'He's one talented guy though, isn't he?' Liam said.

'The tiles?'

'Yeah. I watched him paint the other day. Gifted, no doubt about it. He's raking it in too. Irene says he's the only one in São Francisco de Goiás making any money. The pousadas are empty half the time, the restaurants too. He always has customers. He'll need the money now though. Did you hear his girlfriend's pregnant?'

Fabio asked her out on a date. She told herself it was just pizza and said 'okay.' He beamed and she felt glad to have made him smile.

On the appointed evening, Fabio rang the doorbell right

on time. Freshly scrubbed and shaven, his helmet under his arm, he looked nervous. It amazed her that she could put this accomplished womanizer on edge.

They rode across the highway to the other side of town. Red and white tablecloths covered the plastic tables in the pizzeria. There were two other couples dining. One couple sat in the centre of the dining room, the other by the wall at the far side. Fabio chose a table near the counter. He found a menu. Katherine couldn't read most of it.

'You like cogumelos?' he asked.

'What are cogumelos?'

'Cogumelos? Cogumelos.' He hollered at the pizza chef, who presently appeared at the counter holding a mushroom.

'Mushroom is cogumelos? Yes, I like cogumelos.'

Fabio completed the order without further consultation. His limited English and her non-existent Portuguese made conversation difficult. But he seemed so thrilled and delighted to be in her company that Katherine felt thrilled and delighted too.

He asked her to come back to his house afterwards to watch a film. She thought that might not be a good idea. She remembered that his television was in his bedroom. There would be nowhere to sit except his bed. She wanted to stick to the forty-day abstinence rule.

Besides she didn't think it would be a good idea to get involved with a man whose girlfriend was pregnant.

She reminded him about her operation and the rule.

'No worry,' he said. 'No sex. I like your compagnia.'

Something inside her melted. She let him take her back to his house. If anyone had asked Katherine what film they had watched, she wouldn't have been able to say. They kissed, cuddled and canoodled and just about managed to abstain from sexual intercourse. She did notice the end credits coming up and decided then it was time to go home. He walked her to her gate and kissed her good night.

Somewhere in the back of her mind she was conscious of the ill advisedness of being there in his bedroom with him, touching him, brushing her lips against his shoulder, allowing him to hold her caress her, kiss her.

'Take your clothes off,' he said.

'I can't,' she said. 'Forty days, remember.'

'I want see your body.'

'No, I can't.'

'Please, just looking. I no touch.'

She pulled her t-shirt over her head. Her bra was a lacy blue affair. She hesitated before unclasping it and revealing her small pert breasts.

'Linda,' he said, drinking her in. He eased her back on the bed and helped her out of her shorts. He reached out and very gently ran his finger over her collarbone, along the curve of her breast. He traced a line down to her navel and ran the palm of his hand over her rump. 'Let me see your pusseta,' he said.

Pusseta sounded so much sexier than pussy. She parted her legs slightly.

'I no see.'

She opened them a little more. He bit his lip, then reached out and ran his hand along the inside of her thigh. The air felt thick, heavy with desire, their breathing short, jagged.

The garage door rattled loudly, jolting them out of their reverie.

'Anyone home?' Liam's voice called.

Katherine fumbled for her bra and panties. As she pulled her dress over her head, Fabio went to open the door and let Liam in.

They strolled hand in hand through the cobbled streets of Pirienopolis, once a gold mining town, now a tourist at-

174

traction. The colonial buildings, white walled with red tiled roofs, reminded her of towns she had seem in Portugal. Fabio watched a street artist draw portraits for tourists.

'No bad,' he said, but she gathered from his expression that he thought himself the superior artist.

The stopped for sandwiches at a snack bar before heading out into the hills beyond the town. They turned down a dirt track, soft and boggy. When it became too rough, they parked the bike and went on foot. He gave her his hand as they crossed a river, stepping carefully from rock to rock. They walked along the bank until they came to a waterfall. There, they stripped to their underwear and scrambled down to swim in the pool beneath the cascade.

Later they lay down to dry on the flat rocks. They reached for each other. When they were starting to get too carried away, she reminded him of the abstinence rule.

'But this is sex,' he said.

He had a point, but so long as they refrained from actual intercourse, Katherine could convince herself she was keeping the rules.

Such a nuisance; to meet someone, to feel this intense physical attraction when under orders to avoid sex. And yet there was something quite delicious about this delay. It allowed their desire for each other to grow and intensify.

They dressed and returned to the bike, from where they could see down to the red roofs of Pirienopolis, the woodland, scrub and grassland, the mountains beyond. The path was rough and steep. Fabio had to push the bike for a hundred yards or so, before he could start it. The evening air chilled her arms as they sped back along the highway.

He came in for a cup of tea. Liam joined them and spoke again of his illness and how it both angered and depressed him. Katherine bid them both good night and took a shower to warm herself before sinking into her bed.

She yearned for Fabio's hands on her body. It was a good thing that Liam was in the living room. If he wasn't, she would go out there and drag Fabio into bed with her. She would end up breaking the forty-day abstinence rule, and she didn't want that, not really. She was enjoying this build-up too much.

There had been quite a delay before she and Ichiro first had sex too. With Ichiro the wait had been fraught with anxiety. Because until the night they finally made love, she was never sure whether or not Ichiro wanted to be more than friends and had worried constantly that he didn't see her in a romantic light.

When they'd first started to hang out together, Ichiro had introduced her to the funky neighbourhoods of Daikanyama and Shimo-kitazawa. Together they ate okonimiyakki, man-ja yakki, yakki tori, kushi age. He took her to his favourite kaiten zushi and to several different ramen shops. His mission seemed to be to ensure that she tasted every single type of food that Japan had to offer, to make sure that she returned to Oz knowing that Japanese cuisine was more than just sushi, his way perhaps to repay the kindnesses he had been shown during his time in Perth.

They didn't kiss or hold hands, but then showing affection in public was not a very Japanese thing to do. And they hadn't yet met in private.

He invited her along to Womb one night. His friend was dj-ing there. He suggested she stay in his place afterwards. The trains stopped running around one in the morning. And it would be too expensive to get a taxi all the way back to her apartment in Chofu. She readily agreed, hoping this would be the night.

She spent forever choosing what to wear and getting her make-up just right only to arrive at the club and see that it was choc-full of beautiful people. She couldn't compete.

Ichiro introduced her to his friends, Yuko, Natsumi and Rika. All female, all stunning.

On the dance floor, Ichiro really got into the music, sliding his shoulders from left to right. spinning on his heels, jumping into the air.

'I don't like to dance close to Ichiro,' Rika had to shout to be heard. 'It's embarrassing.' She covered her mouth with her hand and laughed at Ichiro's dance moves.

Katherine didn't find it embarrassing to be seen near him. True, his dance style was goofy, but she admired him for dancing like no-one was watching.

Back at his place, they drank oolong tea at his kitchen table. He showed her photos from his tour of Australia. She failed to stifle a yawn. He decided it was time for bed. He fetched her a towel and showed her the bathroom. She washed and changed into the camisole and shorts she'd brought with her. There was just one futon laid out in the tatami room. A hopeful sign. She snuggled up in it while he took his turn in the bathroom. He turned off the light and got into bed beside her. She waited. He reached across the darkness for her and pulled her to him. More than excitement or desire, what she felt at that moment was relief. He *did* fancy her. He wanted her body. Phew.

With Fabio, it was different. Fabio made it clear that he desired her. That clarity took the stress out if this wait, allowed her to relish it. With him, postponing sex felt incredibly sexy.

BICYCLES AND BIKINIS

Fabio asked if he could draw her.

'Sure,' she said, and struck a pose.

'Nu,' he said. 'Nude.'

She took a deep breath and undressed for him. She reclined on his bed. He sat on the edge, pencil and pad in hand, studying her.

Each stroke of pencil on paper felt like a caress. Her eyes followed his movement. When he looked up and caught her eye, she quivered with excitement.

She thought of all the long, lonely nights of her marriage, of all that relationship lacked: warmth, passion, sex. All of that had been absent from her life for long enough. Fabio was so cute, so funny, so sweet. He told her she was beautiful umpteen times a day. He had told her he loved her before he even knew her name. She wanted to indulge him. She wanted to indulge herself. Fuck the forty days. She was going to have sex with this man.

When the drawing was complete, he knelt beside her on the bed and showed it to her. She looked hot in the pencil sketch. He traced his finger along her collarbone. She pulled him towards her and kissed him on the mouth.

She left his bed while he was still sleeping. Later that morning she heard a knock on the door. Fabio stood on the doorstep holding a single red rose. He handed it to her and blew her a kiss as he returned to his bike. Dazzled, she stood and watched him pull away. None of her past loves had romanced her quite like this.

On her way to the supermarket, she dropped by the pousada to say hello to Irene.

'Hello, you,' Irene emerged from the darkness on the dining room. She pulled out a chair and lit a cigarette. 'How's Liam?'

'All right.' He complained non-stop about his condition, but as far as Katherine could ascertain, he wasn't actually in pain at the moment.

Irene smoked her fag and then disappeared into the pousada. A moment later she returned wheeling out a pedal bicycle with a shopping basket in front. 'I thought this might be handy for you,' she said to Katherine. 'Especially for going to the supermarket.'

'It would,' Katherine said, delighted. The bicycle was similar to the one on which she had whizzed around the streets of Kichijoji. She missed cycling.

'Thank you so much.'

'De nada,' Irene said.

Katherine parked her bicycle in front of the supermarket and went in to buy tea, fruit and the makings of a salad. When she came out, her bicycle was not where she had left it. She saw a man cycling across the wide grassy verge that lay between the row of shops and the highway. Thinking he had to have taken her bike, she dashed towards him. Before she accosted him, she noticed that his bike had a cross bar. Her bicycle didn't have a cross bar. She turned back towards the supermarket and looked wildly around her. Her bicycle was nowhere to be seen. What would she do? Irene would be furious.

She heard a snort of laughter. It came from the bakery next door to the supermarket, Fabio, in his signature Ray-Bans, was watching her, enjoying her predicament.

'It was you,' she said. 'You took my bicycle.'

'I? No.'

The woman behind the counter smiled and shook her head.

'It *was* you.'

He admitted the crime eventually and ducked around the corner to retrieve her bicycle.

'Perfeito,' he said, his eyes lingering on her naked form.

She laughed. Her body was far from perfect. With narrow shoulders, small breasts, wide hips and a big bum, it was pear shaped. Not that she brooded on these imperfections. She was not a model or a movie star; she didn't need a perfect body. She didn't imagine that anyone looked at her body too closely. Certainly, her husband never had. Ichiro had complimented her sometimes on an outfit that she had worn, or the colour of her lipstick, but he had never let his eyes linger on her naked form the way that Fabio was doing now.

Fabio brought her to a local resort. They lay on sun loungers by the pool. To her right, a buxom Brasilera lay face down on a lounger. She wore a thong. Her bare bronzed buttocks glistened in the sun. A woman in a revealing white one piece strode past, her thighs rubbing together as she walked. Her cellulite was worse than Katherine's, but she held her head high, proud of her body. Katherine wore a fifties style tankini, a style popular in Japan. The shorts covered her generous bottom well but did not impress Fabio.

'You beautiful. Why you hide in this?' He pulled at the shorts and made a face.

He was embarrassed by her and no wonder. Her swimsuit was something a nun might choose for day at the beach.

The very next day he took her to Goiana, straight to a small boutique that sold nothing but swimwear.

'No,' she said, turning to leave. She couldn't do that. She

couldn't buy her first, her only bikini in this country famous for the itsiest bitsiest bikinis ever created. She knew her tankini needed to be replaced, but not there.

He blocked her escape. 'I buy for you,' he said. He pulled a bikini from a rack and handed it to her. The bottom was a thong.

'No.' She shook her head. There was no way she would ever go out in public in a thong. He handed her another bikini. She liked the pattern, palm fronds and a variety of leaves in shades of green. It wouldn't do though. She needed something with some padding on top, otherwise she would look flat as a pancake. The cerise pink one was too pink. The yellow would make her look pale. Eventually she found one that she thought might actually be flattering, a halter neck with broad stripes in several different shades of green, the bottoms less skimpy than most of the bikini bottoms in the shop.

She steeled herself to try it on. The assistant adjusted the curtain on the changing room. If it looked too awful, she wouldn't come out in it. She would put her clothes back on and say that it didn't fit.

She appraised herself in the mirror. She thought she actually looked all right. She poked her head around the curtain. Fabio came over and peered in.

'Very good,' he said and yanked the curtain back.

'Bonita,' the shop assistant said.

Katherine leant against Fabio's shoulder and studied herself in the mirror. Her hips were broad and her thighs somewhat flabby, but she looked fine, quite attractive, in fact. All these years she had been covering her flesh, she could have been exposing it.

All her life she had longed for a smaller butt and narrower thighs. All the more so when she moved to Japan where all the ladies had skinny behinds. She had fretted terribly about getting naked in front of Ichiro for the first time, certain that he would never before have seen such an enormous butt.

Had she come to Brazil a decade before, she would have spent the last ten years feeling body confident. She wished she had come here sooner.

Katherine bumped into Irene on the street near the pousada.

'I've been wanting to talk to you,' Irene said.

'Oh?'

'Yes. Oh. What on earth are you doing hanging around with that bloke Fabio?'

Katherine wanted to say that it was none of Irene's business, but she held her tongue.

'You know his girlfriend's pregnant?'

Yes, Katherine knew, and so it did the entire population of São Francisco de Goiás, it seemed.

'What kind of guy chases another woman when his girlfriend is carrying his child?'

Katherine didn't know. But Fabio was kind; Fabio was sweet; Fabio was charming. So maybe kind, sweet, charming men seduced other women when their girlfriends were pregnant. She said nothing though. She didn't want to cause a scene. She let Irene rail on for a moment or two. Then she excused herself and headed for home.

God, why couldn't Fabio and she have met before he impregnated the lawyer from São Paolo?

Liam came into the kitchen, his head down, his brow furrowed. 'I'm after breaking the forty-day abstinence rule,' he said. 'I went for a drink with Irene last night.'

'You had a beer?'

'No, God, beer doesn't tempt me at all. I had sex.'

'With Irene?'

'Christ, would you give me some credit?'

Katherine wasn't sure what Liam meant by that. Irene was interfering and nosey, but despite the white roots and the ever-present cigarette, she was quite good looking. She was in her fifties though, so maybe Liam thought her too old for him. Or maybe the thought of having sex with her was objectionable simply because they were friends, and it would be crossing a line. Whatever. She didn't think Irene would be interested in Liam anyway.

'Do you know Giuliana? She's a friend of Irene.'

Katherine didn't know Giuliana. 'Is she nice?' she asked.

'What does it matter if she's nice? I'm after breaking the forty-day rule.' He shook his head, disgusted with himself.

'I wouldn't worry too much about it,' Katherine said. She had read the Centro guidelines and her understanding was that they advised against sex because they felt that spiritual operations should be regarded with the same seriousness with which regular operations were regarded. Sex could be a strenuous activity and could therefore interfere with healing after an operation. She explained this to Liam.

'You tried to keep the rules,' she said, 'you failed. But now you can just start over and try again.'

'I don't know. I think it's more serious than that,' he said.

'I don't know how you do it. You're so strong.'

Liam believed that the nights she spent in Fabio's bed were chaste. Katherine had no intention of correcting his misapprehension.

'I didn't go looking for it, you know. It was she who chased me, said I was irresistible.'

Katherine raised her eyebrows in disbelief.

'It's the eyes,' he said. 'The Brasileras go crazy for the blue eyes.'

Liam went for a shower and Katherine got stuck into her book. He returned too soon. A waft of deodorant hit Katherine's nose and jolted her out of eighteenth-century France where her book was set.

'Should I tell him?' Liam asked.

'Tell who? What?'

'Dom Arturo, about me having sex.'

'God, no,' she said. She certainly wasn't going to tell anyone about her transgressions. She hadn't even told Liam. 'Just try to avoid sex for however many days are left,' she advised.

Liam was so stressed about the sex, that Katherine began to think that she should be worrying about her own offence. To come all this way, to take up Dom Arturo's time, a man whom so many queued to see, and then to flout his directives. Not good behaviour, not good at all. Yet, sex with Fabio was too much fun to give up. Anyway, didn't it make more sense to obey natural laws and impulses than to obey what Arturo decreed?

She had met a man with lung cancer at Irene's pousada. He had left Brazil looking much healthier and plumper than when he had arrived. And the French woman, Delphine, swore that Arturo had cured her blindness. Yet, sometimes Katherine suspected Dom Arturo of being a charlatan. Her own operation didn't seem to have worked. She had been visited by migraine just the day before. And Fabio was not a fan of Dom Arturo, not a fan at all.

They lay entwined in a blissful post-coital haze. He raised himself onto his elbow and looked down at her pusseta. He scratched his head.

'What?' she asked.

'It's different,' he said.

What was different? Her pusseta? And different from what?

He pulled her up from the mattress and led her into the shower. He waited until the water was piping hot and lathered her crotch in soap. Then he reached for his razor and ever so tenderly began to shave her.

Japanese women had long, flowing bushes. Katherine saw them at the onsen and in the showers at the gym. Cocooned in the Orient, she had been only vaguely aware of the depilation craze sweeping the Western World. She kept her own bush neatly trimmed and she sometimes waxed her bikini line, but she had never shaved before, nor had she ever even contemplated having a Brazilian wax. She supposed Brazilian waxes were de rigeur in Brazil. It stood to reason. To Fabio, she probably seemed like an extra from *Planet of the Apes*.

He placed a finger on the lip of her vagina and with gentleness and care, pulled the razor across her skin until eventually he had removed every last hair.

Katherine looked down at her pussy. She thought it looked like a plucked chicken, most unattractive. But Fabio seemed pleased with his handiwork.

ANOTHER ULTRASOUND

They were sitting next to each other at the same table in Café Gigi where, several weeks before, they had first met. Katherine opened Facebook. A message awaited her. It was from Marina, her Japanese-Brazilian friend in São Paolo. Marina apologised for the delay in replying to her message. She had been very busy. She hoped Katherine was still in Brazil and insisted that she spend some time with her in São Paolo. She promised to take her to the best churasseria in all of Brazil.

It had been six or seven years since Katherine had seen Marina. It would be great to see her old friend again. And to see São Paolo with a local for a guide, that would be wonderful. But leaving Fabio, that would be unbearable. She glanced across at him. He looked weary.

'Look,' he said, and passed his laptop to her. On the screen was an ultrasound.

'It's a boy,' he said. 'She say it's a boy.'

Katherine could never make head nor tail of ultrasounds, but if she said it was a boy, presumably it was a boy. She didn't know how to react. This was too complicated. She passed the laptop back to him and watched him studying the image. He raised his eyebrows, pursed his lips. He didn't look very happy.

She checked flights to São Paolo. They were the cheapest on Wednesday. She emailed Marina to see if Wednesday was okay for her. Marina was online and replied immediately that it was. Katherine purchased the ticket. Wednesday was just four days away. She said nothing to Fabio. He would start work in a moment. Customers were waiting for him in the coffee garden.

Polluted, chaotic, Katherine thought São Paolo a monstrous, difficult city. She yearned for the spaciousness of Goias and for Fabio. Fabio was constantly on her mind. A tour of the Japanese enclave of Liberdade where Marina had grown up provided some distraction. She became sentimental at the sight of the red Torii. And the delicious miso soup that accompanied lunch made her homesick for Tokyo.

During her travels, she'd often fantasized about making her home in Europe or here in South America. As she tucked into delicious gyoza, she thought that returning to Tokyo might be the best thing for her. She had a lot of friends there. And despite her sad marriage, she had enjoyed plenty of good times in that city. It was her home just as much as or even more than Perth was. After the earthquake, she had wanted to quit her job and take a great leap into the unknown. But her boss had offered to hold her position open for her for a year, and ever cautious, Katherine had agreed. A good thing too, she would be broke by the end of this year and would need to start earning again straight away.

But Fabio, how could she be content in Tokyo, with Fabio thousands of miles away in Brazil? While she was in São Paolo, he emailed her daily. He griped about her having left him and begged her to return. She reminded him of his other girlfriend, the pregnant one.

'I no love she. I no marry she,' he said.

Maybe. But a pregnancy complicated things, didn't it? Then one day he sent an email saying he was coming to São Paolo and that he was taking her back with him to São Francisco de Goiás. He'd bought a ticket for her.

She had never felt so desired.

Her heart surged when she saw him sitting, waiting for her

at the airport. He looked different somehow, younger, more vulnerable. She checked in her luggage and they proceeded to the gate. Rummaging in his wallet for his boarding pass, he dropped a piece of paper on the floor. Katherine picked it up. It was a Google Maps print out.

'Do you need this?' she asked.

'No,' he said. 'Is trash.'

For no reason that she was aware of, she scrutinized the piece of paper. The directions appeared to be for a clinic somewhere in São Paolo. She discarded the paper in the next bin they passed but couldn't stop thinking about the clinic.

'Did you meet Selena in São Paolo?' she asked him when they were seated on the plane.

'Sim,' he said. 'I go to clinic with her. She have appointment. She ask me, I go.'

Fair enough. It was the least he could do. The woman was carrying his child. But... 'So, I was not the reason that you came to São Paolo?'

'Sim. You are the reason. I come for you.'

'But you just told me you came for Selena, because she asked you to go to the clinic with her.'

'Two reason. I come for you and I come for Selena. Okay?'

Katherine had momentarily forgotten about his pregnant girlfriend. She hated being reminded.

'Oh, Katarina, minha gattinha,' he said, snuggling up to her. 'No worry. Is you I love.'

RETURN TO SÃO FRANCISCO DE GOIÁS

Little had changed in the eight days she had been away. Dom Arturo received a steady stream of visitors every week at the Centro. Some received healing, others acquired spiritual insights, still more returned to wherever they had come from unaltered by their experience. People from all over the world, and some from just down the street, congregated at Café Gigi to sip lattés and acais and watch the world go by. Fabio painted tiles with his fingers and was paid handsomely for his trouble. Irene sat outside her pousada with a cigarette in her mouth and something to say about all she saw. Liam would return to Ireland in a few days, but for now he was still in São Francisco de Goiás and, according to Fabio, still having sex occasionally with Giuliana, and afterwards beating himself up because he had again broken the forty-day abstinence rule. And of course, he talked about his illness to whoever would listen.

'I think is in his head, the problem,' Fabio said.

Katherine disagreed. Rheumatoid arthritis was a real condition. Still Liam's mental outlook didn't help.

She visited Liam in the house they had shared. He made tea, a strong Irish brew.

'The state of your man when you were away,' Liam said. 'God, was he cut up.'

'Fabio?'

'Who else? He missed you. It was genuine like. He was talking about you the other day, "Katarina is so beautiful." And I said, "Well, she's alright, I suppose." Just to get a rise out of him, you know. He got wicked, pure indignant, like.

"My Katarina *is* beautiful," he said. God, 'twas gas.'

Katherine stared into her tea. 'You don't think I'm crazy coming back here?'

'Why would I think that?'

'Because Fabio's girlfriend is carrying his child.'

'Well shur, it's tough, all right. He really likes you though. It'll never work out with your one anyway. He'll never settle in São Paolo. The big city wouldn't suit him.'

He put the DVD into the player and settled back to watch it from the comfort of his bed. She snuggled up close to him. He wriggled away from her.

'No stay close to me,' he said. 'If you close, I think about sex. I no want sex now. I want see movie.'

She stifled a giggle and edged close to him again. She nuzzled his neck.

'No,' he said. And with one hand on her shoulder, the other on her hip, he pushed her to the opposite edge of the mattress.

She bit her lip to stop herself from laughing out loud and further distracting him from his movie. She wanted to snuggle up close to him, but not if snuggling led too quickly to sex. Her pusseta was still sore from the sex marathon they had enjoyed on their return yesterday.

When the movie came to an end, he pulled her close. He slipped her strap from her shoulder, kissed her breast and flicked his tongue across her nipple.

His phone rang. He ignored it. It rang again. This time he answered it. A female voice on the other end – her, the other woman. Or was Katherine the other woman?

Katherine heard the irritation in his voice when he spoke to Selena. Selena had to hear it too. He stood up and walked to the other room. The phone call didn't last long. And he didn't use a single term of endearment before saying goodnight and hanging up.

For a moment Katherine felt for Selena, pregnant and alone, her boyfriend annoyed with her for calling, unenthusiastic about her pregnancy, grudging even. It had to be awful for her.

On the night before Liam's return to Ireland, they went out for barbecued beef and rice. Fabio told them a story about how he had come home one evening when he still lived in his father's house to find his sister crying. He asked her why she was crying. She said that she was pregnant, and her boyfriend Joao wouldn't marry her.

Fabio fetched his father's rifle. He roused his brother and together they went to Joao's house. He pointed the gun at the man. 'Marry my sister,' he said.

Joao raised his hands in surrender and tried to discuss the issue.

Fabio wouldn't hear any discussion. He simply repeated, 'Marry my sister.'

Joao gave in. But the next day he came to the house to talk to Fabio's sister. Fabio refused to admit him. 'Organize the wedding, then you talk,' he said.

Joao married Fabio's sister. Now, ten years later, they were still married. 'Joao very happy,' Fabio said. 'He love my sister. He thank me.' He laughed at the good of it. Liam laughed along with him.

'What if Selena's brother came out here with a gun and demanded you marry his sister?' Katherine asked.

'Selena no have brother,' he said.

A ROAD TRIP

Fabio showed her Brazil as he had promised. He showed her Brazil as she would have never seen it otherwise. A road trip on his motorbike. Sometimes they camped out under the stars. Other times they arrived unannounced in the gloaming on the doorstep of Fabio's uncle or cousin or old school friend's house. They were always fed and watered, often they were given the best bed in the house.

One night they stayed at the home of an old school friend of Fabio. Rafaela turfed her children out of their cots so that Fabio and Katherine could sleep in some comfort. Fabio tiptoed across the narrow space separating their camp beds and made love to her quietly on the thin mattress before returning to his own small bed. Hours later a gap in the flimsy curtains allowed the moon to shine its light onto her pillow stirring her from her sleep. She saw a child lying next to her: its open eyes, staring and lifeless. Her muddled half asleep brain thought that she and Fabio had rolled onto that child during their love making and crushed it to death. They had killed a child. Her gasping sobs woke Fabio. He flipped the light switch. There was no child. It was a doll. He tossed it into the corner of the room and went back to sleep. Katherine lay awake until morning. The sense of guilt lingered. She could not look their host in the eye over breakfast, this woman whose child she thought she'd crushed to death. Rafaela didn't seem to notice the lack of eye contact. When they were leaving, she told Katherine to come visit again. With or without Fabio, Katherine was welcome, she said.

At his uncle's ranch in Tocantins, Fabio's cousins took

turns riding bulls in a small paddock. The bulls were low sized and didn't seem particularly ferocious. Eighteen-year-old Danilo mounted first. Fabio smack the bull's rump and bit his tail. He sprang and bucked. Danilo managed to stay on for a respectable length of time. Twelve-year-old Lorenço was not so lucky. He hit the ground with a thud and limped away brushing tears from his eyes, poor kid.

Katherine leaned against the fence watching.

'You next,' Fabio said.

'No thank you,' she replied.

'Come. Just sit. I take photo.'

'Just sitting? You'll keep hold of the bull? Promise?'

'Just sitting my love. I promise.'

As soon as she had mounted, Fabio bit the bull's tale and whacked his rump and the bull was off, bucking like a thing possessed.

'Liar,' she screamed. 'You bastard.'

She tightened her legs around the beast and managed to stay on for several more bucks. She came off and landed in a cow patty. She caught a look of concern on Danilo's face. Fabio doubled over in laughter. Soiled, but unhurt, she felt proud of the length of time she had remained on the bull.

If she saw herself now, zooming along the highways and by-ways of Brazil's interior, or stopping for coffee and pão de queiju at a roadside rest stop, she would envy the biker chick with her hot Latin lover. This was living. This was exactly the kind of adventure she had dreamed of and hoped for when as a teenager she had planned her escape from Western Australia. It was the kind of adventure she had sought when on three eleven she had resolved to leave her husband, to leave Japan, to travel around the world. She was living her dream.

Not that this kind of traveling was without discomforts.

Their tent and air mattress were bound in plastic covering and attached to the back of the bike. They dug into Katherine's spine when she leaned back. They covered long distances. Hour after hour sitting in the same position proved challenging. Sometimes she lost concentration, began to drowse. 'Be careful,' he would shout at her. 'You want to die here in Brazil?'

In the mornings, he always wanted to get going early, usually before she had properly woken up. He would shout at her then too. 'Rapido, rapido.'

The vegetation in the jungles of Pará was so dense and the air so humid, she found it hard to breathe. The mosquitoes couldn't get enough of her tasty foreign blood. To them she was a delicacy. They waited in a cloud at the fly screen for her to unzip it so they could feed. Yet, when Fabio suggested they move there, build a shack, get some hens and lead a simple life, her heart thrilled, and she forgot all about the bothersome mosquitoes.

Letting herself in to Fabio's house, she called his name. He silenced her with a finger to his lips. He was on the phone. It was her on the other end – Selena.

'Maybe you should tell her about me,' Katherine said after he'd hung up. It didn't seem such a crazy idea. He'd told Katherine shortly after they first met that the relationship with Selena was over. He hadn't known then that she was pregnant, but still.

'What? She have my baby.'

'So?'

'You no care about my son?' Fabio demanded; his face flushed.

Katherine didn't bear the child any ill will, but as he was yet unborn, he didn't seem real to her.

'After my son born, I tell Selena.'

If he couldn't tell the pregnant Selena about her, she couldn't imagine he would tell a new mother struggling to cope with all the demands of a tiny baby.

'I don't think you will,' she said. 'Not when the baby is small.'

He nodded his head slowly, agreeing that maybe he would not.

'Then when?'

He thought about this for a moment. 'When my son have one year or two years,' Fabio said.

'Two years? I can't wait that long,' Katherine said.

'You no wait?' He said, furious. 'For me? You no wait?'

In two years, he might have forgotten her. Or when the child came, he might fall in love with its mother. How could she wait for him with all these uncertainties?

She had read once about a Swedish princess who had waited thirty years to marry her prince. Because she was a commoner, the king would not give his approval for their marriage. They had waited until his death to wed. Their love story charmed their nation. It charmed Katherine too, the romance of it.

With flowers, dinners and compliments Fabio had wooed her, like no one had ever wooed her before. He charmed and captivated her. 'Don't you know how beautiful you are?' he had said to her just that morning. Being with him intoxicated her. Perhaps after all she could wait.

Selena started to call more often. Fabio would go to the other room to take her calls.

'She say she help me find job in São Paolo,' he told her once after a call. 'Her uncle have airfield near São Paolo. If I work there, I get flight hours. And if I get the license of pilota, Selena say she help me buy small plane.'

She didn't want to hear this. God, Selena infuriated her. Had the woman no pride? Fabio clearly didn't want to be with her. She had used her pregnancy to ensnare him, and now dangled flight hours and the promise of a light aircraft in front of him as added incentives. Disgusting behaviour.

In calmer moments, she felt a kind of kinship with Selena. After all, Katherine had been pregnant when she and Ichiro got married. Ichiro had proposed marriage the moment she broke the news. Katherine had assumed Ichiro felt certain of his love for her, ready to commit to spending the rest of his life with her. She wondered now if Ichiro had felt trapped by the pregnancy. Though they had been together for two years already, they had not spoken about marriage before her pregnancy. It was quite possible he had never seen her as marriage material. Japanese men usually married Japanese women. Perhaps he had asked her to marry him only because it seemed the right thing to do under the circumstances.

The miscarriage had to have been hard for Ichiro too. Instead of a bouncing baby, he had got a disconsolate wife. Her grief had lasted too long and turned into a kind of depression. Ichiro avoided her in her misery, and Katherine resented him for that. But in their carefree days before the accidental pregnancy and the hasty wedding, they had enjoyed each other's company, laughed together, explored the metropolis together. And there had been times during their six-year marriage when that magical feeling had returned to them. Brief and fleeting moments, only. Whenever they had tried to hang on to them, they had vanished into the ether.

A migraine had been hovering for days, waiting in the wings, preparing to strike a crippling blow. She woke in the morning to find her head heavier and more painful than it had been the previous morning. She couldn't face her morning coffee or pão de queijo. Experience intimated that this migraine would get worse before it got better, so when Fabio told her he needed to go to Brasilia and suggested she join him, she declined.

Her headache worsened during the afternoon but had begun to improve before Fabio's return. He showed her the purchases he had made in the capital, tiny t-shirts for a new-born.

Two monkeys cavorting on one, 'Mamãe me ama' *Mummy loves me*, printed on the other. The sight of the t-shirts agitated Katherine. She couldn't bear to look at them. She wished she had never become Fabio's lover. If they had remained friends, she would have been able to get excited with him about those t-shirts and the baby that would come.

She bit her lip to fend off tears. Later, while they made love, she started to cry. Upset by her sobbing, Fabio wanted to stop. She wouldn't let him. She wanted him inside her, his arms around her. She never wanted to let him go.

Katherine and Suzanne rewarded themselves with acais after a double meditation session at the Centro, the first meditation session Katherine had attended in ages.

'What do you make of these rumours about Dom Arturo?' Susanne asked.

'What rumours?' Katherine asked.

'The rumours about him having sex with young women who come here.'

'He has sex with women who come here for healing?'

'If the rumours are true. They might not be.'

'If they're true, well he's a monster... isn't he?'

'Well, I mean, it's not good obviously. But from what I've heard... well it sounds like it's consensual. Nobody has mentioned rape.'

'Even if it's consensual, it's a bit,' Katherine struggled to find a word. 'Icky. He's married, isn't he?'

'Yes, he's been married for forty years. His wife is beautiful too. I mean, obviously, she's not young. But she has a glamourous, Sophia Loren-like quality about her.'

Katherine wasn't very interested in the wife. 'Even if he wasn't married, it's seems like an abuse of his position,' she said.

'Yes,' Suzanne agreed. 'Quite possibly.'

'I'm surprised you're not angrier about this. I mean, you're a devotee of his, right?'

Suzanne nodded. 'I am,' she said.

'You've come all this way and spent all this time here at the Centro. Don't you feel let down?'

'Well, somewhat. But he is just a man. If I put him on a pedestal, then maybe that's my problem and not his. And I'm thinking you know that it's not really him I came to see. It's the spirits he embodies. He is just the medium, the channel.'

Katherine sat back in her chair, ran her fingers through her hair and took a sip of acai.

'Does Dom Arturo have sex with women who come here?' she asked Fabio when she got home.

'Oh yeah,' he replied.

'Are you sure it isn't just a rumour?'

'He does,' Fabio nodded his head vigorously. 'No rumour.'

'How do you know?'

'I see him.'

'You saw him? Having sex?'

'Sim. One day I out walking in one fazenda and there is a car, a big car stopped in the way. I looked. I thought maybe broke down. And there inside Arturo and a girl.'

'A girl? You mean a child?'

'No, no child. A mulher, a woman, nineteen maybe twenty years.'

Katherine tried to take it in.

'Katarina,' Fabio said. 'Arturo makes milagres, but his power is not from Deus, not from God, but from Diablo. He Arturo de Diablo.'

'Arturo of the Devil? Oh, come on.'

'Really Katarina. One day one girl she go to see Arturo at the Centro. He tell her to come his office later. She go. He have sex with her. She come to me. She crying. She hurt.'

'He hurt her? Physically?'

'No, no violent. She very sad, very angry. She no come here for sex. She come here for healing. He take advantage.'

After these revelations, Katherine chose not to attend the meditation sessions at the Centro de Dom Arturo any longer. But she continued to go there sometimes to sit in the gardens. Fabio's house didn't have a garden.

She came home from the gardens one afternoon to find the house empty. Fabio bustled in moments later.

'She coming,' he said. 'I think she coming.'

'Selena?'

'Sim.' He rushed into the spare room. All the crap that was on the bed, he threw on the floor. 'If she come, you say you sleep here.' He flung a pillow onto the narrow single bed. 'You say you my friend. Ok?'

Katherine stood in the doorway watching him. 'No,' she said.

'Please Katarina. She have my baby.' Fabio dashed off again

Katherine wasn't staying around to witness this reunion. She quickly packed her suitcase, then walked to Irene's. She plastered a smile on her face and asked Irene for the number of a taxi driver.

'Wouldn't Fabio organize that for you?' Irene asked.

'His guy has a puncture,' she lied.

She followed Irene inside. Irene handed her a card with a picture of a black sedan on it and a phone number printed underneath. She would get the taxi driver to take her to a pousada in Brasilia tonight. Time to get back on the tourist trail. She resolved not to think about Fabio. She could see Brasilia. She would take a city tour. And the next day she would fly to Foz do Iguacu.

She chatted to a French lady on the tour bus and thought that she was managing to come across like a normal human being. Inside was turmoil. She did not hear anything that the tour guide said about the National Congress. The cathedral barely registered.

What a creep, expecting her to sleep in the spare room when he and Selena were sleeping next door. Did a woman need to be pregnant to command his respect? She knew she had done the right thing in leaving and yet it hurt to be apart. Her heart had shattered into tiny fragments. She longed for him.

She hadn't said goodbye to Suzanne or even told her friend that she was leaving. Perhaps she would be able to find Suzanne on Facebook or, failing that Liam would have her contact details. She wondered how Liam was getting on back in Ireland, whether the symptoms of his illness had returned and whether he had met up with Fiona who had left Brazil several weeks before. Liam and Fiona came from different parts of Ireland, but it was a small country, so they might get together.

Katherine failed to understand Liam, Fiona and Suzanne's devotion to Dom Arturo, especially since hearing about the sex scandals. But each to their own, she supposed.

Suzanne had not yet left São Francisco de Goiás but was already planning the next visit. Liam too, though broke, was hoping to return in a year or two. And Fiona was a regular visitor of the Centro.

Fabio was waiting at the pousada when she returned. How he had found her, she didn't know. He looked pale, subdued.

'I understand,' he said. 'You go, I understand.'

She went to him, wrapped her arms around his neck. They spent one last night together. They fell asleep with their bodies entwined but moved apart during the night. He woke in the early hours. He reached for her and pulled her close.

He wouldn't let her go until the PA announced the last call for her flight.

The flight attendant helped her put her carry-on bag in the overhead compartment. She sat in her aisle seat and fastened her seatbelt. She strained to see out the window, hoping in vain for one last glimpse of him.

There were too many tears for any handkerchief to cope with. She let them flow. She wished it could have lasted forever and yet it had not been the lack of a lasting, enduring love she had regretted when the earthquake struck, but the lack of passion, the lack of excitement. For the brief period they had spent together, Fabio had filled her life with passion and excitement. He had given her so much.

The Japanese valued cherry blossom all the more because of the brevity of its bloom, In the same way, her love affair with Fabio was all the more precious for being short lived.

PART FOUR
IN AMERICA

A FAMILY IN EXILE

Yearning for some real Japanese food, Lauren had made the daring decision to take her children to the Yamamori for lunch. Bringing two-year-old Ken to a restaurant was a high risk venture, but so far so good, and they had almost finished their meal.

Emi popped the last piece of korokke into her mouth and beamed across the table at her mother.

'Dou datta?' Lauren asked. *How was it?*

'Oishikatta,' her daughter answered. *It was yummy.*

Lauren smiled. So good to see her children eat well, and they had both behaved impeccably too. Just as that thought was flitting through her mind, Ken threw his plastic spoon onto the floor. Best to get going before he got cranky. Lauren lifted Ken out of the highchair, strapped him into his buggy and manoeuvred the buggy towards the door.

Just then, the door of the restaurant pushed open. An attractive wide-eyed Japanese woman breezed in. Dressed in skinny jeans and a plaid shirt, she looked effortlessly chic. Lauren was similarly attired but didn't look nearly as stylish. Lauren looked like a dumpy American Mom which, she guessed, was exactly what she was.

The Japanese lady beamed at Emi and Ken and looked from them to Lauren. She seemed curious about those two hark haired, dark eyed children with their blond, green eyed mother.

Distracted by the newcomer, Lauren almost forgot her Japanese etiquette. She turned towards the counter, bowed slightly in the direction of the chef and said, 'go chi sou sama deshita.' *It has been a feast.* Emi copied her, enunciating the phrase perfectly.

'GO.CHI. SOU. SA.MA.DE.SHI.TA,' Ken bellowed from his buggy.

'Kawaii!' the pretty Japanese lady said. *Cute.* 'Hafu desu ka?' *Are they half-Japanese?*

Lauren hated to hear her children referred to as hafu. But the woman was smiley and friendly and clearly meant no harm. 'Sou desu ne,' she replied. *That's right.* 'Oto wa ni-hon-jin desu.' *My husband is Japanese.*

Ken started to grumble loudly. He leaned his body towards the door and simultaneously turned his head around and look up crossly at his mother. Lauren took the hint and pushed the buggy towards the door. The Japanese lady held it open for her and followed her outside.

'I'm Yuka,' she said. 'My husband is the chef and manager.' She pointed at the Yamamori's signboard.

'It's a great restaurant,' Lauren said. 'The best Japanese food in Santa Fe.'

'Thank you. I tell my husband you like.'

'Please do. I'm Lauren, and this is Emi and that's Ken.'

'Yoroshiku onegaishimasu.' Yuka said with a bow. *Nice to meet you.* 'Are you living in Santa Fe?'

'For now, yes. We came here after the earthquake.'

'Me too. Same, same. And your husband, he is here?'

'No, my husband stayed in Tokyo.'

Yuka nodded gravely at this piece of information. Then she reached into her purse, found a business card. 'It's old one, from Tokyo,' she said. She scribbled her American phone number on it and handed it to Lauren.

'Thank you,' Lauren said. 'I don't have a card, but I'll call you when I get home.'

'Please, we can get a coffee or do something.'

'That would be lovely.'

Lauren pushed the buggy to the car park feeling pleased to have made this new acquaintance. She hardly knew anyone in Santa Fe. She hadn't really tried to make friends because Santa Fe was temporary. Tokyo was home.

'Get on the first plane out of there,' Lauren's mother had pleaded when news of the earthquake and tsunami broke. 'I don't care how much it costs.'

Lauren had hesitated. She didn't want to leave without her husband. She felt her family should stay together, but her husband refused to go anywhere. Naoto had school to teach on Monday. He would not abandon his third graders at a time like this.

'Besides,' he said. 'The crisis is not here. It is in the North.'

But when the Metropolitan government distributed bottled water to babies under twelve months, Lauren bolted. How had the government lighted on twelve months as a cut-off? If they thought the water unsafe for an eleven-month old baby, how could they be sure it was fine for a thirteen-month old to drink it? Or a twenty-four month or thirty-month old for that matter. How could she give bottled water to her baby boy, and expect her baby girl to drink water from the tap? She flew with her babies back to the States, to her mother and stepfather's home in New Mexico.

When the school year ended in April, Naoto followed her to Santa Fe. He hoped they would all return to Tokyo together after Spring Break. Things were returning to normal in the capital. People worried about the origin of the food they ate and avoided food grown anywhere near Fukushima. Others worried about the Fukushima farmers and felt duty bound to eat their produce. There were rolling blackouts, but you got used to those, worked your way around them. The unremitting aftershocks were harder to get used to, but fifteen million people continued to live in Tokyo. Fifteen million men, women and children were coping. Lauren agreed that she and Emi and Ken could cope too.

'But the radiation,' her mother said.

'The whole country could implode at any moment,' her stepfather asserted.

Russell had a point. Japan was a high-risk zone and, as her mother reminded her, radiation caused more harm to the very young whose cells were swiftly multiplying. Her children were still so small, Ken only seven months old. It was her job to keep them safe.

Behind her mother and stepfather's house sat a two-roomed casita. Their tenant had recently given notice.

'You could stay there,' her mother said. 'I know it's small, but you're used to small places.'

Naoto returned to Tokyo alone. He sent the lion's share of his salary to his wife each month.

Lauren and the children had been living in the adobe casita for eighteen months now. There Ken had grown from a baby into a toddler. He was two years old and Emi had turned four.

HIROAKI AND YUKA

Hiroaki removed the tempura prawns from the hot oil and put them on the kitchen paper next to the tempura vegetables, before placing them gently on top of the rice. He ladled miso soup into bowls and placed one on the tray next to the tempura donburi and another on the tray with the sushi bowl. Waitress Megumi swiped both trays from under his nose and delivered them to a table by the window. Next Hiroaki plated the tonkatsu and gyoza orders. The Yamamori seated only fifty but got very busy at lunchtime. A party of four entered the restaurant, followed by a party of three. Megumi was under pressure. Yuka grabbed a cloth from the kitchen and began clearing some tables. Hiroaki's wife often helped out in the afternoons – she didn't have much else to do. The conditions of her visa didn't allow her to work.

Hiroaki liked it when Yuka came into the restaurant. He might be able to give her a job here when her green card came through. He thought she would be happier if she had a job.

Just one couple remained at the table by the window, the lunchtime rush was now over, Hiroaki could listen to Yuka and Megumi chatting and teasing each other as they cleared the tables.

'Five toots on my way here today, Megu-chan. Beat that if you can,' Yuka said.

Here, the men tooted at women as they drove by in their trucks. Hiroaki had married a good-looking, younger woman. He was not surprised by the attention she attracted.

'It's because you walked. I would get just as many toots if I walked,' Megumi said.

Yuka walked everywhere. She had never learned to drive. In Tokyo she hadn't needed to. In Santa Fe walking along the crumbling sidewalks, she was an oddity.

'Okay, I challenge you. Walk tomorrow and see how many toots you get.'

'It's too far,' Megumi wailed.

'Cycle?' Yuka suggested.

Hiroaki's wife liked to cycle. There were some nice cycle paths along the railway line and by the Santa Fe river (a tributary of the Rio Grande, it rarely held more than a trickle of water.) Hiroaki knew that his wife often felt nervous cycling on the road with the traffic. In Tokyo cyclists could cycle on the sidewalks if they wanted. Here you were not allowed to do that.

Seeing Yuka joking with the waitress, you would never guess that some mornings his beautiful wife couldn't drag herself out of bed. When she breezed into the restaurant, she brought sunshine and light with her. She left the darkness and despair at home.

Yuka used to be a customer at Hiroaki's yakkitori-ya in Togoshi. That was how they met. She would drop in on her way home from work, order a chicken skewer and a beer and regale him with gossip about her co-workers and stories about her boss. Her boss farted constantly, she said. Yet, despite this problem of his, one of her co-workers had slept with him after an office party. According to Yuka's friend the hotel room smelt foul the following morning.

Yuka was cute, pretty and she made him laugh. Hiroaki would refill her beer without charge and give her the occasional complementary bowl of edamame.

One evening she drank more than usual and grew weepy. She told him that her ex-boyfriend had married her old school friend. She didn't love that ex-boyfriend, not anymore, but she worried that she would never get married herself. Even her younger brother was married now, but Yuka was still single.

Hiroaki had been married once and knew that marriage was no guarantee of happiness. He told her this. She nodded, said she was sure he was right, but she felt marriage would give her life meaning. She didn't want to work forever, to be stuck at the same dead end job without any hope of parole.

'You're young,' he said. 'You have plenty of time.'

'I'm not so young,' she said. 'I'm thirty-six.'

He had put her at twenty-seven or twenty-eight and was pleased to note that there were only eight years between them after all.

Several nights later, she stayed until all the other customers had left. Then she asked him to take her to his bed. Hiroaki obliged.

On his next night off, he took her to a little Tapas Bar he knew in Meguro. She was not familiar with Spanish food. He ordered for them: chorizo, patatas bravas, a jug of sangria. She enjoyed every morsel. They fantasized about visiting Spain together.

That big beaming smile of hers. It did him in.

When her friends organized a barbecue on the banks of the Tama River, he went with her, bringing plenty of chicken skewers. And when Ryuji's band played a gig in Shibuya, she went along with him and supported his friend.

After just six months of dating, she suggested they get married. His first marriage had taken so much out of him; he hadn't planned on remarrying. But he couldn't refuse those wide eyes of hers.

Her smile began to fade several months into the marriage. They were trying to conceive, but she wasn't getting pregnant. She read that stress could affect fertility, decided her job was stressing her out and quit.

Then the earthquake struck. She spent day after day in front of the television watching that dark water devastate village after village along the Tohoku coast. Again, and again the wave came, surging through streets and highways, infiltrating schools and businesses, destroying everything in its path. He encouraged her to turn off the television to find something to take her mind off the tragedy in the North of the country, a new job perhaps. But jobs were hard to come by in those post three eleven days.

She weaned herself off television by going online. There she read reports about Fukushima and discussions about Sieverts and micro Sieverts and what constituted safe levels of radiation, accounts of how the government was hiding the truth about the disaster and scary tales about dangerous levels of radiation found on street corners right there in Tokyo. She developed a conviction that radiation poisoning was the reason why she wasn't getting pregnant. Yuka began to talk of moving to America. She thought that in America, away from the radiation which was contaminating them, where the air was clean and fresh, the food untainted, they would conceive a child.

Hiroaki thought it unlikely that Fukushima was to blame for his and Yuka's failure to conceive. Many of these stories on the internet were not verifiable. And after all his cousin Natsue was pregnant and she lived in Ibaraki, closer by far to the stricken nuclear power plant than they were in Tokyo.

Still, things like radiation, they affected different people in different ways. You could not be sure. You could never be sure.

Though Tokyo had not suffered, not really, not in the way Tohoku had, everything had changed on March the eleventh 2011. You could say that in the metropolis things returned to normal within weeks, but it was a different normal. Fear lingered. The aftershocks persisted. People downloaded earthquake-warning apps for the phones. Anxiety reigned: it hung over the city like a cloud. And because of that cloud, he thought it might not be a bad idea to get away from Tokyo for a while.

Hiroaki had spent the first two years of his life in New York where his father had been a sushi chef. He was entitled therefore to a US passport and to return to work in the land of his birth. In his twenties, he had worked in Los Angeles for a couple of years. He could find a job there again, or in some other part of that vast country.

The yakkitori shop that he managed in Tokyo belonged to his uncle. Hiroaki would inherit it one day. He had a good staff at the yakkitori-ya. Tetsu in particular was dependable and steady. Tetsu agreed to take on the position of manager for a year or so, with the understanding that the position would be Hiroaki's again if and when he returned from the States. Hiroaki's uncle wasn't all that happy about the arrangement, but eventually he acquiesced.

An old friend in little Tokyo told him about the job in Santa Fe. He said New Mexico was beautiful, which indeed it was. But neither he nor Yuka had lived in a city as small as Santa Fe before. Hiroaki's job kept him busy, but Yuka was bored and lonely.

They had been there for six months, and still they hadn't conceived.

COFFEE

Lauren spotted a parking space right in front of Betterday Coffee. Yes! She wouldn't have to take the children out only to strap them back in again five minutes later. She could wait for Yuka in the car.

She unbuckled her belt and turned around to face the kids in the back. Her tummy caught her attention as she turned, the uncomfortable bulk of it protruding over the waistband of her jeans. She hadn't yet lost the baby weight and her 'baby' was almost two. When they first arrived in Santa Fe, she had thought she and the children would be able to get around on foot and public transport as they had done in Tokyo, but buses were infrequent and grit and gravel spewed out of yards and onto the sidewalks which were cracked and broken and so narrow in places that they were treacherous for a mom, a four-year-old and a toddler in a buggy. She had traded in the notion of walking for a used Toyota. A great little car but driving everywhere wasn't doing her figure any favours.

Lauren hoped Yuka understood that coffee meant take-out. Ken could not be trusted to behave in a coffee shop. Far better to take the coffee to the park and let the children run around, while she and Yuka got to know each other.

Lauren felt a bit nervous. She hoped she and Yuka would get along. It would be so nice to have a female friend. Apart from her mom and the cashier at Trader Joes, she rarely talked with other adults nowadays. And she didn't even talk to her mother all that much. Ironic that when they lived in Tokyo her mom had complained constantly that she never saw her grandkids. Now that they lived in her back yard, she avoided the children as much as possible. She flinched at the sight of Ken's grubby hands coming towards her Donna Karan casuals. Rather than wipe a runny nose clean, she averted her eyes whenever either child had a cold.

An Asian woman wheeled her bicycle to the front of Betterday Coffee. Lauren bent her head to get a better look. It was Yuka. She rolled down the window and waved her over.

'Hello.' Yuka waved excitedly at the children in the back. They responded by shifting slightly in their car seats and widening their eyes. Lauren explained about getting takeout and going to the park.

'Okay, okay,' Yuka said. 'I think I can park my bike over there.' She wheeled her bicycle over to the bicycle rack.

Ken started to fuss, reaching to be taken out.

'We're going to the park, Ken,' Lauren told him. 'You can get out at the park.'

'It's taking a very long time,' Emi said.

Yuka came back, sat into the passenger seat and removed her bicycle helmet. 'I hate this thing,' she said.

'Horrible, aren't they? I think they put people off cycling.'

'Me too. Only the fitness fanatics cycle in this country.'

'Dressed head to toe in Lycra, their cycling shoes strapped to the pedals.'

'Ugh.' Yuka shivered at the thought of all the Lycra clad American cyclists. 'I think I am the only person in Santa Fe who understands that a bicycle is not just an exercise machine, it is a means of getting from A to B.'

'Practical Japanese,' Lauren said.

Yuka nodded. 'Okay, let's go to the park.' She beamed back at the kids.

'Don't you want coffee?' Lauren asked.

'Coffee,' Yuka slapped her forehead. Ken, who'd been watching her intently, did the same. Emi giggled.

This was going to be fun.

At the playground Yuka pushed Emi on the swings and cheered for Ken when he zoomed down the slide. She took one side of the see-saw, while Emi and Ken sat together on the other. Lauren and Yuka didn't get much of a chance to chat, but it was all good. With Yuka running around after the kids, Lauren was able to sit back, sip her latté and watch the world go by. She'd always enjoyed people watching, or if there were no people around, staring into space served just as well. She hadn't had much time for either since becoming a mother, especially since her flight to the States had effectively made her a single mom.

That morning became the first of many mornings that Yuka spent with Lauren and the children at the playground. She started bringing Middlemarch to the playground and would get through a chapter or two while Yuka played with the kids. Middlemarch was incredibly long winded, but Lauren was starting to get into it and to understand why it was so highly regarded. She'd brought the book all the way from Tokyo with her after the earthquake, but only started reading it when Yuka entered their lives.

Yuka also joined them at the swimming pool. Lauren had actually managed to swim a couple of laps while Yuka stayed with the children in the kiddie pool. It was wonderful having Yuka around.

Adobe house followed adobe house. Some of the clay had a warm pinkish or purplish tint, others were orange flavoured, but most were mud brown. Not that it mattered, even when painted green, the walls retained their muddy character. Each clay home was separated from the next by a clay wall or a wooden fence. And they built their fences high in Santa Fe.

Yuka had found Santa Fe so charming when she and Hiroaki arrived first. The plaza delighted her: the open green at its centre, the Indians selling their wares under the canopy of the Palace of the Governors. Canyon Road and its art galleries enchanted. The snow-capped mountains so close you could almost reach out and touch them. But she had seen it all in a day or two. Now she was fed up with the place. It was all the same. Adobe and dust. Even the trailers strived to look like adobe. Mud attempted to disguise their aluminium panels.

One... two... three... third right. This was it. Yuka had slowed down so much before turning right that she couldn't take the steep incline on Moore street. She dismounted and pushed her bicycle up the hill. This was her first time to visit Lauren, Emi and Ken at home. They'd invited her for lunch.

Yuka and Emi had been talking about their favourite food. Emi said that mac 'n cheese was her favourite lunch.

'Macen cheese? What is macen cheese?' Yuka had asked.

'You don't know mac'n cheese?' Emi's eyes opened wide in surprise. 'Mom, Yuka doesn't know mac'n cheese.'

'Well, we must have her over to try some,' Lauren had said. 'It's an American classic.'

Number seventy-six. An adobe-coloured adobe house,

back a bit and to the right, a smaller house just as Lauren had described. She walked past the casa and knocked on the door of the casita. Emi opened it. Ken toddled over to greet her.

'Just in time.' Lauren was stirring something on the stove.

Bookshelves, a fireplace, a TV, toys scattered around the floor. A three-seater sofa separated the living area from the kitchenette. Cushions surrounded a large square coffee table. A doorway led presumably to the bedroom and the bathroom. Lauren had told her that there were just two rooms. It was a little bit smaller, than the apartment she and Hiroaki shared, Yuka thought. In Japan, everyone thought that all Americans lived in large houses. It simply wasn't true.

Lauren put a large bowl of pasta on the table next to a bowl of green salad, sat on a cushion and gestured for Yuka to sit too. Emi sat down next to Yuka and smiled up into her face. Ken took his time waddling over. Then a tassel on his cushion distracted him and he bent over, bum in the air to fiddle with it. When he finally sat facing his food, Lauren, Yuka and Emi bent their heads and said 'itadakimasu.'

Ken chanted 'I.TA.DA.KI.MA.SU,' punching the air with his fist.

Emi giggled and copied him, 'I.TA.DA.KI.MA.SU.' She wiggled from side to side as she did so.

Lauren ladled pasta onto the children's plates.

'Pasta?' Yuka enquired. 'I thought we were having makin cheese.'

'This is Mac'n cheese.' Emi pointed emphatically at her plate.

'Makin cheese is pasta?'

'Yes. Macaroni with a cheese sauce,' Lauren laughed.

'Ah, macaroni and cheese. Sou ka.'

Emi took her first bite. 'Oishii,' she said. *Yummy.*

Yuka tucked in. 'It's good,' she said. She took a few more bites. 'I know why children like it. It's..., how do you say, it's bland.'

Lauren nodded in agreement. 'Comfort food,' she said.

While Yuka was clearing away the dishes, Emi brought Yuka a Japanese storybook to read. She sat on the sofa. Emi snuggled up next to her. She had just read the title page when Ken toddled over and clambered into her lap.
'They really like you,' Lauren said. 'They were so excited about you coming over.'
Yuka sighed. 'I really like them too,' she said.

'Owari,' Yuka said when they reached the last page. *The End*.
'Let's play hide and seek,' Emi said.
'Outside,' Lauren told her.
Emi took Yuka by the hand and led her out to the yard. Ken came charging after them.
'I know a really good hiding place,' Emi said.
'Do you?'
'Yeah, over there, behind that tree.'
'Wow.' Yuka stifled a laugh. Emi seemed to not quite understand the purpose of the game.
'You count,' Emi said.
'Ichi... ni... san...' Yuka counted slowly to give Emi plenty of time to settle herself behind her tree. 'Nana... hachi... kyu... jyu. Ready or not, here I come. I'm coming to find you.'
She could see Ken's bum sticking out from behind the tree. She imagined Emi holding him tight, trying to keep him still.
'Are they under the slide, I wonder,' Yuka said and made a demonstration of looking under the slide. 'No. Maybe they're in the sandbox.' She lifted the lid of the sandbox. 'No. They could be behind the house.' She sauntered around to the back of the house. 'Nobody there,' she called. She turned back around the corner.

Emi and Ken jumped out from behind the tree. 'Haha. You couldn't find us,' Emi shouted.

'You're too good at this game,' Yuka said.

'Now, you hide,' Emi said.

'One, two, five,' Ken said, his eyes wide open. He had no idea. But Emi knew how to count, and she covered her eyes more or less.

There weren't many places to hide, not a lot of vegetation in New Mexican yards. Yuka crouched down between Lauren's car and the main house. When Emi reached ten, Ken took off, thundering across the yard. He tripped over a stone and pitched forward onto his head. He screamed. Yuka jumped up and ran to him. She picked him up and studied him for injury. Just a graze on his forehead.

'MOMMMY,' he wailed. Tears wet his face and dropped from his chin.

Lauren had heard the commotion and hurried out to him. She took her son in her arms, petted and soothed him, as only a mother could.

Quiet now, he reached up and stroked his mother's cheek, ever so gently. So sweet, it broke Yuka's heart. She yearned for this special connection, longed so much to be that magical person, the one to stop a child's tears, the only one who would do in a crisis, the one who could turn everything to right.

She couldn't stay here watching them, feeling so left out. 'I've got to go,' she said.

'So soon?'

She bit her lip and nodded. She stroked Ken's hair and bent to hug Emi, then grabbed her bicycle, pushed it out the gate, and took off down the hill.

Once home, she crawled into bed and under the covers.

Hiroaki had told her that if Fate chose not to bless them with a child, he would be okay with that. It was enough, he said, just to have her.

Hiroaki was such a good man. She knew he liked her from that very first evening when she stopped at his yakkitori-ya for some chicken skewers and a beer. She had made his shop a regular haunt and had decided to have an affair with him. Why not? An affair would break the monotony of her life. Soon after they became lovers, she decided to marry him. They had fun together. They were compatible and that seemed to her a solid basis for a marriage. She couldn't wait for ever for some grand passion, she wanted a child. Then after they were wed, this love for him grew inside her. It overflowed and took her completely by surprise. She had not expected to feel so deeply for him, not at all.

It should be wonderful to be married to the man you were in love with. But sometimes it just made life more difficult. Because sometimes she wanted to give up, to stay in bed for a week or more. But when she stayed in bed too long, Hiroaki looked so worried and sad, and she hated to upset her honey.

Despite this great love she felt for him, it wasn't enough. She couldn't accept that the Gods might not give them a child. She couldn't bear the idea that she might never carry a child in her womb, hold her own tiny baby in her arms.

They would conceive. They had to.

The desert surrounded them. Imposing mountains in the background as they drove to Cerillos petting zoo.

'The wild west,' Lauren said. 'It's mesmerising, isn't it?'

'Yes,' Yuka agreed. 'I'm waiting for a few cowboys to ride by and there could be some Indians perched on horseback, really still, on that ridge over there.'

'I know, right? I couldn't get over it when I first came here, I felt like I'd landed on the set of a Western.'

'Didn't you grow up here?' Yuka asked.

'No. I grew up back East, in Philadelphia. My Mom moved here with Russell around the same time I moved to Japan.'

Lauren pulled into the parking lot at Cerillos petting zoo. It looked like an old-style ranch. It promised goats, llamas, and fancy chickens to pet. As she opened the back door to release the children from their car seats, a large and shiny SUV pulled up next to her battered old Toyota.

'Hello Neighbour,' said the woman emerging from the passenger side.

Lauren turned around to see a tall brunette in her late thirties, or early forties, her hair pulled back into a ponytail. She knew her... It was... from a few doors down. What was her name?

'Hi... Rachel.' The name came to her just in time. 'This is my friend, Yuka,' Lauren said.

'Hi Yuka. Are you visiting from Japan?'

A puzzled expression crossed Yuka's face. She didn't seem to have caught what Rachel had said. She never had any trouble understanding Lauren. But then Lauren had worked as an ESL teacher when she first arrived in Japan and was used to speaking so as to be understood by non-native speakers of English. Also, herself and Yuka often used a mixture of Japanese and English, with Yuka speaking in Japanese and Lauren answering in English.

'Yuka lives here,' Lauren answered for her. 'Her husband runs the Yamamori; you know, the Japanese restaurant on Marcy.'

'Oh, yes. We've eaten there.'

'Great restaurant,' her husband said. 'I love the yakkisoba.' A bulky fair-haired man, he wore chinos and a check shirt. He was some of kind of lawyer, or perhaps he was an accountant, Lauren couldn't remember.

Emi waved into the SUV at Rachel's little daughter who was waiting patiently for someone to let her out.

'We should get these two together for a play date sometime,' Rachel said. 'Trini loves playing with older children.'

'She is quite advanced for her years,' the husband said.

'She knows all her numbers already,' Rachel.

From what Lauren had seen of Trinity, she seemed like quite a normal three-year-old. But from what she'd seen of Rachel and her husband, she thought they were the kind of parents for whom normal would never be good enough. Lauren took her time getting Ken's buggy out of the trunk. She didn't want to be tied to Rachel & Co as they made their way around the petting zoo.

YUKA BABYSITS

Exposed beams stretched across the living room ceiling. Two large and sumptuous sofas faced each other across a coffee table. There was no television in the living room. Instead, the Mitchells watched TV in their den. Adobe, like all the other houses on the street, looked quite small from the outside, but inside it had a surprising number of rooms, as well as the den, it had a computer room each for the adults and a play room for Trinity. Yuka hadn't figured out her way around the place yet.

'So, if you give her a bath about seven and put her to bed at eight…' Rachel said.

On the previous two Saturdays, when she'd babysat for Rachel, Trinity had already been bathed and in her pyjamas when Yuka arrived. She supposed that Rachel now felt she could trust her enough to give her more responsibility.

'Okay,' she said.

Lauren had organised this babysitting gig for her. Rachel had mentioned she needed somebody, and Lauren had suggested Yuka. It was good to have some kind of job, even if it was just one evening a week.

In Trinity's playroom, they made playdough cakes and towers that toppled and had fun together until bath time when the hitherto angelic child turned into a demon. She screamed 'no' and ran out of the playroom and up the stairs. Rachel had told Yuka that Trinity loved bath time.

Through the railing on the landing, Trinity peeped down at Yuka.

'I see you,' Yuka said.

She pulled her head away, then poked it forward again.

'You can't get me,' she said.

Reluctantly Yuka gave chase, but when she caught the child, Trinity squirmed out of her grasp and ran away again. Yuka had to resort to candy to lure her into the bathtub. Although Rachel claimed never to give the child candy, there was a big tub of the stuff in the kitchen cabinet.

Happily ensconced in the warm bubbly water, Trinity stuck her chin into the bubbles then thrust her face towards Yuka for comment.

'You look like Santa Claus,' Yuka said.

'You come in too,' Trinity said, pointing at her.

'No.' Yuka shook her head.

'Please.'

'It's your bath time, not my bath time.' Yuka didn't want to get in the bath. The water temperature was not high enough for her. In America, children bathed in lukewarm water. Americans had some notion that hot water would damage children's skin. Yuka had told Rachel that Japanese children bathed in piping hot water at home and at hot spring baths and it never did them any harm, but Rachel had insisted that Trinity's bathwater be lukewarm.

'I said please,' Trinity pouted.

'And I said no.'

'Please, please, PLEASE.' Trinity was not going to give up.

'Okay,' Yuka conceded. She took off her clothes, hung them on the hooks at the back of the door and stepped into the bath beside Trinity. The little girl grinned in delight.

Yuka relaxed back into the bubbles. Her breasts protruded above the water.

With a mischievous look in her eye, Trinity poked first one breast and then the other. 'Boobies,' she said.

Yuka tickled the yellow-haired child under the armpits. The child slid around the bath. Oops. No tickling at bath time, she must remember that.

She blew bubbles at the child, sailed the plastic boat along the foam.

She'd loved bathing with her own mother as a child. Her little brother often joined them too. Yuka had not wanted him there. She'd wanted it to be just herself and her mother.

After about five minutes she'd had enough of the tepid water and stepped out of the bath and wrapped herself in a large bath towel. She really liked this those big fluffy American bath towels, although they didn't dry as effectively as the small, thin Japanese variety.

She let Trinity stay in the bath a little while longer before she pulled the plug. She was taking the child out of the bath and wrapping her in her own special hooded bath towel, when she heard the front door open.

'Yoo hoo,' Rachel called.

'We're in here,' Yuka shouted.

Rachel opened the bathroom door. 'Hey sweet pea,' she bent and stroked her daughter's hair. 'I forgot my phone and thought it best to come back for it,' she told Yuka. 'Did you have a nice bath?' she said to her daughter.

'Yes, Yuka take a bath with me.'

Rachel looked quizzically at Yuka, taking in the bath towel wrapped around the babysitter's body. 'You took a bath with Trinity?'

'Yes, Trinity beg me to get in.'

'You got in the bath with her?'

Yuka wondered if she had mixed up her vocabulary. Perhaps she shouldn't have used 'beg' in this context. 'Yes,' she said.

'You took off your clothes and got in the bath with my little girl?' Rachel's face was flushed, her voice high and tight.

Yuka nodded slowly.

'Jonathan,' Rachel called. 'Jonathan.'

Her husband stuck his head around the bathroom door.

Rachel spoke to him; her words came fast and furious. Yuka couldn't catch them.

'Just wait a second here,' Jonathan said. 'Yuka, did you wear your swimsuit in the tub?'

'No.'

'Or leave your underwear on?'

'My underwear?'

'Yeah, you know, your bra and panties?'

Yuka glanced at the hook where her bra and t-shirt were hanging. 'You mean did I wear bra and panties in the bath?' she asked.

'Yes,' Jonathan said. He looked relieved to have gotten through to her at last.

'No, of course not,' she said.

Then Jonathan started jabbing his finger at her, his face all screwed up, his words no longer decipherable. Rachel was shouting, her cheeks horrible and red. Trinity started to cry.

'Get your clothes on,' Jonathan yelled. 'I'm taking you home.'

They left her alone in the bathroom. She pulled on her clothes and emerged meekly into the hallway.

'Come on,' he said, jangling his keys.

'It's okay. I can cycle.'

''Your bike's in the trunk.'

They drove in silence until he pulled up in front of her apartment building.

'We could prosecute,' he said as he threw her bike down on the sidewalk.

LAUREN CLEARS UP A CULTURAL
MISUNDERSTANDING

Lauren was still in her pyjamas when her phone rang on Sunday morning. Yuka's name came up on the screen, but Hiroaki's voice greeted her when she picked up. He told a garbled story about Yuka taking a bath with Trinity, the Mitchells getting upset and threatening to call the police. Hiroaki wanted Lauren to talk to the Mitchells persuade them not to inform the police. Lauren groaned. She hadn't yet had her morning coffee. But she agreed to go and talk to the Mitchells. She had to. She felt responsible. She had set Yuka up with the babysitting gig after all.

She felt sure it was all perfectly innocent – Yuka taking a bath with Trinity. Having spent a decade and a half in Japan, communal bathing seemed completely normal now to Lauren. She could see though how it might seem odd to the Mitchells. And she could imagine them getting all hot under the collar and overreacting.

Poor Yuka.

Still, she shouldn't be too hard on the Mitchells. A long time ago, when Lauren was still new to Japan, Natsumi, a colleague, had invited her to visit her summer house in Karuizawa. Natsumi's four-year-old son had asked Lauren to join him for his bath. Lauren had been totally freaked out by the idea and had refused. Natsumi had been baffled by Lauren's reaction.

Lauren threw on leggings and a t-shirt, knocked on her mother's kitchen door, asked if she could keep an eye on the children for ten minutes, then dashed out the gate before her mother had time to refuse.

Jonathan opened the door.

'I hear you had some kind of misunderstanding with Yuka last night,' Lauren said.

'You could say that,' he said and led her through to the kitchen to where Rachel sat, a mug of steaming coffee on the table in front of her.

'You,' Rachel said. 'How could you recommend that, that, that, that deviant to take care of our precious little daughter?'

'Rachel, I think you've got the wrong idea.'

'Maybe it's you that's got the wrong idea,' Jonathan said

'I bet you've never left her alone with your children,' Rachel.

Lauren tried to remember if she ever had left Yuka alone with her children, then stopped herself. She trusted Yuka. Her new friend could be a bit scatty, but she wasn't a pervert.

'Maybe you don't know your little Oriental friend as well as you think you do.' Jonathan tapped at the table, hammering out his point. 'That is one screwball that friend of yours. She gets into the bath naked with my daughter and she doesn't even know she's done anything wrong.'

'And has she... done something wrong?'

'She let Trinity touch her breasts,' Jonathan screamed, his face red as a ripe tomato.

'Ken and Emi often touch my breasts. I'm sure Trinity touches Rachel's breasts.'

'But I'm her mom,' Rachel whined.

'When I worked in a Japanese elementary school the first and second graders would poke my butt. And one little boy, if ever I crouched next to his desk, he would lean his head back and let it nestle in my bosom.' Lauren smiled at the memory.

Jonathan and Rachel scowled.

'I've a good mind to contact the police,' Rachel said. 'Her name should be on a list. She shouldn't be allowed around children.

Lauren scrambled around in her mind, searching frantically for an argument, a thread something to make them see that Yuka was not a monster. She tried explaining the customs around bathing in Japan.

'In Japan there are onsen – hot spring baths and public baths, and some of them are unisex. Men, women and children all taking a bath together.'

Rachel and Jonathan looked horrified.

Lauren backpedalled. 'Most of the baths are single sex nowadays. Children usually go to the female baths, but sometimes they go with their dads to the male baths. It's all perfectly normal over there.' She babbled on for a while. 'I sometimes take baths with my children,' she said. 'And my husband used always bathe with Emi when we were in Tokyo.'

Whether or not she managed to convince them that it was all a cultural misunderstanding, Lauren was not sure. Thankfully, they agreed not to inform the police.

'She is not coming to babysit anymore,' Jonathan said.

Lauren felt pretty sure that Yuka wouldn't want to babysit for the Mitchells ever again. 'I'll let her know,' she said.

Yuka sat on a swing kicking at the dirt. 'What did they think I would do?' she asked.

'I have no idea. Put it out of your mind,' Lauren said.

'I could understand their reaction if I was a man, but I'm a woman,' Yuka said. She sighed heavily. 'I don't think I'll ever fit in here. I'll always be the weird Japanese lady. If I ever have children, they'll feel ashamed of their mother with the funny accent.' She pulled the swing back and started to swing higher and higher.

'Mom,' Emi called. 'Mom, come push us.'

Lauren stayed up late, hoping to Skype her husband.

Eventually he came online. He looked tired. He talked about Tohoku. He had been there the previous weekend. He and several colleagues made occasional trips up to the stricken region. They shovelled mud from homes to make them habitable again.

Lauren told him about Yuka, the trouble she had with the Mitchells.

His brow creased. 'Is it so strange for adults and children to bathe together?' he asked.

'Well, I guess it's un-American,' Lauren said and laughed.

Naoto did not join in her laughter. 'Time for me to go to school.' He hung up without telling her he loved her or blowing her a kiss.

He had lost interest in her. He never wanted to talk to her anymore. He wanted to talk only to his children. He was probably having an affair. Not that she could blame him. She had abandoned him after all.

He had visited in the summer. He came over whenever he could, but this was not the family life they had imagined when they wed.

Naoto's dad had left the child-rearing to his wife. Working late, traveling a lot for business, he rarely saw his sons and couldn't tell one from the other. Naoto had planned to be a present, involved father, the very opposite of how his own father had been.

The earthquake had got in the way of this desire. Or perhaps it was just Lauren with her fear and paranoia that had got in the way. Would he ever forgive her for taking his babies away from him?

Emi studied the menu, pretending it made sense to her. Lauren let Ken play with her phone in the hope that it would keep him quiet. Yuka had asked them to come and meet her here today. They hadn't seen Yuka in over a month. The last time Lauren had suggested meeting up, Yuka had been evasive. Then she and Hiroaki had taken a trip to San Francisco.

'California must have been good for you,' Lauren said. 'You look great.'

Yuka looked radiant. 'I'm pregnant,' she said.

'Wow, Yuka, that's fantastic.'

'I know. I'm so excited.'

'How far along?'

'Twelve weeks. I felt very sick for several weeks. That's why I didn't reply to your texts. Just yesterday or the day before I started to feel better.' She turned to Emi and took hold of her arm. 'I'm going to be a Mommy, Emi.' she said.

'A Mommy?' Emi looked baffled.

'Yep. I'm going to have a little baby.'

Megumi brought their food to the table. 'Itadakimasu,' they said, all but Ken, who was concentrating intently on the phone.

'It's so great to be able to enjoy food again.' Yuka ate quickly and when she had completely devoured her meal, she made an announcement. 'I've decided to go back to Tokyo,' she said.

'What? Now? Aren't you worried about the effects of radiation on your baby?'

'A little, but I found out that they carry out nuclear testing here in New Mexico. Did you know about that?'

Lauren had known about the nuclear testing but had somehow managed to put it out of her mind when she decided to make New Mexico her safe haven.

'And a few weeks ago,' Yuka continued, 'I spoke to a customer here whose husband used to work in the uranium mines. He died of cancer when he was 46. That's Hiroaki's age. The uranium is the reason he got cancer. And this woman, she has health problems too. Also because of the uranium.'

'She worked in the mines too?'

'No, but she washed her husband's clothes and things like that. So, I think maybe New Mexico is just as dangerous as Tokyo.

Lauren rubbed her forehead. God. Was Yuka right? Was Tokyo just as safe as Santa Fe? Had she done the wrong thing bringing her children there? Should they all have stayed in Tokyo?

It had been so scary when the earthquake struck. She had felt hopelessly inadequate, ill-equipped to deal with mothering in the Pacific Ring of Fire. Both her babies screaming. She'd held the two of them in her arms and had had to crouch down to stop herself from falling over. Frozen to the mat in the centre of the living room, she couldn't for the life of her remember what it was she was supposed to do in these circumstances. Where was the safest place?

'Besides, it's not like I'm going to Fukushima,' Yuka said. 'And if I my baby goes to elementary school in this country, he could get shot. At least in Japan we don't have the guns.'

Lauren didn't want to send Emi to elementary school in the U.S. either. She fiddled with her chopsticks. 'Is Hiroaki going back with you?'

'He's going to follow me later. I need to go soon because it's best to travel in your second trimester. I'll stay with my mother in Saitama until Hiroaki gets back.'

'And is he going to be able to return to his old job?'

'Yes, it's his restaurant more or less.'

Yuka chattered with the children. Lauren finished her meal in silence, wondering why on earth she had split up her family to come to this barren place.

Hiroaki came over to say hello. Lauren congratulated him. He blushed. Ken started to act up. No long lazy lunches with Ken around.

'I'll miss you,' Lauren said when they were parting.

'We'll see each other before I leave,' Yuka said. 'Anyway, you'll be back in Tokyo soon, right?

PART FIVE
GOING TO GOA

SINÉAD AND PAUL ARE GETTING MARRIED

They met halfway up Galtee Mór one chilly Sunday morning. Neither was a member of the hill walking club. Paul had come as his brother's guest and Sinéad was Tricia's. Tricia had warned Sinéad against taking photos or chatting too much. The East Munster Hill Walkers considered these activities a hindrance to the business of walking. No one had warned Paul. He paused to appreciate the panorama and was reaching for his camera when the leader barked at him: 'We're not here to be admiring views. Get a move on.'

Paul's bewildered expression amused Sinéad. She caught his eye, jerked her head in their leader's direction, and cast her eyes to heaven. Paul laughed and introduced himself; Paul Maloney, born and raised in Bishopstown, now living in Kinsale. They chatted as they walked and arrived at the summit when the rest of the group was already starting the descent.

The following Thursday evening Paul drove all the way to Cashel and took Sinéad out to dinner at Chez Hans. He impressed her when he ordered mussels to start with. So many Irishmen feared shellfish.

Over dinner they shared each other's recent histories. Paul had lived in the Middle East for eight years and then moved to Canada for love. But 'things hadn't worked out', so he had returned to Ireland eighteen months previously. He was in IT and did freelance work from home. He had plans to set up a small company, create a few jobs, help get the economy back on track.

Sinéad too had lived abroad. She had taught in an English conversation school when she first arrived in Japan, and later had found a job as an English teacher in a Japanese kindergarten. The kids were just gorgeous and were always telling her how much they loved her. She'd even received marriage proposals from a couple of four-year olds. She had a good life in Tokyo, but when the big earthquake struck, she decided it was time to move on. Not that she had had to leave; she had lost neither her job nor her apartment. In Tokyo things had returned more or less to normal several weeks after the earthquake. But the aftershocks were frequent and each one scared her half to death. All the talk about radiation freaked her out too. She didn't want to live somewhere where she was constantly reminded of her own mortality.

Paul sympathized. He had experienced a couple of minor tremors himself. They'd terrified him. He understood too, Sinead's sense of her world shrinking since she moved back to Ireland. He too felt that he'd lived a bolder, more exciting life abroad.

Sinéad finished scraping play dough off the Thomas the Tank Engine jigsaw. She stood up, stretched her aching neck and rubbed her tender back.

'See you tomorrow,' Sophie said before breezing out the door. The lucky classroom assistant was free to leave as soon as the children had been collected.

This job wore her body out. The skin on Sinéad's knees had become rough and red because of all the time she spent kneeling in order to be at eye level with her charges. And too many children hanging out of her caused the backache.

One child had soiled his pants today. Another had wet himself. Neither had a change of clothes in their backpacks. She sat at the computer and typed a note to the parents to remind them about the need for spare clothes.

Returning to Ireland after eight years in Tokyo, Sinéad had decided that she wanted to continue working with small children, so she did a Montessori course in Dublin. It wasn't all she'd hoped it would be. In fact, she found it boring. There was a lot of coursework, all very dull and repetitious. While Montessori education encouraged independent thinking and creativity in children, these attributes were actively discouraged in budding teachers. Their files had to be created in the same way students of Montessori had created files for generations. There was no room for modern innovations. Taking photographs of the Montessori equipment with digital cameras was considered sacrilegious. Each learning tool in the Montessori classroom had to be drawn by hand. And after drawing the pink tower, the long rods or the brown stairs, the trainees had then to write a detailed description of the thing, as if the picture didn't describe it well enough. The instructor didn't like her students to ask too many questions either. The stiff, grey haired lady viewed questioning of the Montessori method as blasphemy against the Blessed Maria Montessori. Disillusioned though she was, Sinéad completed the course and found a job at Rainbow Montessori School in Clonmel.

There were certainly worse things you could do for a living. You could be down the mines, or stitching jeans together in a sweatshop in Bangkok. She did like the children, but sometimes, when changing one of the younger kids' nappies, or wiping vomit from the floor, she wondered if she wasn't wasting her honours degree in English literature and sociology. She felt particularly exhausted today, but she felt worn out every day. Small children required so much care and attention. Thankfully she lived with a mother who spoiled her and often had her dinner ready when she got home. Poor Tricia, who was in charge of the classroom next door, had to cook dinner for herself and her elderly mother when she got in from work.

Her phone beeped as she was unlocking her car door. She read the text before starting the engine.

"Fancy a walk this sunday? without the east munster hill walkers, this time. slievenamon maybe?"
Paul x.

She texted back saying she would love to climb Slievenamon with him and drove home with a smile on her face.

As well as long walks, Paul and Sinéad's courtship involved plenty of fine dining. Paul would text her mid-week asking if she'd ever had the taster menu at the Convent, or if she fancied a drive to County Clare. He'd heard of a hotel there that served sushi of which even a former resident of Japan would approve.

Sinéad enjoyed spending time with Paul. His tendency to whip out his camera every five minutes got on her nerves though, especially when they were on a wet and windy mountain and he spent ages trying to get just the right shot. She found it a drag too to have to look at his photos afterwards. He took photos of the oddest things: cattle sheds, half-built houses, hand ball alleys. Sinéad did her best to feign interest. Tricia joined them occasionally for a walk or a pint. She took the pressure off by showing genuine appreciation of his photographs.

Sinéad and Paul didn't rush into a sexual relationship, but when they became lovers, Sinéad had no complaints about the sex, it was very pleasant. Paul was no Adonis. At 5ft 7, he was barely an inch taller that she was. He was losing his hair, and he was starting to bulge around the middle. But he had nice broad shoulders, strong arms and he was always clean.

Sinéad had been trying to meet a decent man since the earthquake and her subsequent return to Ireland. She'd gone speed dating and given online dating a shot, but the men she'd met had either been incredibly dull or just looking for a quick shag. Until at last she met nice, normal Paul. A man who, like herself, enjoyed a good walk and good food.

Eleven months after they first met, Paul and Sinéad went to Inis Mór for the weekend. They rented bicycles and cycled from one end of the island to the other, taking in Dun Aengus and many of the little temples, where early Christian monks had lived in prayer and isolation. He got down on one knee and proposed to her at the edge of the Atlantic. He had a ring. He said it could be changed if she didn't like it.

Sinéad looked out at the ocean. She remembered the day when another ocean had stolen the lives of thousands less fortunate than she. And in Tokyo, out of sight of that ocean, she'd had to struggle to keep her balance as the ground had swelled beneath her feet. While the earth was heaving, the thought had occurred to her that she should get married, that she should have a baby, that she should do all those things that normal people do. And now almost three years later Paul, good, sweet, decent Paul, was on his knees offering all that to her. How very thoughtful he was. How nicely he'd planned everything. Sinéad got all weepy. She said yes. She saw no reason to say no.

'You skinny bitch,' Tricia said, when Sinéad told her the news. 'I've been walking faithfully with that shower of dry shites for the past four years, and it has done nothing whatso-ever to enhance my romantic life. And you, you come along to one, just one of the East Munster Hillwalkers' walks and you snap up the only eligible man that's ever joined us on a walk. There is no justice in the world.'

Sinéad smiled sheepishly.

'Ah come here,' Tricia said, giving the bride to be a big bear hug. 'I'm happy for you. I really am. He's a lovely fel-la. Have ye set a date?'

'November 22nd,' Sinéad said.

'So soon?'

Paul's sister would be home on holidays from New Zealand in November, and that was why they had decided to have the wedding then. It suited Sinéad. She had no desire to plan anything lavish. And she was anxious to start trying to get pregnant as soon as possible. Just that morning she'd read another newspaper article banging on about how hard it was for women over thirty-five to conceive. Tricia told her that her mother was forty-five when Tricia was born. That gave Sinead heart, but not much, because Tricia was not the first-born, she was the youngest of six.

PAUL FEELS ANXIOUS

Paul enjoyed their walk in the Glen of Aherlow, his first time in the Glen. In fact, until he started seeing Sinéad, he'd hardly spent any time in Tipperary at all, even though the county neighboured his own native Cork.

They needed refreshments after their walk and found a pub in Tipperary town. While they were waiting for their drinks to arrive, Tricia picked up Paul's camera and idly perused its contents. Paul thought a lot of Tricia. She had travelled the world. She'd been to every continent bar Antarctica and had worked on several as well. She'd returned to Ireland to take care of her mother, now too frail to cope alone in the house. But if after years spent in Sao Paolo, Beijing and Doha, Tricia found life in South Tipperary dull, she didn't let it show.

Sinéad returned from the loo and slid into the seat beside him. Tricia switched off Paul's camera and put it down on the table.

'I'm mad with you, you know,' Tricia said, looking straight at Paul.

'What?' Paul reddened. Had she caught him looking at her bosom earlier? Tricia had lovely generous breasts, and that V-neck sweater exposed quite a lot of cleavage.

'Taking my friend away from me,' she said, looking mournfully over at Sinéad.

'Ah, Tricia, you'll still see plenty of me. I'm only going to Kinsale,' Sinéad said.

'There'll always be a bed for you in our house,' Paul said, relieved.

'Not if this one has anything to do with it,' Tricia laughed.

'Sinéad can't wait to fill all those beds up with babies. Can you Sinéad?'

Paul nearly choked on his Guinness. Sinéad had barely mentioned children before their engagement. She told him the occasional funny story about something one of her little charges had gotten up to, but that was it. And then suddenly, babies were all he heard about. The previous week it was baby names, the day before plans to refurbish his house to make it more child friendly. What a nightmare.

They were getting married in November, just six weeks away now.

LUKE MAKES A PLAN

Luke Brentwood got a couple of beers from the fridge, switched on his computer and wandered aimlessly from one site to another. His nephew's birthday party this year had been even worse than the year before. With his going nowhere job, his rented accommodation and his bachelorhood, he was an embarrassment to his brother. His sister-in-law seemed to have given up on trying to set him up with anyone. Julie no longer considered him eligible for even the sorriest single females.

When he'd started out at Direct Insurance, he told himself it was just until he found something more suitable. That was eight years ago. Something more suitable had never come up. He had interviewed for other jobs. He'd been hopeful about a PR position in a green energy company eighteen months back. He'd done well at the interview. He'd been called back for the second round, but someone else got the job. Somebody else always got the job.

Had he stayed in Japan, life might have been better. He might have married a Japanese lady and fathered a child or two. If he had children to support, there would be some point in being a company slave. For a single man, it was ridiculous.

He went to bed a 1:30 am. There was no point in staying up all night moping about his situation. Work was pretty awful every day, but on the days after he stayed online half the night, it was even worse. He fell asleep quickly but awoke with a start an hour later.

The night was still and silent around him. His chest felt tight, his stomach uneasy. It had been happening a lot recently, this waking up in a panic in the middle of the night. Cold and sweating, alone in the dark stillness. Lonely nights, worthless days. His life was empty, null, void. He couldn't take it anymore. He couldn't take it and he didn't have to. Enough was enough.

He got the keys to his beat-up '98 Volkswagen Polo and went for a drive. He found himself driving towards Barton-under-Needwood, where Sharon had lived. Sharon: he'd seen hope in her eyes when Julie had introduced them. The hope had gradually faded the more time she spent with him, until eventually she had come to realize that he just wouldn't do. He wouldn't fit into the role she had in mind for him. He had disappointed her, just as he had disappointed anyone he had ever come in contact with. He was a disappointing bloke, disappointing even to himself.

On a quiet and narrow Staffordshire lane, Luke passed a sharp bend, framed by a stone wall. He turned at a farm gate and drove back towards the bend. He accelerated and aimed straight for the wall. He came to when a policeman shone a torch in his face. The policeman breathalysed him and asked what he was doing driving around those lanes late at night. Though dazed, Luke managed a coherent lie. He said he was going to see an ex-girlfriend and that he must have fallen asleep at the wheel. An ambulance arrived and brought him to the hospital. His injuries were minor, a concussion, some bruises and a couple of stitches to his forehead. He wasn't sure why he had failed. He must have taken his foot off the accelerator too soon. His car was a write-off.

His mother gave him long penetrating looks and said how lucky he was, they all were, that he had not been more seriously hurt. She wondered aloud, while preparing Sunday lunch, what they would do without their Luke. Luke suspected they'd be better off without him.

He tried for a while to adopt the position that he was indeed lucky to have this second chance at life. He tried to believe that he could turn things around, or that something marvellous was waiting for him just around the corner. He even tried talking to people about how low he'd been feeling. But no-one seemed to hear or be willing to listen. Whenever he broached the subject of his crappy job, he was told he was lucky to have one. Think of the lengthening dole queues. Count his blessings.

He raised the subject of his failures in the relationship department with his sister in law. 'I feel bad about how things ended with Sharon,' he said.

'Sharon will recover. She's resilient,' Julie replied.

'The thing is, I don't have a clue about how to love someone,' he continued. 'The whole idea of being in love seems a complete fantasy to me, like a fairy tale, or a sappy Disney movie.'

'When the right woman comes along, you'll understand,' Julie said, patting him on the knee. It sounded more like something you'd say to reassure an adolescent. He didn't think she meant what she said either, 'cos she didn't try to send any potential right women his way.

His mates were all in relationships. Many of them were married. 'You're lucky not to be tied down,' they said, 'to be still out there playing the field.'

'But I'm not playing the field,' he replied. 'The only woman who touches me these days is my mother when she kisses me goodbye after Sunday lunch.'

They seemed to go deaf.

He went along with his friend Gemma one Saturday to hear an Indian guru speak at the Civic Centre. The bearded Hindu was witty and amusing at first, and Luke began to hope that there was something to this spirituality business, but when the guru started wagging his finger at his audience, telling them how unbalanced their culture was with its huge emphasis on material wealth, he switched off. He had been to India, seen the squalor, the deprivation. He thought it might be Indian culture that had got the balance wrong.

Now that he had lost his car, he couldn't even go for a drive in the country. He had to take the bus with all the other losers. He went to the park sometimes. But sitting near the playground watching the children play, as he sometimes did, he'd noticed parents throwing hostile glances in his direction. And there he had been thinking that he looked like a nice guy, a normal bloke. He was wrong. People could see the big hole inside him. 'I'm not a pervert. I'm just dead inside,' he muttered to himself as he left the park and walked back to his gloomy flat.

It was too late now to start carving out some new path for himself. Life was not for him. He would never find purpose or meaning in it. Death was preferable. It was time to accept that. It had been an impulsive act, that first attempt to end his life. That was why it had failed. If he made a plan, he could succeed.

In Japan, salary men threw themselves under trains. It worked, but it was messy. There was hanging, but he couldn't bear the thought of his mother or his father finding him dangling and having to call someone to cut him down. One of his parents would be the most likely to find him too, if he slit his wrists, and anyway the method had a high failure rate. Then the answer came to him: Beachy Head. It was a popular jumping spot. And the idea of taking a giant leap appealed to him.

Fifteen years before, when he was a young man of twenty something, he had brought Cecile to Beachy Head, wanting to show her some of England's charms. He had gone out with Cecile for three and a half years, his longest relationship yet. They met when he was in his final year at university. She was an Erasmus student and had returned to France in the summer. They were long distance lovers for two years. The long-distance thing worked really well for him. It was when Cecile decided to join him in London that he started to go off her. She was beautiful and smart, but she was also very touchy, feely, kissing and caressing him in public, even in front of his parents. It had made him uncomfortable. And her long dark hair was forever clogging up the shower drain. He would find those long dark hairs everywhere, on the counter tops, pillow covers, trailing along his computer keyboard. Those stray hairs repulsed him.

His friends had thought him an idiot for breaking up with her. They were amazed that she'd ever gone out with him in the first place. Cecile had not seen it coming at all. He'd told her it wasn't her; it was him. He was the one with the problem. He hadn't realised the truth of his words at the time. He did now. He *was* the problem. It *was* him. He was a freak, incapable of ever really loving anyone.

That was it then. Beachy Head. He had a week's holidays coming up towards the end of November. That's when he would do it. His death would cause less inconvenience to his colleagues if it came at the start of his holidays. He would have his mother's lawn raked free of autumn leaves by then too. His mother would appreciate that, and he enjoyed raking the leaves.

Sinéad had only nine days left at work. She couldn't wait to get out of the classroom. She had half -heartedly looked for some jobs around Kinsale and Cork city, but secretly hoped she'd get pregnant so soon she wouldn't have to bother about finding a job. Paul had seemed perturbed when she suggested throwing away their contraceptives and trying to get pregnant straight away, but Sinéad didn't let his reaction put her off. It was a typical male response. He'd get used to the idea.

She and Paul had agreed on her being a stay at home mum at least until the child had started primary school. If she had one baby next year and another three years later, she could keep herself out of the workforce for at least seven years. And by then she may have actually figured out what she'd like to do career wise. She certainly didn't want to spend the rest of her working life dusting pink towers and teaching other women's children how to wipe their noses. She could escape it all if she went ahead with the wedding. The only problem was she was starting to have serious doubts about her relationship with Paul. He was a nice guy, but the thought of happy-ever-afters with him totally unnerved her.

It had all seemed like a great idea just a few short months before. But now, Sinéad wasn't sure if she wanted to leave her little bedroom in her parents' house on the outskirts of Cashel. She'd had to share it as a child, but now she had it all to herself. She'd replaced her sister's bed with a comfy armchair. She had her books neatly arranged on her bookshelves, a hardback copy of Middlemarch, her favourite novel, acted as a bookend. Her laptop and her ceramic cats on her desk, and the Daruma and Kokeshi dolls from Japan sitting on the windowsill. She could move everything with her to Kinsale of course, but it wouldn't be the same. She wouldn't be able to hear her parents pottering about downstairs or see Hoare Abbey from her window and wonder whether the distant figures there were tourists or Dan Ryan and his sons checking their sheep. Kinsale was a picturesque, coastal town. And even though it was often overrun with day trippers from Cork city, she'd enjoyed the weekends she spent there with Paul. But she did always look forward to coming home to her own bed. Soon she would have to share Paul's bed with him every night and for the rest of her life. She didn't know if she could stand it.

He was so methodical about everything. Got up at the same time every morning and did his bloody morning stretches. And as soon as Sinéad got out of the bed, he smoothed down the sheets, and fluffed up the pillows and the duvet. He was far too tidy for her liking.

Sinéad and Tricia were in the school kitchen washing the dishes, the building blocks and anything else that could be thrown into hot water.

'I don't know if I can go through with it' Sinéad said.

'Go through with what?' Tricia asked, turning to face her.

'The wedding, I'm dreading it.'

'You could always elope.'

'No, it's not that, not the wedding itself.' She took a deep breath. 'I don't think I want to spend the rest of my life with Paul.'

'Did something happen?'

'No, but when I try to picture me and Paul five years from now, ten years from now, I feel sick to my stomach.'

'It's probably just pre-wedding jitters. I wouldn't worry about it.'

'Pre-wedding terror more like. I'm terrified.'

Tricia took off her rubber gloves, leant back against the radiator and gave Sinéad her complete attention. 'What is it that frightens you?'

'I don't know I can't explain it. It's just, you know, he gets on my nerves sometimes.'

'If you spend a lot of time with someone, they're going to get on your nerves occasionally. Paul is a good man.'

'Yes, he is.'

'The two of you get on so well. You have a lot in common. And his house in Kinsale is lovely. You'd be a long time trying to find someone as good as Paul. He's a catch.'

'I know.'

'What's more, if you want to have children, you need to do it while you still can. I don't regret not having children myself. I mean, I have all the little ones in my class. But having children of your own is very special and there's only a limited window of opportunity to do that. That window does close.'

When Tricia spoke, Sinéad listened. Tricia was a sensible, sassy fifty something year old. She had lived in New York, Amsterdam and Beijing. She had worked with street kids in Sao Paolo and spent a year in an ashram in Tamil Nadu. There wasn't a spot on the planet that Tricia didn't have some connection with, some story to tell about. Her words were sane and logical. They resonated with Sinéad.

Sophie's contribution was unhelpful; 'You love Paul, but you're not in love with him,' the young classroom assistant said. A lot of nonsense, Sinéad thought. She didn't set much store by this 'in love' business. It was gooey, elusive and most probably a complete fiction. She'd believed herself to be in love with Kotaro. But after it was all over, she saw she'd been deluding herself. The guy had never made her happy. He'd never called when he was supposed to. He was always broke. He'd laughed at her whenever she mispronounced anything in Japanese. And sex with him was over before it had even begun. She'd been dazzled by his hot surfer body and conned herself into thinking there was something more to it.

Sinéad then made the mistake of telling her young classroom assistant that recently she'd been thinking a lot about Luke, an old friend of hers from her first year in Japan. Sophie got all excited and said that maybe *he* was *the one*. She urged Sinéad to get in touch with him. Sinéad wasn't sure if she had a valid email address for him, but Sophie assured her that she would find him on Facebook.

Tricia thought it was a bad idea. 'You're fixated on him because he's the one who got away,' she said.

Sinéad explained that they'd only ever been friends; friends with a mutual attraction, who had smooched one time, but still just friends. Tricia thought that was all the more reason to stay away from him.

'Think about it. If you'd actually gone out with this Luke guy, you'd have realized that he had faults and failings like any other human being. Because you didn't go out with him, you never discovered those little things about him that would drive you nuts. You have an image of him, and it's not the full picture,' she said. 'It's half fantasy. Paul can't compete with that. You've found a good man and he wants to marry you. Don't go messing it up. How would you feel if he contacted an old flame just weeks before your wedding?'

Sinéad didn't think she'd mind if Paul looked up an old friend on Facebook and she couldn't see any harm in looking Luke up. So, later that evening, she typed his name into the friend finder and clicked search. There was only one Luke Brentwood on Facebook and it was her Luke Brentwood. He looked good. His hair, which when she knew him had had blonde streaks, was now streaked with grey. It suited him and he had much more of it than Paul had. He was considerably taller than Paul too, she remembered. And one of his shoulders was higher than the other giving him an endearing, lopsided appearance. She'd love to talk to him again. She crossed her fingers and sent him a friend request.

Luke switched on his computer as soon as he got home from work. Waiting for him was a friend request from Sinéad Conway. There she was, with her cute little button nose and friendly hazel eyes. Her hair was short and blonde when he knew her in Tokyo. Now it was a more natural reddish brown and almost shoulder length.

He wasn't sure if he should accept her friend request. Now that he had set a date for his departure from the world, it would be better not to rekindle any old flame.

Flame? Who was he kidding? Nothing had ever happened between them. They had had a bit of a snog once. That was all. She'd probably only ever thought of him as a friend or a friendly co-worker, had only hung out with him, because she didn't know anyone else in Tokyo at the time.

The snog had happened one night when, after a long karaoke session, everyone headed to Jonathan's place. Sinéad and Luke had escaped the crowd and gone back to Luke's instead. He made her a cup of tea while she flicked through his Japanese textbooks. Luke studied the language diligently. He had developed a love for kanji in his earlier sojourn in Japan, when he was on the Jet program in Kyushu. His goal was to pass level one of the Japanese proficiency test. He had taken the test for the second time in December. The results were due soon.

Sinéad had picked up only a handful of Japanese phrases in the six months she'd been in the country. She was trying to learn it using Romanized texts. Luke advised her to master the kana.

They gossiped about their co-workers and laughed about the drunken capers of their night out. He kissed her. She kissed back, leaning her body into his. They made out with enthusiasm on the legless chairs in his little six mat room, until she excused herself to go to the bathroom. When she returned, he suggested they might be more comfortable in the loft. Sinéad got flustered then, said she needed to be getting home, bolted out the door and had fled the apartment building before Luke had time to get his shoes on to walk her to her door.

He felt confused. He really liked her. He had been attracted to her since she first started at Ben's English School. He thought the attraction was mutual. They sought each other out during coffee breaks. They had a similar sense of humour and were never at a loss for things to talk about. He'd hoped their friendship could develop into something more.

Perhaps she thought they were moving too fast. Taking things slowly was fine with him. He was in no rush, was not by nature a fast mover. Or maybe she was worried that a one-night stand was all he was after. It wasn't. One-night stands didn't particularly interest him. He would see her at work on Monday. They could talk, straighten things out.

She was chatting with Jonathan and Jennifer when he entered the staff room on Monday morning. She smiled at him. She seemed her usual self. But when Jonathan went off to make photocopies and Jennifer went to the kitchen to get coffee, she scarpered. Later in the day she was approaching the kitchen, but when she saw that he was alone there, turned on her heels and headed in the opposite direction. She was avoiding him. He was offended. If she didn't like him, if she didn't think of him in that way, couldn't she just say so? He wasn't an ogre. He wasn't going to hound her. They were mates. She didn't need to act this way.

Sinéad had kept giving Luke the cold shoulder for an

entire week. The following week his exam results arrived. He'd failed the Japanese test and badly. His contract was up for renewal, and his supervisor arranged a meeting to discuss his progress and sign a new contract. Luke surprised them both by saying he wouldn't be renewing his contract. He had decided to leave. He was going to travel around South East Asia for a couple of months before heading back to England. Sinéad looked upset, when she heard the news, but she didn't seek him out, didn't try to speak to him.

Now here she was, a decade later, seeking him out on Facebook. It probably didn't mean anything. She might just want to increase her quota of friends. In all likelihood, she would never send him a message, write on his wall or comment on his posts. Not that he posted much on Facebook anyhow. He wouldn't be posting anything at all there come November.

He accepted her friend request. She wrote on his wall the very next day. Soon they were messaging each other on a daily basis. She sympathised about his crappy job and told him about her doubts about her upcoming nuptials. He encouraged her to go ahead and get married. Society showed more respect to married people than it did to singles and he thought that that in itself would make life sweeter. Plus, if she didn't take this chance, she could find herself a single octogenarian.

They chatted sometimes when they were both online at the same time. One evening Sinéad explained her strange behaviour towards him before he left Japan:

Sinéad

Do you remember that night we almost did it? We'd been kissing on those little legless chairs, then I left abruptly.

Luke

Yeah, I remember.

Sinéad

It wasn't because I didn't like you. I did like you.
Luke
But you didn't think of me in 'that' way. You liked me, but you didn't fancy me.
Sinéad
I fancied you all right. That wasn't the problem.
Luke
What was the problem? Were things happening too fast?
Sinéad
No, not really. Well maybe. I don't know. But we did work together. We'd seen each other every day for months, so the speed should have been just right.
Luke
So, why did you dash out of my room as if it was on fire? Why did you ignore me until I left the country?
Sinéad
It was terrible. Really childish of me. Sorry.
The thing is
I was a virgin.

A virgin, who'd have guessed? She would have been twenty-five or six back then. A twenty-six-year-old virgin. Unusual. But then she was an Irish Catholic. She'd had virginal role models. She had been educated by nuns.

Luke
So, are you saving yourself for marriage? Are you going to be a virgin bride?
Sinéad
God. No. I'm not a virgin now. I lost my virginity ages ago, shortly after you left Tokyo actually.
Luke
Who was the lucky guy?
Sinéad

Just some guy I met in a bar in Roppongi. You see I wasn't a virgin by intention, I was a virgin by accident. And by my mid-twenties I was just so eager to lose it.
Luke
I would have been happy to deflower you.
Sinéad
Yeah, but the thing is I was embarrassed by my virginity. I really liked you. I didn't want you to know I was a virgin. You'd have thought I was weird.

Luke tried to recollect his twenty something self. He probably would have thought her weird, but he might just have been gentlemanly enough not to let it show.

Luke
You are weird, but I kinda like weird.
Sinéad
Thank you. I like you too.
Luke
Got to go, weirdo!
Sinéad
See you.

He didn't really have to go anywhere, but this warm fuzzy feeling he got whenever they chatted online made him uncomfortable. He had been numb for so long.

It had been a shock to hear that he had a low sperm count. Zoe had presumed she was the reason they couldn't get pregnant. If that had been the case, it wouldn't have changed the way Paul felt about her. It wouldn't have bothered him that much at all really. Paul didn't mind if he never became a father. He'd never been particularly interested in kids. Zoe had reassured him, said she loved him, but her attitude towards him changed the day they discovered he was infertile.

He should have told Sinéad ages ago. The poor girl was already trying to get pregnant. He'd contemplated not telling her at all. After they'd been married for few months, she'd probably see a doctor to find out why she wasn't getting pregnant. The doctor would suggest a fertility clinic. Paul could pretend he'd never been to one of these places before. He could pretend it was news to him when the doctor revealed that his low sperm count was the reason Sinéad wasn't getting pregnant. No one need ever know that he'd been told this before in a fertility clinic in Toronto.

But it would be wrong. It would be a lie. He should have never let things go this far. If they were to have any chance at a happy marriage, they needed to be honest with each other. He got into his car and drove, hoping that he wouldn't chicken out before he reached Cashel.

He had asked her once, when their romance was new, if working with small children had put her off the idea of having children of her own. She had said it hadn't affected her feelings about motherhood one way or another. She hadn't expanded, and Paul had left it at that, assuming from her response that she wasn't too pushed about having children.

He realised now that he should have delved deeper. He'd been so eager to get off the whole roller coaster ride of relationships, to commit himself to one woman and stay with her forever. And he liked Sinéad. He liked her a lot. He liked it, so he put a ring on it, as the song said.

Sinéad was still in her pyjamas when he arrived. 'I thought we weren't meeting until later at Tricia's birthday thing in Tierney's' she said after greeting him with a kiss.

'There's something I need to talk to you about' he said.

'Oh, Okay.' Paul followed Sinéad into the kitchen, where she filled the kettle and started making tea. She dawdled at the kitchen counter, fiddled with the tea caddy and the mugs. She looked anxious, wary of whatever words were about to come out of his mouth.

'I can't have children,' he said when they were at last sitting at the table. 'I have a very low sperm count. It is unlikely that I will ever be able to father children.'

She shook her head, as if to shake off the information he was giving her. 'What? How do you know?'

Paul rubbed his forehead. 'Zoe, my Canadian girlfriend, she was a few years older than me, so when we moved to Toronto, she wanted to try to get pregnant straight away. We weren't having any luck, so we went to a clinic and it turned out that I was the reason we couldn't get pregnant.'

Sinéad stood up, but she didn't move away. She stayed there holding onto the table-top. 'You've known all this time and you tell me now, five days before our wedding?'

'I know I should have told you sooner. But, at first, I didn't think that you had your heart set on having children. You seemed ambiguous about it.'

'But we've talked about having children. We've discussed it.'

'Yes, but only recently. Until a month or so ago I had no idea how important having children was to you.'

'You can't ask somebody to marry you and not mention that you can't father children.'

'I'm sorry,' he said. He had hoped to find a woman who liked him for himself, not just for his sperm. Was that too much to ask?

'You should have told me.'

'I know. I know. I almost did many's the time, but I just couldn't seem to get the words out. I suppose I was afraid of losing you.'

He thought that might be a good time to make the suggestion he had rehearsed in the car. 'We could adopt, a little girl from China, maybe.'

He wasn't sure if she heard his suggestion. Her eyes drifted to the dresser behind him and then down again at the tabletop. She wouldn't look at him. This was going even worse than he'd expected.

He heard a car pulling into the driveway, Sinéad's parents back from mass, most likely. Sinéad fled up the stairs leaving Paul to make his own way out.

'Well, Paul,' Sinéad's father said, 'are yourself and Sinéad going off somewhere for the day?'

'No, no I just dropped by for a quick chat,' Paul replied, getting into his car.

WHAT SOPHIE SAID

Sinéad lay on her bed staring at the ceiling for some time after his car pulled away. The dog was barking. She should really take him for a walk, but she couldn't seem to rouse herself. That bastard. She had wasted a year of her life with him, a year she could have spent looking for another man, one with viable sperm.

Life was such a let-down. As a student at Scoil Mhuire, she'd dreamt of an exciting career, fairy tale romances and babies to nurture and love when the time came. What had she got? A draining job that she couldn't wait to leave. Disappointing romances. And now even her hopes of having a child of her own were evaporating. It was so unfair. Some people had it all, babies, big love stories, exciting careers. What did Sinéad have? A big fat nothing.

'What should I do?' she asked Sophie. They were driving into town to pick up Tricia's birthday cake in Sophie's ancient Micra. (Sinéad was too upset to be behind the wheel.)

'It would be so mean to leave Paul now,' Sophie said. 'It's not his fault he has a low sperm count.'

'I know, but...'

'Are you sure you really want kids?' Sophie asked. 'You've been counting the days until you get away from the kids in our classroom.'

'I might not like my job very much, but I love kids. I've always liked children. That's the reason why I got into this kind of work.'

'You could adopt.'

'We could, I suppose. But it's not the same, is it?' Sinéad

yearned for a baby. Ever since her teens she'd dreamt of a child growing inside her, an infant, *her* infant cradled in her arms, suckling at her breast.

'What about a sperm bank?' Sophie asked.

'Do we have sperm banks in Ireland?'

'I have no idea. If not, ye could go abroad for some fancy foreign sperm. Paul could pay for it. He has money, hasn't he?'

'He's not poor. You know, he's the only decent, eligible man I've met in the last half decade. If I leave him, I don't fancy my chances of finding another eligible man any time soon. So, the sperm bank could be the way to go. Of course, I might get pregnant if I started going to nightclubs, picking up random men and having unprotected sex with them.'

'When was the last time *you* went to a night club?'

'Yeah, I know it would require a big lifestyle change,' Sinéad said. 'But it could work, if I drank copious amounts of alcohol, and went clubbing on my most fertile nights of the month.'

'Poor Paul,' Sophie said.

'What do you mean poor Paul? He lied to me.'

'I know he should have told you sooner, but I feel sorry for him. I mean, the poor guy. That Canadian ex of his went off him when she found out his sperm was no good. And now you.'

Sophie had a point. This wasn't all Paul's fault. Sinéad hadn't been completely honest either. She hadn't told him she wanted kids, not until after he'd put an engagement ring on her finger. Afraid that it would scare him off, she had kept her yearning to herself.

'You're not really in love with him,' Sophie continued. 'I mean, if Darragh told me he couldn't father a child, I wouldn't leave him. I wouldn't dream of it. He's my man, my lover. And if I couldn't have children and he left me to go impregnate some other woman, I'd have to kill him.'

Sinéad looked at the slip of a girl behind the wheel and thought how good it must feel to love so intensely. She didn't think she'd ever loved like that. She suspected that she wasn't capable of it. She sniffled and wiped the tears from her cheeks.

'There are tissues in the glove compartment,' Sophie told her.

THE SNUG

Paul looked shook when he entered Tierney's. Tricia went to him to see if he was all right.

'I think Sinéad's going to call off the wedding,' he told her.

Tricia was getting really tired of Sinéad's dithering. 'She'll marry you, don't worry. She's just got pre-wedding jitters.'

The look on Paul's face told Tricia there was something more. She drew him towards the snug so they could talk about it in private. Behind the closed door, he told her about his infertility and how he had kept it from Sinéad until now. The poor guy looked so distressed; Tricia wanted to make it all better. She wrapped her arms around him. He smelled good when she pulled him close. He turned his face towards hers as if to say something more. She could feel his breath on her cheek. His lips were quivering. They looked so soft and tender, so inviting. She kissed him. He kissed back, reaching for her head, grabbing her hair between his fingers.

'Where's the birthday girl?' Sinéad asked when she arrived in Tierney's.

'She's in the snug with your fiancé,' Sophie said.

'Paul?' Sinéad hadn't expected him to make an appearance, not after the bombshell he'd dropped earlier. She walked towards the snug. She thought it best to face him. She didn't know yet what she was going to do, but they needed to talk things through. She opened the door of the snug. She saw Tricia's back and her blonde shoulder length hair. There were hands gripping the blonde locks. Male hands. They were Paul's hands. Paul's hands were in Tri-

266

cia's hair and his lips were touching her lips. They were kissing. Her fiancé and her so-called friend were kissing each other in the snug. Sinéad pulled the door shut behind her and walked out of the pub. She could hear someone calling her name. It was Paul. He caught up with her, attempted to explain. He tried to hold onto her, prevent her getting into her car. She shrugged him off. She turned her keys in the ignition and drove towards home.

She couldn't believe Paul kissing Tricia. The woman was over fifty and looked it too. She was glad they'd planned a small wedding, so much easier to call off. She'd ring the hotel in the morning and the priest too. There was the photographer, the flowers and the hair and make-up girl and of course the guests. Well, Paul could deal with his half of the guest list. God, it would be embarrassing ringing people up and telling them the wedding was off. Hopefully her mother and sister would help.

She could hear the sound of the television coming from the living room, but she didn't put her head around the door to say hello to her parents. Instead, she walked straight up the stairs to her room.

Just yesterday morning she had started to pack for her move to Kinsale. Too soon as it turned out. She had to remove a box of books from her chair before she could sit down at her computer.

She took her copy of Middlemarch from the box and returned it to its place on her bookshelf. Marriage hadn't turned out so well for Dorothea and Causabon or for Lydgate and Rosamund. Why had she been so hell-bent on marriage? Why so determined that her life take that particular path? It seemed crazy now, a mania that had taken her over.

She might as well go on her honeymoon. It was she who had booked it. She had the tickets. She didn't have a job anymore. And two weeks in the sun would be good for her.

She didn't fancy going to India on her own though. Luke had mentioned he was taking some time off soon. She sent him a message inviting him to come to Goa with her.

LUKE'S DILEMMA

Luke was online and read Sinéad's message straight away. Funnily enough, his chosen date for his departure from this world was the same day that Sinéad would be heading off on her honeymoon. He'd booked his holidays for the whole of that week, so as to lessen the inconvenience his death would cause for his co-workers. He had told his family, his work mates and Sinéad that he intended to spend the week in the South East and in London, catching up with old friends. The truth was he hadn't actually contacted any of his friends in London for ages.

He replied to her email straightaway saying he already had plans, and that in any case he had only booked a week off work. Sinéad wrote back coaxing him to change his plans and ask for an extra week off work. It wasn't every day you were offered an all-expenses paid trip to Goa after all.

'Besides, you hate your job,' the message continued. *'You could meet me at Heathrow. Come on, do something crazy.'*

An all-expenses paid trip to Goa with an attractive red head. It was the most enticing invitation Luke had received in a very long time. He didn't know what to do. Thinking about it gave him butterflies. He rubbed the back of his head and looked up at the ceiling, hoping to find the answer there.

The strap of his rucksack dangled over the edge of his wardrobe. It caught his eye. It seemed to be beckoning him. That rucksack had accompanied him through Rajasthan, Shikoku, Thailand and Vietnam. It was old and worn, but it might just do for a trip to Goa.

PART SIX
ANOTHER EARTHQUAKE

When Ken finally drifted off to sleep, Lauren pulled her arm out from under his body as gently as she could, got up quietly and went to the kitchen to make tea. Any minute now, her brother and his fiancée would be back from their day trip to Kamakura. They would like tea.

Jack and Amanda had flown in from Chicago a week before. Such a treat to have family visiting. She heard the spare key turn in the lock. Here they were.

They joined Naoto in the living room. Lauren arranged the tea things on the coffee table while on the television screen emergency workers stretchered victims out of the rubble of a collapsed tower in Kathmandu.

'It's not as big as the earthquake here a few years ago, is it?' Amanda asked.

'No, it's not,' Naoto answered, 'but it's big. And Nepal, it doesn't have the infrastructure Japan has. And I think the buildings are not constructed to the same standards.'

'You mean it could be just as devastating?' Jack said.

Naoto tilted his head to the side, thinking it through. 'Well,' he said. 'Nepal is inland, so they won't have to worry about a tsunami.'

'They might not have nuclear reactors to worry about either,' Amanda said.

Naoto shrugged. 'I don't know,' he said.

'Fukushima was so scary. The radiation and all. When Jack first suggested coming to Japan for a holiday, I was like 'no way.' I mean, I want to be a mom someday. And I don't want to ruin my chances of that happening just for a foreign holiday.'

'I told her we wouldn't be going anywhere near Fukushima,' Jack said. 'And if Tokyo is okay for the Olympic athletes in 2020, then it should be okay for us.'

'Tokyo seems fine,' Amanda said. 'It is fine, right?'

Naoto shrugged again. 'Who knows?' he said. 'I read an article the other day about a doctor who moved to Western Japan. He said that Tokyo was no longer safe for human habitation.'

Lauren hadn't seen this article. But then she might not have been able to read it. Chinese characters flummoxed her.

'But there are nearly forty million people living here. And they look fine. It must be safe,' Jack said.

Naoto nodded. 'Well, we hope it's safe. We think it's safe, but sometimes I don't know if we are deluding ourselves. Fukushima is an ongoing problem that no one knows how to handle.'

'But Fukushima is hundreds of miles away right?'

'Two hundred and forty kilometres,' Naoto said. His fingers tapped the armrest. 'You know, I hated being separated from my children, all that time they spent in New Mexico. But then when they returned, I worried. Was I selfish to want them here? What if my children develop cancer?'

Lauren had never heard her husband express these fears before. She had always believed he thought she had overreacted in taking the children to the States. Now she saw that his feelings were more complex than that.

'Time for sakura mochi and tea,' Lauren said.

Amanda stood and peered at the tray of Japanese treats. 'You're so good to us, Lauren,' she said, 'making sure we try all these exotic delicacies.'

Their week in Tokyo had come to an end. The next day the couple would embark on a week-long rail tour of Japan. Atami Hot Spring Resort was their first stop. Lauren, Naoto and the children would join them for the first leg of their journey. After that they would be on their own. On their return, they would spend one last night in Tokyo before flying back to Chicago. And then when would Lauren see her brother again?

Lauren felt tears pricking her eyes. It hadn't been easy hosting Amanda and Jack. She'd had to keep reminding Jack to remove his trainers in the genkan. And Amanda had several times paraded around the living room in the bathroom slippers. But worse than either of these faux pas, were the noises that had woken Lauren several times during the week, noises that had rattled and discomfited her, the sounds that her brother and his fiancée made having sex. She was glad that her brother and his fiancée had an active sex life. She really was, but she would have preferred not to have had to hear evidence of it.

Lauren led the way through the split curtain which marked the entrance to the hot spring baths. Inside the portiere, the walls were lined with wooden pigeonholes.

'Leave your slippers in one of those cubbies,' Lauren told her guest.

She took off her own slippers and placed them in a cubby at shoulder height. Her brother's fiancée followed suit.

Lauren then stepped into the changing area and took one of the laundry baskets down from a shelf.

'Put your big bath towel in here and take off your yukata and leave it here too,' she instructed.

'My yu- what?' Amanda asked.

'Your yukata, your bathrobe.'

'Oh, the kimono,' Amanda said.

It was not a kimono, but Lauren decided against explaining the difference between a kimono and a yukata at this point. 'You can use the small towel to protect your modesty, if you wish,' she said.

'That won't hide much,' Amanda said, holding up the thin strip of white towel.

Jack's fiancée had wide hips, a broad back and a large bosom. Jack had always been attracted to hefty peasant types. Amanda was attractive though, her skin a creamy white, alabaster, and she had a great head of luxuriant, rust coloured hair.

'Don't worry,' Lauren said. 'The place is almost empty.'

But Amanda looked very worried. 'I don't know about this,' she said. 'Your brother is the only person who has seen me naked in years.'

'It's just women in here,' Lauren tried to reassure her guest.

She hoped Amanda wouldn't hate the onsen. She so wanted Jack and Amanda to experience the real Japan, but she worried that she was forcing them to do things that they really didn't want to.

Amanda followed Lauren through the glass doors and into the steamy room. She kept one arm crossed over her boobs and the hand of the other arm placed in front of her crotch.

A long fogged up mirror covered one wall. Above it hung shower heads, beneath it tapped. An old Japanese lady sat on a low plastic stool, a basin of water at her feet. She massaged her arms and shoulders with a soapy mitt. Amanda looked petrified. But she hadn't bolted. At least there was that.

'Okay, so we need to wash ourselves before we get into the bath.' Lauren hunkered down on a plastic stool and filled a basin with water. Amanda followed her example. The Mid-West native still looked uneasy.

Outside in the night air, gazing at the stars while luxuriating in the hot waters of the rotenburo, Amanda appeared much more relaxed.

'All that tension in my neck, I can feel it dissipating.' Amanda raised her shoulders to her ears and let them drop back into the water.

'I knew you'd like it once you got over the whole being naked with other people thing.'

'Well, I don't know how comfortable I would feel if there were more people here.'

It was just as well Amanda hadn't come earlier in the day when Lauren had come with the children. The baths had been crowded then.

Tomorrow, Lauren, Naoto and the children would return to Tokyo and the recently engaged couple would continue to Kyoto, Hiroshima and Miyajima. They had a guidebook, and Lauren and Naoto had made lots of suggestions and recommendations, they should manage alone.

Lauren felt herself overheating, raised herself out of the waters and sat on the ledge. She noticed Amanda's face turning crimson and warned her against staying in too long. 'It can make you lightheaded,' she said.

Half an hour later, they emerged from the onsen wrapped in their yukatas, towels protecting their shoulders from their dripping hair.

'So, is that the ideogram for woman?' Amanda asked, pointing to the character on the red curtain in the doorway they had passed through.

'Yes, and that is the character for man.' Lauren pointed to the character on the navy-blue curtain in the doorway across the hall.

'So those are the men's baths.'

Mop and bucket in hand, an elderly member of staff came towards them along the corridor. Written in hiragana on a badge on his breast pocket was his name; 'Tanaka Tadashi.' He bowed low and welcomed them. He said that there was no-one in the men's baths at this time and suggested that Lauren and Amanda take the waters there briefly. He told them that the view was beautiful. These baths looked out to sea.

Lauren translated for Amanda.

'Wow, could we? Just for a moment.'

Lauren didn't really fancy having to dry herself off all over again, but she was thrilled that Amanda wanted to, so she said that they could.

Amanda soaked up the waters and the ocean view. 'Do men always get the better baths?' she asked.

'Actually, they usually change around every few days. This side will be for men for three days and then they'll switch the curtain and the women will get the sea view.' Lauren sat naked on the edge of the bath. She had had enough steaming hot water for one day.

'Oh, not as sexist as I thought then.'

Looking back through the glass doors, Lauren saw Tadashi mopping the floors inside. She had assumed he would wait until they left, but she guessed the old man wanted to finish cleaning so he could get home to bed. They were delaying him. Perhaps it had been inconsiderate of them to take him up on his suggestion that they take a dip in these baths. Perhaps he had not expected them to. Perhaps she had yet again made some kind of cultural faux pas. Almost two decades in this country and she still didn't get all the social mores.

Moments later, she looked back over her shoulder again and saw that Tadashi had stopped mopping. She thought he must have left and was startled to spot him standing half hidden by a pillar peering out at herself and Amanda. His eyes bulged with excitement at the sight of their naked flesh. And though she couldn't be certain, she thought he had his hand down his trousers.

She turned to tell Amanda they were being watched, but Amanda seemed so completely enchanted by the ocean view and so very much at one with the world, that Lauren didn't want to break the spell. Lauren felt a twinge in her left shoulder. It often bothered her, a consequence she thought, of her children hanging out of her all the time. She massaged the site of the twinge, kneaded her neck, then rubbed her shoulders again. She stroked her right breast and then her left before letting her hand rest on her breastbone. She gave a surreptitious glance back at the old man. He was rubbing his lips together drinking in her naked image. She was appalled, but also weirdly gratified.

No eyes had lingered on her body like this in a very long time. She had been back from the States for over two years, but she could count on one hand the number of times she and her husband had made love.

Once, after the children had been put to bed, she had wrapped her arms around her husband from behind and planted a big sloppy kiss on his neck. He had flinched.

That flinch had put her off initiating anything amorous again. And Naoto certainly didn't initiate anything. He seemed to have lost interest.

She thought he might have had an affair during her exile in New Mexico. But since she'd returned to Japan, there had been no unexplained absences, no mysterious phone calls, no lipstick on his collar. If he had had an affair, it was over now.

She fantasized about other men sometimes. The barista in her local Starbucks had a smile that lit up the room. And Emi's gym teacher was really cute. But Lauren didn't want the barista, or Emi's gym teacher, not really. The only man she wanted was her husband.

A woman in her prime, such a shame that all her sexual and amorous feelings should be left to waste away. Now it had come to this – getting her kicks from touching herself in from of an elderly peeping Tom at an onsen.

'Oh, my God,' Amanda shrieked.

'What?'

'He's staring at us. The creep. Ugh. He has his hand down his trousers.'

Lauren turned in time to see the old man skedaddle taking his mop with him.

Amanda's breath came heavy and fast. They got dressed and gathered their belongings. Lauren kept her head down. She felt guilty. She should have alerted Amanda. She should have been the one to scream.

They walked back along the corridor and caught the lift down to their floor.

'Do you think he lured us in there just so he could watch us?'

'I don't know, maybe,' Lauren said. 'Or maybe he just caught sight of our bare bodies as he was mopping the floors and couldn't help himself.'

'He shouldn't even have been in here,' Amanda said. 'Yuck, I feel soiled.'

Lauren didn't feel soiled. She felt more or less unaffected.

'We have to complain,' Amanda said. 'He could be peeping at all the women who come in here.'

'Not many women enter the men's baths.'

Amanda glared at her. 'We have to report him,' she insisted

Lauren was not convinced that they *had* to report him. Perhaps they should. A complaint would, she guessed, discourage this type of behaviour. And obviously, women should be able to bathe in peace without having to worry about peeping Toms. But who knew what consequences a formal complaint might have? Amanda's shrieks had probably done enough to put Tadashi off peeping for some time to come. If he had been leering at children, or at younger, more vulnerable women, Lauren would agree that they had to report him. But what danger did a little old man pose to two sturdy, strapping women like herself and Amanda?

As they neared their hotel rooms, they saw Naoto and Jack, sitting in an alcove next to a vending machine, each with a can of beer in his hand.

'You will never guess what happened to us,' Amanda said, and proceeded to tell her fiancée and his brother in law all about peeping Tadashi.

'Oh, my God, honey. Is he still up there?' Jack stood up and made to move towards the lifts.

'Wait,' Lauren placed a hand on her brother's forearm. She felt an inexplicable urge to protect Tadashi san from her brother. Not that Jack was a violent type, but he could get loud when he was angry. It could get ugly.

'I've got to sort this guy out,' Jack said.

'I'm sure he's left by now,' Lauren said.

'Where's the manager? We got to find the manager.'

'Could be better wait 'til morning,' Naoto said. He looked very worried. He would blame himself, Lauren knew, for any difficulties or inconveniences Jack and Amada suffered on Japanese soil.

'You know, it would be best to do it in writing,' Lauren said. 'Japanese people are very bad at confrontation, so a complaint in writing would work best.'

Jack ran his fingers through his hair. 'Would it need to be written in Japanese?' he asked.

'Of course,' Lauren said. 'Don't worry. Naoto and I will take care of it. You two just forget about it and enjoy the rest of your holiday.'

Eventually Amanda and Jack retired to their room. Lauren flopped down on the bench next to Naoto.

'What will we write?' he asked.

'Don't worry,' she told him. 'They'll have forgotten all about it by the morning.'

'You mean you don't want me to write a complaint?' Naoto asked.

Lauren couldn't bring herself to complain. 'No, he is a very old guy. I don't want to get him in trouble,' she said.

Naoto's whole body relaxed when he heard this.

In the morning, when Lauren, Naoto and the children emerged from their hotel room, Jack and Amanda were already in the corridor, pulling their large suitcases towards the elevators. Ken ran after Jack and charged straight into his uncle's butt.

'Hey buddy,' Jack said.

Lauren loved Ken's exuberance but worried he would hurt himself and others. Naoto scooted ahead, caught up with the four-year-old and held his hand to prevent him jumping down the elevator shaft.

Having Naoto around made parenting easier. In New Mexico, she'd rarely taken the children further than the local playground. Trying to keep two tots safe anywhere else had proved too much of a challenge. Just preparing lunch or dinner had been testing. She'd ended up sticking the kids in front of the telly far more than was healthy for them. When she'd met Yuka, she'd started to get out and about a bit more, but that had been towards the end of her time in New Mexico. Parenting was so much more doable since she'd returned to Tokyo. She and Naoto worked well as a team. Two friendly co-workers united in the task of raising Emi and Ken. The problem was that all traces of their former intimacy and romance had gone. She had excused Naoto's frostiness at first. She knew it must have been hard for him being left behind in Japan. But she had expected a thaw long before now.

They had been such a good couple once. They had been together for eight years before they married, and it had been another two before they welcomed Emi into the world. Lauren had thought their relationship strong enough to survive whatever life threw at them. She hadn't reckoned on an earthquake.

She had imagined them touring Europe together in their late fifties or early sixties. A handsome, older, mixed race couple, they would cut a dash on Parisian boulevards and Spanish sea fronts. Her husband would be elegant and graceful, his thick black hair streaked with grey. He would wear the same type of Gap Chinos and Uniqlo shirts and sweaters he wore now. A couple of more decades in Japan would have knocked the sloppy American out of Lauren. She would be neat and sophisticated, her hair still blonde, even if she needed Clairol's help to keep it so.

But how could they be that attractive couple fifteen years from now, if they never regained any of their former intimacy? What would hold them together after Emi and Ken had grown?

They waved Jack and Amanda off at the station before boarding the shinkansen back to Tokyo.

'You know, I bet it was you that ojiisan was looking at in the onsen,' Naoto said. 'You are more attractive than Amanda san. You have a better body.' He took her suitcase from her hand and put it in the overhead rack.

Lauren felt her cheeks blush red. She pulled Emi to her in a bear hug to hide her confusion.

A FUNDRAISER

Lauren waited for Yuka at Toranomon subway station's ticket gates. She had invited Yuka to come with her to a fundraiser for Nepal.

The fundraiser was being organized by an Italian guy called Alessandro. Lauren didn't know him. Apparently, he was a friend of Fumiko. Lauren had deduced from the event's Facebook page that Katherine and Charlotte knew him too. They would also be there tonight. She looked forward to seeing them. It had been a while.

Yuka arrived looking flustered. She whined about how difficult Shouta had been all day. The two-year-old had thrown a tantrum when it was time to leave the park. He lay down the path and wouldn't budge. So many tantrums lately, Yuka worried that Hiroaki would not be able to cope all by himself.

'I'm sure he'll be fine,' Lauren said. 'Hiroaki is great with Shouta. And you need a break.'

Yuka agreed. 'But you know, when Shouta's not with me, I feel so strange, like I'm missing a limb or something,' she said.

Yuka asked how Jack and Amanda had enjoyed their holiday and commiserated when Lauren said she felt lonely after them.

Lauren consulted her phone to check if they were headed in the right direction, then she spotted the signboard. 'Pizzeria da Angelo, 3F,' it read.

They entered the lift and pushed the button for the third floor. Seconds later the doors opened into the restaurant. Despite getting little natural light, the restaurant had a bright and airy feel. Its turquoise and white painted walls were decorated with seashells. A large pizza oven dominated the far corner of the room. The cashier's desk was situated in front of the elevator doors. The cashier demanded 5,000 yen from each of them and reminded them that all of the money raised tonight would go to help the victims of the earthquake in Nepal.

Guests stood around in small groups chatting, ignoring the baskets of bread on the tiled tabletops. Head and shoulders above most of the other attendees, Charlotte was easy to spot. She was talking with an equally tall, bespectacled foreign man whom Lauren thought she recognised from the event's Facebook page as the organizer of this fundraiser. A far shorter, bearded Japanese man stood with them.

Charlotte glanced up, saw Lauren and crossed the dining room to greet her. She talked about calling over to see Emi. She had brought back some children's books from her recent trip home to England that she thought Emi might enjoy. She wanted to give them to the child before she moved.

Charlotte had been talking about moving to the countryside since quitting her job at the British council some twelve months before. She now worked freelance and felt that her income would stretch further in a rural area and, apart from financial considerations, she had grown weary of city life and felt she needed a change.

'So, have you found a place yet?' Lauren asked.

'Yes, didn't I tell you? We found a place in Ibaraki,' she said. 'A big old house surrounded by rice fields for just 30,000 yen a month.'

'We?' Lauren asked.

'Satoshi and I,' Charlotte said.

'Satoshi?'

'My boyfriend.'

'B-boyfriend.' Lauren felt her jaw drop in astonishment, but quickly closed her mouth and tried to look composed.

In the fifteen years that Lauren had known Charlotte, the English woman had never had a boyfriend. She'd never mentioned any guys she was interested in, nor had she ever complained, as so many foreign women did, about the difficulty of meeting men in Tokyo.

'That's him over there talking to the tall gaijin.' Charlotte blushed a little as she gestured towards the man in her life.

'He looks nice,' Lauren said. And he did look nice. He had a neatly trimmed beard and hair speckled with grey. A good head shorter than Charlotte.

'Lauren san, Charlotte san,' came a voice from the entrance.

They turned to see Fumiko and Morioka san.

'Hisashi buri desu ne,' Fumiko said. *Long time no see.*

Lauren introduced Yuka to everybody.

'Strange to have a fundraiser for Nepal in an Italian restaurant,' Yuka said. 'But then many foreigners helped Japan after the Tohoku Earthquake.'

'Yes, like Alessandro,' Morioka san said. He nodded in the direction of the tall foreigner who had been speaking to Charlotte earlier. 'Ale volunteered for a long time in Tohoku.'

Morioka san suggested that they sit. 'My legs are tired,' he said.

'Ojiichan,' Fumiko teased. *Grandpa.*

Charlotte returned to her boyfriend and Morioka led the way to a corner table set for six. He positioned himself in the inside corner. Fumiko sat opposite him. Lauren and Yuka took the next two seats.

'Have you met Charlotte's boyfriend?' Lauren asked.

'Charlotte has a boyfriend?' Fumiko said. 'I didn't know that.'

Fumiko spotted Katherine and waved her over to join them. She sat opposite Lauren. With her pixie haircut and the polka dot scarf, the Australian looked effortlessly stylish, as always. 'Did you know Charlotte had a boyfriend?' Lauren asked her.

'Yes, I did,' Kathrerine said. 'That's him over there.'

'I didn't think she ever bothered with men,' Lauren said.

'I don't think she did until she met Satoshi. Waiting for the right guy, I suppose. Satoshi's lovely.'

Katherine told Lauren that Charlotte and Satoshi had met while volunteering in Tohoku. Satoshi had quit his boring office job to help the stricken region and Charlotte had taken several months leave of absence to do the same thing. As far as Katherine knew, their relationship had started as a friendship, and then grown into something more.

She explained that Alessandro, who had organized this Nepal fundraiser, had volunteered with the same organization, *Disaster Relief Japan.*

'Charlotte introduced him to *Disaster Relief Japan,*' Fumiko interjected.

'Did she?' Katherine said. 'She put me in touch with *Disaster Relief* as well.'

'You volunteered too?' Lauren asked. She was beginning to worry that she was the only person present who had done nothing to help Tohoku after the earthquake and the tsunami.

'Just for a week when I returned from my travels,' Katherine said. 'Not like Charlotte, Satoshi or Alessandro. They volunteered for months.'

Alessandro appeared at their table. He greeted Katherine with kisses on both cheeks. Fumiko received the same attention. Morioka san stood and bowed to the Italian. Alessandro bowed in return, then slapped Morioka on the shoulder.

Waiters brought platters of cured meats, olives and cheeses to the tables. Alessandro pulled out the remaining chair and sat with them. Lauren loved the antipasto. The primo followed shortly. Platters of fettuccini, gnocchi and risotto landed on their table.

Yuka spoke to Alessandro. She told him how impressed she was to hear how he had volunteered in Tohoku. 'I am a Japanese, and I did not go to Tohoku,' she said. 'At that time, after the earthquake, I thought mostly about myself. I think I must be selfish person.'

'If you are selfish, so am I,' Lauren said. 'I am married to a Japanese. My children are Japanese, and I didn't go to Tohoku either. I ran away to America.'

'But it's your duty to protect your children,' Alessandro protested.

'And the earthquake was so scary,' Katherine said. 'Nobody knew what would happen with Fukushima. It made sense to leave, if you had somewhere to go'

Alessandro agreed. 'And I think we all act out of selfish motivation,' he said. 'Me more than anybody. It was to help myself that I volunteered in Tohoku.'

Yuka shook her head in disbelief. She could not see how volunteering in tsunami-stricken Tohoku could be in anyway self-serving.

Alessandro explained that Fumiko and Morioka had invited him to visit Japan. And on a whim, he had booked a flight. 'I was a mess at the time,' he said. 'I was probably drunk when I booked the flight. I was drinking every day. When I landed in Tokyo, I had a choice, I could stay here drinking cheap saké, or I could go to Tohoku and try to do some good. I was curious to see Tohoku. It had been on the news so much in Italy. So, I went. I felt useful there and I stayed for six months.'

'I shovelled mud,' he continued. 'Ten months after the disaster and there was still so much mud. I worked on several construction projects too. The physical labour, being around the tsunami survivors. They had lost everything, and they appreciated me being there. It helped me deal with my own loss.'

He told them that he still visited Tohoku when he could but was based in Tokyo. He was working for Angelo at the restaurant while improving his Japanese.

'I admire you,' Yuka said.

'Kochiro koso,' Alessandro replied. *I should be the one to say it.*

'No, no. no. I am selfish,' Yuka insisted.

Lauren wondered what loss Alessandro had suffered. She saw sorrow lurking still behind his handsome eyes. His grief had not left him, but perhaps he had learned to live with it. When Alessandro got up to greet some late arrivals, she asked Katherine about it.

'His girlfriend died a few years ago,' Katherine told her. 'She was travelling in Thailand at the time, or was it Bali? Her death was ruled to be accidental, but there was a suspicion of foul play.'

Lauren lost her appetite on hearing this story, which was just as well she had already eaten too much. Alessandro returned from the bathroom and soon he and Katherine were deep in conversation.

Katherine speaking, Alessandro listening closely, his hand on her upper arm. Lauren wondered if there was something between them. They would make a handsome couple. But then the hand on the arm might signify nothing more than the fact that he was Italian and touchy-feely by nature.

Lauren looked over the tables to where Charlotte and Satoshi were seated. They were giggling about something. She saw Charlotte put her hand to her nose. She had probably snorted. Charlotte often snorted when she laughed. Satoshi doubled over in mirth. So cute, the pair of them, totally immersed in each other's company, deriving so much enjoyment from each other. Lauren and Naoto had been like that once.

The tables had turned. Lauren had always been the one lucky in love, happy in a stable relationship. Now Lauren worried constantly that her husband no longer loved her, that his heart would never thaw. And Charlotte had a beau who seemed besotted with her. And Fumiko, who had constantly obsessed over men who didn't know she existed, was happily married to the charming Morioka san.

Sinéad was probably happily married by now too. At least the last Lauren had heard, her Irish friend was supposed to be getting married. No wedding photos had ever appeared on Facebook though, she wondered if the wedding had ever taken place. She asked Fumiko who told her that Sinéad had cancelled the wedding. She didn't know the reason why but said that Sinéad seemed fine about it.

Lauren couldn't think of Sinéad without thinking of the book club and how Sinéad used to dictate what books they would read. Sinéad's book choices had often been ill-considered. Middlemarch, for example, more than eight hundred pages long. Who had the time for that? And it must have been a huge struggle for Fumiko. Sinéad had started the book club and organized their get-togethers. But Lauren never understood why they couldn't choose reading material democratically. That's what Lauren would do if she ran a book club. Those book club meetups seemed so long ago.

'So much has changed since three eleven,' Lauren said.

Katherine sighed. Morioka san grimaced. Fumiko stared off into the middle distance.

'The world seems a scarier place,' Yuka said. 'More terror, more natural disasters.'

'I don't think we can blame three eleven for that,' Katherine said.

'The world shifted on its axis,' Yuka said. 'The earthquake moved it somewhere between ten and twenty-five centimetres.'

'I guess that could have some kind of knock on cosmic effect,' Katherine conceded.

'Who knows,' Alessandro said.

'Sometimes, I think I have been reeling ever since Three Eleven. Like I lost my balance and haven't quite regained it yet,' Lauren said.

'I know what you mean,' Katherine said. 'My life's been quite rocky these past few years.'

'We thought Tokyo was so safe,' Morioka san said.

GREG REAPPEARS

Yuka boarded the Asakusa bound train, while Lauren and the Moriokas waited for the Ginza line towards Shibuya.

The train pulled into the station. They boarded and sat together. A Eurasian teenager and a middle-aged Caucasian man ran and caught the train just before the doors closed. They remained standing near the door trying to catch their breath and congratulating themselves on making it. Lauren studied the young man, searching in him for clues as to how her own mixed-race children might turn out. Freckles dotted his cheekbones. His floppy hair was dark but not quite black. He was taller than his father and much better looking.

Fumiko nudged her husband and pointed at the foreigner. They spoke in hushed but animated tones and threw excited glances in his direction. Lauren could not make out what they were saying. But the way they stared at the foreign man made her uncomfortable.

There was nothing remarkable about him, nothing she could discern that might attract so much attention. He looked to be his mid to late fifties. His fair hair was sparse. He wore a blue polo shirt and a navy sweater draped across his shoulders. His bulging stomach strained the waistband of his cream coloured chinos.

As the train approached Aoyama Itchome station, Lauren stood up and said goodbye to Fumiko. Fumiko was so intent on glaring at the balding foreign man that she didn't hear. Morioka also rose to his feet. This was not his stop. Lauren gave him a quizzical look. He ignored her and stood quietly at the door of the train.

The train came to a halt. The doors opened. Both Lauren

and the young Eurasian man alighted on the platform. Out of the corner of her eye, Lauren saw Morioka stick his leg out. The foreign man tripped over it. He put his hands out to break his fall, but too late, the side of his face smacked against the concrete. Lauren's heart lurched in fright.

'Daijoubu? Otōsan, daijoubu?' the young man said. *'Are you okay? Father, are you okay?'*

The train doors closed, then opened again. The man's feet were still inside the train. His son pulled him clear.

The doors closed once more, and the train continued towards Shibuya. Lauren hurried to catch her connecting train, her heart beating uncomfortably in her chest.

Why would Morioka trip up that man? It made no sense.

There was some anti-American sentiment in Japan. And there were Japanese people who assumed that all white foreigners were American. She had heard of people spitting at Westerners on the subway, but such incidences were extremely rare. And Morioka san did not seem the type. She had met Fumiko's husband only once before tonight, but he seemed gracious and kind. She guessed you never knew what lurked inside people's hearts.

'Tadaima,' Lauren called from the genkan. *I'm home.*
'Okaeri,' her husband replied from the kitchen. *Welcome back.*

She was surprised he was still up. Naoto would usually be sound asleep at this time on a Sunday night. He started work early in the morning.

She took off her shoes, went into the living room and collapsed onto the sofa.

Naoto came from the kitchen with two glasses of oolong tea.

'Thank you,' Lauren smiled, pleased that he had thought of her.

'How was it?' he asked.

'Fun,' she said. 'I saw so many people I hadn't seen in ages.'

'Did they raise a lot of money?

'I think so,' she said. Then she told him about the strange occurrence on the subway, about how Morioka san had tripped the gaijin, and how the man had smacked his head on the platform.

'Morioka san? Are you sure?'

'Yes, I was standing right next to him.'

'Did you have a lot to drink?'

'Several glasses of wine, but Naoto, I tell you, Morioka san tripped him up.' Even as she said the words, she began to doubt them herself, to wonder if her mind had not played tricks on her. Perhaps Morioka had been standing at the door just to get a better look at the subway map. Perhaps he had stuck his leg out absentmindedly. Perhaps he felt terrible about the man tripping but couldn't do anything because the train pulled out of the station. Or perhaps the man had been drunk and had fallen without any help from Morioka san.

Lauren sank further into the sofa and placed her head on her husband's shoulder. He put his arm around her. She closed her eyes. She felt safe, protected. They sat there in comfortable silence as the city slept outside their window. Her husband placed a kiss on the top of her head. Another on her forehead. She daren't open her eyes, in case she was sleeping, and this was a dream. He kissed her eyelids, then her nose. He rubbed her cheek. She felt her insides liquefy. He had thawed towards her at last.

She and Naoto were going to be okay. Yes, they were going to be all right.

ACKNOWLEDGEMENTS

I am grateful to Anna Cellamare, Camelia Bezzola and Georgia Grasso at Europe Books, and to Emanuele Tranchetti for proofreading the manuscript.

For all sorts of support and encouragement thank you to my mother, Norah Grant, my sister, Claire Grant, my aunties: Margaret Tedders, Anne Maher, Helen Grant and the late Peggy Grant.

Thank you Anne Cooke, Deirdre O'Mahony and Seosaimhín Nic Eachaidh for egging me on.

I very much appreciate the mentoring and writing advice I received from Dianne Highbridge in Tokyo many moons ago and more recently from Fay Weldon my tutor at Bath Spa University who couldn't have been nicer or more astute.

A big thank you too, to all my cohort at Bath Spa, especially Jen Leggo, Dixie Darch, Morag Shuaib, Christine Stephenson, Zhenia Webster and Linda Pinsom. I couldn't have done it without you, Linda.

Index